The Vows We Break

Sicilian Mafia Wars
Book 1

Meaghan Pierce

Pierced Soul Publishing

Editing by Comma Sutra Editorial

Cover Design by Books and Moods

For Chelsea. You are a constant inspiration to me. I'm so glad I don't have to do this life without you.

Dear Reader,

Please be aware that *The Vows We Break* contains content that may be triggering for some. For a list of triggers, please see the next page.

Chapter One

The bastard was finally dead.

And by his own hand, no less. He deserved worse than to die in that expensive leather chair in his study that smelled like cigars and wood polish and paper. He deserved worse than a single bullet to the temple. But at least he was dead. At least she was free from him.

"Carina."

Her brother's voice was a whisper in her ear, the squeeze of his hand on her elbow a gentle reminder. She was still playing a part. The part of the dutiful daughter mourning a father gone too soon.

The rich scent of damp earth filled her nose as she bent to collect a handful, dropping it into the gaping cavern of the freshly dug grave where it pelted the dark cherry casket with a dull plop. She stared down into the cavity for a moment more, grateful the black lace veil hid her face from other mourners, that it prevented her from leaning over and spitting on his final resting place. Good fucking riddance.

Rain-soaked grass squelched under the heel of her stilettos when she returned to stand next to her brothers. Luca gave her arm another squeeze, and she made the sign of the cross while the priest prayed, slipping her fingers over her mother's rosary beads.

She was an orphan now. And even though she wouldn't mourn her father, wouldn't miss him for a second, nothing could fill the empty space left by her mother's death. The cancer had taken everything. It had even taken Matteo.

Carina let her eyes drift to her oldest brother in his black three-piece suit. It looked tailored, and she wondered, not for the first time, what he'd been doing in the seven years since abandoning them. Whatever it was, it paid well.

He'd arrived the night before in a cherry-red Alfa Romeo, his car growling up the driveway. She'd watched from her balcony as he ordered around the maids and butler he'd roused from sleep with all the confidence of the lord of the manor. Though she supposed he was. With their father dead, Matteo was head of the family now.

The thought left a bitter taste in her mouth. Matteo might be the oldest, but he'd walked out on them. All she remembered of that night, through her haze of grief, was her father and brother screaming at each other in the courtyard before a door slammed and she never saw her brother again. Until now.

She didn't know what to make of him being back. It never occurred to her while she grit her teeth through the preparations for this godforsaken funeral she didn't care about that he would show up at all. There was no love lost between Matteo and their father. Even before their last fight, the two had been at odds. Always screaming at each other over how to run the family businesses. Matteo had been far more ambitious than their father had the patience for.

It was likely Matteo was here to sign some paperwork, check on the health of the casinos, and pretend at pleasantries before he disappeared again to wherever the fuck he'd been before. Maybe he'd pass on the title and the money and the responsibilities to Dom as next in line and wash his hands of them completely. She could only hope.

The priest began the last incantation, and she bowed her head, eyes trained on the dark rectangle that swallowed up her father's body. Her hands trembled, and she clenched them until the wood cross from her mother's rosary bit into her skin. She couldn't afford to show emotion here. There were too many eyes. She had to keep up the act a little longer.

She made a final sign of the cross, glancing up at Luca with a tired smile when he gave her arm a gentle pat. They'd grown apart over the last few years since she'd been married off to the Romano Don and dumped at his sprawling villa in Cefalù. But they'd been close as children. As close as their father allowed them to be anyway.

"You managed that well," he whispered into her ear, and she had to bite back a grin. "Not a single tear, though. You'll have to work on your acting skills."

"And where were your tears?" she murmured, barely swallowing a laugh when he raised a brow.

He helped her into the back of the limo and climbed in behind her, settling on the opposite seat and pulling out his phone. Dom joined them next, taking the seat beside Luca. She was ready to get the fuck out of here. Guests would arrive at the house for the reception soon, her father's men and their families. She wanted a minute of solace before she had to greet them and make painful small talk, accepting condolences for grief she did not feel.

Unpinning her veil from her head and smoothing a hand over her hair, she reached for the car door to close it, shooting an irritated look at her brother for leaving it open. A hand reached out to grip the frame as she eased it shut, and she gave an exasperated huff.

She was really not in the mood for whatever business one

of their capos couldn't wait a few damn hours to discuss. But it wasn't one of their men; it was Matteo's face that filled her vision and blocked out the light. He looked so much like their father it made her uneasy.

"What are you doing?" she demanded when he started to get in.

"We're all going to the same place, aren't we?"

"Unfortunately," she mumbled, scooting back from the door and pressing herself against the other side of the car to leave as much space between them as possible.

The door closed, plunging them into shadows, the light filtering weakly through the tinted windows. The silence was thick, stifling. Luca reached up to knock on the window separating them from the driver, and the car lurched into motion.

Matteo tapped a finger against his knee and cleared his throat. "You look well, Carina. All grown up."

She snorted. "Some of us had to."

"And what does that mean?"

She heard the irritation in her brother's voice. Good. It wasn't her job to make him feel better about showing up here again as if nothing had changed.

"It means not all of us had the luxury of running away from our responsibilities. You left." She flicked a hand at Luca and Dom, who watched them but didn't intervene. "And we stayed to pick up the pieces."

Matteo shifted, angling his body toward her, but she refused to tear her gaze away from the window. Watching the buildings give way to trees, the bright blue of the sea peeking through the stretch of green.

"Clearly the empire didn't crumble without me."

The car climbed the long, tree-lined drive toward a hilltop villa overlooking the Tyrrhenian Sea and pulled around the fountain pouring water from baskets that looked precariously stacked. The house rose behind the thick wall of the courtyard with its wrought iron balconies and white stone.

In the summer, the windows would be thrown open to catch the breeze coming off the water, her mother's favorite turquoise curtains billowing like searching fingers. It had been a long time since she'd seen home. It was nice being back these last few months.

The car pulled to a stop in front of the courtyard gate, and a moment later, the driver opened her door. Carina carefully folded her veil and pressed out the wrinkles with her fingers.

"The empire might have survived without you, Matteo. But you have no idea what price was paid to keep it afloat."

She slipped from the car, nodding to the driver, then to the butler who opened the gate and the maid who kept pace beside her, prattling in her ear about all the arrangements for the reception. Guests would be arriving in less than half an hour. She needed a moment of peace.

"I trust you have it all in hand, Giulia. I'm going to freshen up, and then I'll be down."

Dismissing the maid, she rounded the corner for the stairs, her heels clicking across the tile floor. At the top, she turned toward her bedroom, easing the door closed and leaning back against it.

She'd fully expected her father to gut her room once she'd married, but it was exactly how she remembered it. The same four-poster bed covered in pale green linens, the delicate table and chairs framing the fireplace in the corner, the rug her mother had given her as a gift for her thirteenth birthday spread out over the patterned tile.

Crossing the room, she kicked off her heels to rest her feet and pulled open the balcony doors. If she craned her neck, she could see the courtyard below like she had last night, but she was more interested in the view of the sea and the breeze on her face.

Closing her eyes, she let it ruffle her hair and wash over her skin, raising goosebumps along her arms and legs. She was ready for the heat of summer, ready to start fresh and put herself back together again. Ready to leave her past where it belonged and forge her own future.

Whatever Matteo's plans for the Bianchi territory and businesses, Carina would make damned sure she wasn't a pawn in any of it. She'd been forced into that game once, and she refused to play it ever again. Whatever her destiny, she was going to forge it with her own two hands if it killed her.

Chapter Two

He stood in the shade of the cabana at the far end of the pool, one hand tucked into the pocket of his slacks, and watched. He'd been watching her all day. Reading her moods through her tells. She smiled without showing her teeth when she was tired, played with her hair when she was annoyed, pressed her lips together when she was trying to hold her tongue.

He'd mapped every bit of her over the years. Always watching, never touching. Never allowed to touch. But the one thing that had always stood between them was gone now. And he might finally be able to get close enough to claim the only thing he'd ever really craved. Carina Bianchi.

She stood on the balcony outside her bedroom, eyes closed, arms wrapped tightly around her perfect body sheathed in black. Her dark brown hair, tinted with reds and golds, blew around her face in the breeze, and he knew her eyes to be an equally rich shade of brown. Eyes that were sad when she'd shown up on the doorstep a few months ago asking to come home.

Her father wanted to turn her away, but Alexei never

would have let that happen. Whatever the price, he would have paid it to have her near again, away from that fucking husband who never deserved her in the first place. The man was old enough to be her father, for fuck's sake.

She opened her eyes when someone called her name, but before she turned to go inside, she caught sight of him. His favorite tell of hers made his mouth tick up at the corner. Whenever she saw him, she swallowed hard, the beautiful column of her throat contracting with the effort. A throat he wanted to get his hands around, wanted to squeeze while she writhed against him, under him. He wanted to feel her pulse under his fingers while he slid in and out of her.

She held his gaze for a long beat, longer than she would have when she was younger, before she married the man who put steel in her spine and distrust in her eyes. She'd left Bianchi territory a shy, sweet, innocent girl who expected the world laid at her feet. A world he'd happily have given to her.

But she'd come back different. Harder. Less willing to trust and more willing to stand up for herself and have her say. He didn't know what had changed her, but it only made him want her more.

Shoving away from the cabana when Carina disappeared inside, Alexei crossed to the wide glass doors and let himself into the great room. Guests had already begun to arrive, loyal Bianchi soldiers and their wives glancing around at their Don's opulent villa, so rarely opened for visitors.

Alexei kept to the edges of the room, ears trained on the conversations he passed. There were whispers about the suicide. People wondering what caused Lorenzo to lock himself in his study, pull out a silver-plated pistol, and blow his brains all over a priceless da Vinci painting.

Another group wondered about Matteo and whether he was back for good. Alexei wanted to know the same. No one had seen or heard from the oldest Bianchi son in years, and suddenly he was here, looking every bit the spitting image of his father, right down to the hard stare permanently fixed on his face.

A murmur went through the crowd, and Alexei glanced at the door. Not Carina. It was the three Bianchi sons. Matteo in his expensive three-piece suit with Dom and Luca at each elbow. They looked like a force, but Alexei knew they were hardly united. Lorenzo delighted in pitting his sons against each other. The more they fought among themselves, the less likely they were to gang up and overthrow him.

It would be interesting to see what came of this. A power struggle? A violent grab for the top spot? Or maybe Matteo would simply wash his hands of the family once and for all and choose a successor in one of his brothers. Whatever the outcome, Alexei wondered if his days serving the Bianchi Don were over. Matteo had never liked him. And the feeling was entirely mutual.

His phone signaled, and he dug it out of his pocket, ignoring how guests scurried out of his way as he moved through the party toward the pool for some privacy. People had always given him a wide berth, whether because of the jagged scar that ran the length of his face or the blood on his hands, he wasn't sure. He didn't care either way. Better they were afraid of you than underestimating you.

He accepted the call once he was alone and pressed the phone to his ear. "Sokolov."

"Sorry to interrupt the festivities." Alexei snorted. "I've got someone you've been trying to find."

Alexei paced away from the door and kept his tone bored. "If it's anyone other than Cappelletti, you're wasting my time."

Muffled sounds drifted through the receiver, then the dull thwack of a blow landing on soft flesh and a pained groan.

"What did you say your name was again?" The question was muffled. Another punch, another groan.

"Eduardo." A cough. "Eduardo Cappelletti."

Alexei's grin was quick and wicked. The father instead of the son. Excellent. "He's mine, Berto. Don't touch him again until I get there."

It sounded like Berto was sulking when he said, "You're coming now? I thought you'd at least wait until after the reception."

Alexei glanced over his shoulder at the door and the people he could see through the glass. "They won't miss me. Besides, Eduardo's son owes us quite a bit of money. And I intend to collect."

Ending the call, Alexei decided against going back through the party and instead rounded the side of the house. This was business that predated Matteo's return on his white horse, and Alexei didn't need his permission to handle Bianchi matters. Not yet. Or at least not for this.

Jogging down the steps to the lower garage, he entered the code for the door and climbed behind the wheel of the classic Aston Martin he'd bought for a steal at auction and fixed up. He careened down the driveway and toward the casino nearest the house. It was the one with the biggest basement, and it was where Alexei liked to do his work. Lorenzo had never much cared where or how Alexei did what needed doing as long as he got results.

The casinos were closed for the day out of respect, and Alexei angled his car by the rear entrance marked Employees. Letting himself in, he took the steep stairs down to the damp cellar. It smelled like the earth, musty and rich. The air was thick; he could feel it filling his lungs before he hit the bottom.

The room closest to the stairs was for storage in case a civilian wandered down where they shouldn't to poke around. The other rooms were for more…unsavory activities.

Stopping by the last door, the light spilled under the crack to brighten his shoes. Alexei rolled his sleeves up to his elbows and cracked his neck.

Eduardo was bound to a wooden chair in the center of the room, a bruise already forming across his jaw, blood trickling down from his nose and over his lip. Berto was relaxed against the wall with his arms crossed over his chest. The single overhead bulb cast harsh shadows on the concrete floor as Alexei strode in, and Eduardo's eyes widened at the sight of him.

"You…you're…" he stammered.

"Yes," Alexei said simply, reaching into his pocket and pulling out the knife he always kept there.

He'd prefer his full tool kit, but he'd left that in his cottage back at the villa. A knife would have to do. He flicked the blade open, and the man flinched, shrinking away from Alexei when he took a step forward and crouched in front of him.

"What are you going to do to me?"

"I'm going to get the money your son owes this casino."

Eduardo blanched. "But I don't have any money. Not enough to cover what he owes."

"Hmm," Alexei replied, pretending to think. "I guess you'll have to tell me where he is, then."

The man hesitated, then swallowed. "I don't know where he is."

Keeping his eyes trained on the tip of the blade, Alexei drew it lightly down the length of his first finger. "Eduardo, this will hurt so much more if you lie to me. You don't want that. Do you?"

Eduardo shook his head violently. "Please. My son is just going through a rough patch. He didn't mean to take so much. Can't we negotiate?"

Berto snorted from his post in the corner, and Alexei

grinned. "The Bianchis aren't interested in a negotiation. Your son borrowed money from this casino to gamble, and now he needs to pay what he owes."

"You can't get something from nothing," Eduardo spat, a little fire coming into his voice. "How's he supposed to give you money he doesn't have?"

Alexei placed the tip of the knife against the pulse in Eduardo's throat, a little thrill going through him when he saw it quicken. Eduardo's fear was a scent on the air so thick he could almost taste it. It was his favorite drug.

"I can be very persuasive. You can tell me where your son is so I can collect, or I can send you to him so he can be reminded of the deal he made. In pieces."

Eduardo swallowed again, the knife pressing into his skin enough to well a drop of blood that slid down the blade, shining in the light.

"What does it matter if I tell you or not? You're going to kill me anyway."

Alexei leaned in until their noses were almost touching, Eduardo's wide eyes staring back into his. "Because I can keep you alive but in unimaginable pain for days. It would be fun to see if I could break my record."

"Y-your record?"

"Mmm," Alexei murmured. "What is it again, Berto?"

"Five days?" Berto tilted his head. "No, it was six. Definitely six."

Eduardo whimpered, and Alexei clicked his tongue in sympathy. "That is your choice. I'll get what I want either way. And you can choose whether you die quickly or slowly." He traced the knife down Eduardo's throat, drawing a thin line of blood. "Which is it going to be?"

"He's my son."

The words were defiant, but Alexei knew by Eduardo's

tone he'd already won. Disappointment flared in his chest. He'd have preferred the slow and painful way.

"Last chance."

Eduardo inhaled a deep, shuddering breath, and his voice shook when he spoke. "Camporeale. He's got a cousin there. They're innocent in this. You'll leave them out of it? They've got childr—"

Alexei didn't let the man finish, drawing the blade across his throat so his sentence faded into sputters and gasps. He stepped back to watch the blood drip down the front of Eduardo's shirt, turning to Berto when he started to twitch.

"Camporeale. You know it?" Alexei wiped the flat of his blade against Eduardo's pants to clean it.

"Well enough. It's not very big. Maybe about an hour's drive from here."

"Good. I want that son of a bitch in this room in forty-eight hours or less."

"Consider it done." Berto followed Alexei into the hall. "I heard Matteo's back."

"He is." Alexei inspected the blade before flipping it closed. "He was at the funeral today."

"What do you think that means?"

Alexei pinned Berto with a bland stare. "How the fuck am I supposed to know?"

"You live there, don't you? Haven't you heard anything?"

"I live on the grounds. In a guest cottage like the other staff. I'm hardly in the inner circle."

"Still, the men are nervous. They don't like not knowing who's in charge. Matteo? Dom? Luca? If they don't choose someone soon, the other families will smell blood in the water. You know Varda has wanted to get his hands on Bianchi territory for years."

"I know." Alexei sighed. "I'm sure we'll have an answer

soon enough. Until then, don't worry about it. Clean up this mess and go get me that little shit from Camporeale."

Leaving Berto to his task, Alexei climbed the stairs and started for home. Berto was right. The men would be anxious without clear leadership. Either Matteo needed to claim his place as the new Don or appoint another.

Until then, they were leaving themselves exposed to anyone who thought they could run this territory better.

Chapter Three

Carina was awake and staring at the ceiling, her eyes tracing a tiny fissure across the plaster she'd never noticed before, when someone knocked on the door. Pushing herself up against the pillows, she ran a hand over her hair and reached for her robe at the end of the bed. Slipping it on and belting it loosely, she cleared her throat.

"Come!"

When Giulia entered without her usual breakfast tray, Carina frowned. Every morning for the last three months, Giulia brought a perfectly prepared cappuccino and her favorite pastry to her room. Carina had no idea why today would be any different. She tilted her head to study the maid wringing her hands, refusing to come any further into the room.

"Is everything all right, Giulia?"

"I'm supposed to say breakfast will be served in the family dining room in an hour."

Carina's eyebrows winged up. No one had eaten in the family dining room since her mother died. She picked at an imaginary piece of lint on the bedspread. "And if I would prefer my usual cappuccino in my room?"

"You may..." Giulia paused to take a deep breath. "You may only have breakfast if you come down to the family dining room in one hour."

Carina's eyes narrowed on the maid's face, and Giulia took a quick step back. "And who gave this ridiculous order?"

"*Il Signore* sa—"

"Don't call him that," Carina snapped, and Giulia winced. Of course this was Matteo's doing. Carina massaged at the headache quickly forming behind her eyebrow. "Did my brother ask you to address him that way?"

"N-no. I just assumed since your father is...since he..." Giulia hung her head. "I just assumed. I'm sorry."

Motioning for Giulia to leave with a flick of her wrist, Carina sighed when the door closed with a gentle click. Not back a full forty-eight hours, and Matteo was already ordering everyone around, terrifying the staff into calling him lord, for fuck's sake. Her hope that Matteo would breeze out as unexpectedly as he'd breezed in was rapidly dying.

She knew he'd have to stay for at least a little while. There was paperwork to sign, assets to see to. The lawyer would be coming by in a day or two to read the will. But she'd prefer he take care of business and leave her the hell alone.

Picking at the lace edge of the coverlet with her fingernail, she debated refusing to come down for breakfast. But Matteo had issued a challenge with this command, and she wouldn't hide from it. She wouldn't back down from a man's challenge ever again. Besides, going down for her morning cappuccino didn't require politeness. She could drink it in silence in the family dining room as easily as she could in her bed.

Throwing back the covers, she set her feet on the cool tile floor and let the goosebumps wash up her calves and over

16

her thighs. Crossing to the bathroom, she sat at her vanity and carefully applied a light layer of makeup. She fully intended to spend most of her afternoon by the pool, soaking up the sunshine the weather was promising, deciding what came next in her life now that she was free from the men who would use her for their own gain. She just had to get through this stupid breakfast first.

After painting her lips a neutral pink, she moved to the closet, running her fingers over the small collection of clothes she'd managed to take with her from her husband's estate. She'd left most of them behind. Gifts from her husband because he preferred she dress a certain way. These clothes were the only thing she'd arrived with that he hadn't thrown away or torn to pieces.

She slipped a deep pink fitted sundress over her head, smoothing the fabric over her curves, and stepped into a pair of casual black flats. With one last appraising look in the mirror, she turned toward the door. Time to get this over with.

The house was quiet as she descended the stairs, the familiar dull roar of the waves hitting the rocks below the villa echoing in the silence. Was she too early? She glanced at the antique clock that hung over the ornate oval mirror in the front hall. No. Matteo would be expecting her any minute if he was being strict about punctuality.

She turned at the sound of a door opening and relaxed a bit seeing Luca coming in from the courtyard. His eyebrow went up at the sight of her downstairs at this hour.

"You were summoned too, I take it."

"I was. Do we know what he wants?"

Luca's brows drew together, but he shook his head. "No."

Carina looked down the hall toward the family dining room, gripping her hands in front of her. "I didn't speak to him much yesterday. I kept myself busy with guests. Did he say anything to you?" She glanced at Luca out of the corner of her eye. "About…everything?"

"No. And not to Dom, either," he said before she could voice the question. "If his mood this morning was any indication."

"Hard to tell," Carina replied. "Dom is never in a good mood."

Luca chuckled and motioned ahead of them for Carina to go first. Taking a deep breath, she crossed the hallway into the family dining room, her steps faltering only slightly at the image that flashed through her mind. Her mother seated at the far end of the table directly to her father's left, laughing into a glass of wine, her black hair cascading over her shoulders and down her back. How old that memory must be, since her mother had died with her naked head wrapped in colorful scarves.

Luca squeezed her shoulder and held a chair out for her at the opposite end of the table, claiming the one next to her as Dom strode in. Dom plopped unceremoniously into a seat across the table, sprawling back against it and looking as irritated as she felt at being ordered around by a brother who hadn't bothered to show his face in nearly a decade.

Matteo was the last to enter, and his smug look at seeing the three of them already waiting around the table made her want to rake her nails across his skin just for the satisfaction of drawing blood.

"I'm glad you all decided to join me." He claimed their father's place and motioned to the butler.

"You didn't give us much choice," Dom pointed out.

"Of course I did. Skipping breakfast wouldn't have killed you."

"Speak for yourself," Luca piped up, reaching for his latte as soon as a maid set it in front of him. "You haven't seen Carina without her cappuccino."

Matteo's grin was easy, his gaze shifting to Carina. "I don't remember you being much of a coffee drinker before."

Carina studied him over the rim of her mug. "A lot has changed since you stormed out."

The grin fell from Matteo's lips and a muscle ticked in his jaw. "Christ. Can't we get through a single hour without you reminding me of how I failed you?"

"Apparently not." Carina shrugged at her brother's narrowed stare. "What did you really want out of this breakfast, Matteo? I can't imagine it was family bonding. We've never been very good at that."

Dom snorted in agreement, and Matteo sighed. "I wanted to see how everything was going at the casinos and—"

"You don't need me here for that."

"And see how you were," he ground out. "To find out what you've been doing since I left."

The laugh bubbled out of her before she could stop it. "You can't be serious. You lost the right to know about my life a long time ago. It'll take a lot more than a command to join you for breakfast to get it back. If that's even possible."

Matteo's jaw clenched, and he stared at her with an unflinching gaze that might have intimidated her once. But she'd been through too much these last few years to cower in the face of one of his tempers.

"Then you can go," Matteo said through clenched teeth.

Carina pushed back from the table and strode toward the door. "Enjoy your day, gentlemen."

When she passed Matteo's chair, his hand shot out and gripped her wrist, squeezing until it ached. "Watch yourself, Carina. You may not like me, but you're damned sure going to respect me."

She tried to wrench her arm away, but he tightened his hold. Looking down at his fingers on her skin, she fought against the anger enveloping her. "Get the fuck off me, Matteo."

He gave her arm a little tug, causing her to lurch forward half a step. "You are my sister and my responsibility. I can't make that disappear any more than you can."

"You sure as hell tried when you walked out on this family after my mother died." Sadness lit Matteo's eyes, maybe a bit of regret. She hoped it was a lead weight around his shoulders. She hoped he drowned under it. "You are nothing to me. Now let go of my fucking arm."

Every head turned at a noise in the corner of the room, and Carina saw her father's man, Alexei, step out of the shadows, his gaze trained on where Matteo still gripped her wrist. The rage on his face might have scared her if it hadn't been directed at her brother.

"I suggest you do as she says and let her go."

Matteo shot to his feet, releasing her in the process, and Alexei moved across the room in quick strides, stopping short when Carina positioned her body between them. "Enough."

She felt the heat of Alexei at her back, and the urge to lean into him instead of away caught her off guard.

"Do your business and make your choices, Matteo. I can't stop you. But don't think just because you're here, just because you're sitting in Father's chair, you can snap your fingers and expect me to obey."

Breezing out of the room without a backward glance, she crossed to the archway leading to the courtyard and pulled open the heavy wooden door. The air washed over her, and she pulled sea air deep into her lungs, turning her face up to the sun. If she had to take what little money she had and start over far from Sicily, she would do it. She would do anything to ensure her freedom again.

The door opened and closed with a heavy groan, and she knew without turning around it was Alexei. He didn't speak, just watched in the same intense way he had ever since they were children. The memory of the day they first met was as vivid as her memories of her mother.

Her father had brought him home dirty and covered in blood. Alexei had been left in the hall outside her father's study while her father and his favored capos shouted on the other side of the door. He had a fresh cut down the side of his face but wouldn't say how he got it.

It's not your kind of story, he'd said. *It doesn't have a happy ending.*

Alexei had always intrigued her, had always called to something deep inside her that she couldn't explain. She'd often wondered if her father knew of her fascination with the boy who became his deadliest weapon. If that was why he sent her to boarding school and then married her off entirely too young to a man entirely too old.

It hardly mattered now. It didn't matter how much Alexei called to that unseen part of her or how her body warmed when she felt his eyes on her or how she yearned to know the deepest, darkest parts of him to see if they matched the deepest, darkest parts of her.

She could never allow herself to get close enough to any man ever again. She could never allow herself to lose control.

Chapter Four

Alexei sat at a small table in the little kitchen area in his quarters, cleaning and sharpening the tools in his kit. A craftsman was only as good as his equipment, and he prided himself on taking care of his things. Wiping the scalpel's honed edge with a soft cloth, he slipped it into its pocket and picked up a pair of long, thin tweezers.

There was still no news from Berto about the Cappelletti thief hiding out in Camporeale. Berto had twelve hours left to find him and bring him back to Palermo, but Alexei was eager to work out his frustrations. Especially after his confrontation with Matteo this morning. Or his almost confrontation.

He poured cleaning solution onto a rag and ran it over the tweezers, careful to get it into the grooves and wash away any evidence that might remain from their last use. It had been years since he'd stood that close to Carina. Close enough to smell the delicate floral scent of her hair, to feel the heat of her skin. Close enough to touch.

Then there was the look in her eyes when he'd followed her into the courtyard. Want. Something he'd never expected to see from her. At least not without a little encouragement. But it had been there in her gaze, her eyes traveling down the length of his body and back up to his face.

He would have closed the distance between them, crushed her body to his, and finally claimed her mouth if not for Luca interrupting them. Soon. All he had to do was deal with Matteo first.

The door to his two-room cottage flew open, and without looking up, Alexei knew it would be Matteo framed in the doorway. Speak of the fucking devil. Matteo said nothing, simply waited to be acknowledged. The man grew more and more like his father with each passing second.

"Your father was also immune to knocking."

"This is my property."

Alexei carefully set the tweezers back in their spot and leaned back in his chair before meeting Matteo's gaze with a casual tilt of his head. "Is it?"

Matteo's scowl deepened. "It is until I say otherwise."

"Of course. Boss." Alexei sneered the word. "To what do I owe the honor?"

"Do you enjoy your job?" Matteo shoved his hands into his pockets, his eyes traveling over the sparsely furnished space. "Enjoy working for the Bianchi family?"

Alexei's hands curled into fists in his lap, but he forced himself to relax, to clear his mind of every murderous thought that wanted to flit through it. His ability to completely detach and remain calm is what made him so good at his job. A job the Bianchi Don, whoever it ended up being, needed him to keep doing if they wanted to maintain control over this territory.

It would take absolutely no effort for Alexei to defect to another family. The Antonettis, who ran the Syracuse territory, had tried to poach him several times. Even the Gallo Don had approached him about contract work a few years ago. Being able to get information out of even the most stubborn target or kill someone and make it look like an accident was a very marketable skill.

"I'm not interested in being threatened today, Matteo. Did you have something you needed to say?"

"Something that obviously should have been made clear to you a long time ago. Stay away from my sister."

Alexei glanced down at the neat row of implements glinting in the light from the window. It wouldn't take much effort to bury one of them, any of them, into the side of Matteo's neck, cutting off his air supply so he couldn't even scream for help. His body would weaken quickly with that much blood loss.

He allowed himself a brief moment to picture watching this smug son of a bitch bleed out all over his floor. But as much as he might enjoy it, he wouldn't do that to Carina. Unless she asked him to, of course.

"No."

"Excuse me?" Matteo demanded.

"No. I won't be taking orders from you. Not where Carina is concerned. You want to aim my blade and my skill at a target who threatens the Bianchi businesses? Fine. But that's where your influence over me ends."

"Maybe I'll get rid of you, then."

Alexei laughed. "You could try to kill me. But you won't."

"No?" Irritation laced the single word, and Alexei grinned.

"Your father is dead. The alliance with the Romanos is tenuous at best, and Varda is eager to make a move. You can't afford to look weak now. And how do you think getting rid of me makes you look?"

Matteo was quiet for a long moment, his fingers reaching up to twist his watch around his wrist. Alexei let him have his silence, carefully rolling up his leather tool kit and securing it with thin ties.

"What Romano alliance?"

"No one's briefed you on that?"

Alexei's eyebrow shot up when Matteo shook his head. The Bianchi brothers were really going to have to work on their communication if they wanted to keep this territory afloat.

"She was married to the Romano Don a couple years after you left." The thought of it still made his blood boil, but he shoved that down too.

"Giuseppe?" Alexei nodded. "Fuck. He's three times her age."

"He was."

Matteo's head swiveled from the spot he was examining on the far wall, and he met Alexei's gaze. "Was?"

"Died of a heart attack about three months ago." Served the greedy, disgusting bastard right.

"And so she came home."

Alexei stood, storing his tools in a cabinet over the sink. "She did. Your father wanted to turn her away. Send her back to Cefalù to see if she could charm her way into the new Don's bed, act as his mistress to keep the alliance intact since they didn't have any children."

He gripped the edge of the counter so hard he thought it might splinter in his fingers. The idea of Lorenzo pimping Carina out to another Romano had enraged him so much it had taken everything in his power not to wrap his hands around Lorenzo's throat for even suggesting it.

"Let me guess. You talked him out of it."

Turning, Alexei leaned back against the counter, crossing one ankle over the other. "I did. Why? Would you have preferred she become a Romano whore?"

Matteo's jaw clenched, a muscle ticking away. "Of course

not. She should never have been married to that fuck in the first place."

"Maybe she wouldn't have been if you'd stayed. But," he went on when Matteo opened his mouth to hurl a retort, "it's done, and he's dead. All that matters now is what you plan on doing about it."

"About repairing the alliance?"

"About all of it. The alliance, the casinos, the family, the territory. Are you going to man up and be the Don these people need, or are you going to run again? Whatever you decide, you need to choose soon because the men are getting restless."

"The last person in the world I want to be taking advice from is you," Matteo snapped, taking a step back over the threshold, then pausing. There was reluctance in his voice when he asked, "What have you heard?"

Alexei shook his head. "About what you'd expect from men who've just lost their Don and don't know who's calling the shots. Dom, who's been here all along but prefers to serve as a Bianchi general? Luca, who has a good head for business? You? The long-lost son finally returned home to take his rightful place?"

His phone signaled an incoming message, cutting through the mounting tension, and Alexei dug it out of his pocket. Berto. "Business doesn't stop while you figure your shit out."

"I'm aware of that," Matteo bit off. "Go handle whatever that is." He nodded his chin toward the phone in Alexei's hand when it trilled again. "You can brief me about it when you get back."

"Sure thing, boss," Alexei replied with a sarcastic smirk, firing off a quick text to Berto and reaching behind him for his tool kit.

Matteo turned on his heel and disappeared, leaving the door swinging on the hinges. Alexei rolled his eyes. Tucking his kit under his arm, he stepped onto the small front walk and secured the lock. The breeze carried a scent to his nose he'd recognize anywhere, and he took a slow, deep breath.

"Carina," he said into the silence. There was a pause, then the rustle of a nearby tree before she emerged. "Were you eavesdropping?"

She crossed her arms over her chest and cocked a hip, her eyes alight with defiance. "I saw Matteo coming down here, and I wanted to make sure he didn't do what he always does."

Alexei raised a brow. "And what is that?"

"Make his poor choices everyone else's problem."

"And you stayed because?"

Her cheeks flushed an enticing shade of pink, but she didn't break eye contact. "Because no one ever tells me anything."

"Mmm," he murmured, turning toward the lower garage, pleased when she jogged to catch up and kept pace with his long strides. "And what did you learn?"

"I didn't know you knew all of that. About the Romanos." Her voice was soft, and something in it made him want to comfort her.

"I know about a lot of things. You can learn quite a lot when people forget you're standing in the shadows."

She waited with him while the garage door lumbered up the tracks and stepped in behind him, laying a hand on his arm when he moved to open the car door. "Did you really talk my father out of sending me back to them?"

He glanced down at her fingers on his bare skin, the heat radiating up his arm from the contact. The heady scent of her shampoo in his nose was distracting. "I did."

"Thank you," she said softly, her hand lingering a moment more before she dropped it to her side, curling her fingers into her palm. "Matteo needs you, you know."

He reached up to tuck her hair behind her ear, then captured her chin gently in his hand and dragged the flat of his thumb over her lower lip. When she didn't pull away, he moved closer until their bodies were almost touching.

"I know." His eyes dipped down to her mouth, then back up to meet her gaze. "I suspect he'll figure that out soon enough. And you?"

"Me?" she asked breathlessly.

Another step, his hand slipping to cup her jaw and tilt her face up. "What do you need?"

Her eyes didn't leave his, didn't wander to trail a path down the jagged scar painting the length of his face from eyebrow to jaw. The fact that she could hold his gaze, that she didn't shrink from it, only made him hungrier for her.

"I need—"

The ring of his phone sliced through her words, and he silently cursed the interruption when she stepped out of his reach, hugging her arms tightly around herself. He'd have to punch Berto in the throat when he saw him.

"We'll finish this later," he assured her, grinning when her eyes darkened.

Climbing behind the wheel, he gunned the engine before peeling out of the garage. He watched her in the rearview mirror until he turned the corner and she disappeared. He'd have to find her when he got back and coax from her exactly what she needed.

He would give every bit of it to her and then some.

Chapter Five

Carina hadn't seen Alexei in days. Not since he'd almost kissed her. Not since she'd almost let him kiss her. It was just as well, since kissing him would be a huge mistake. Giving into Alexei and all he might offer her was a terrible idea. One she hadn't been able to stop thinking about.

When they were children, he intrigued her because he seemed like a wounded animal. When she was a teenager, it was because he was forbidden, her father forever warning her to stay away from Alexei and let him do his work. Now he intrigued her because she wasn't the girl she'd been. Life had changed her, darkened her, demanded too much.

He might be able to give her all the things she craved, pluck her secrets out of the deepest parts of her soul and hold them up to the light and see them for exactly what they were without turning away. That was precisely why she couldn't let herself go there with him. She could never be that naive and unguarded with someone again. Least of all someone like Alexei. Someone who could ruin her and make her love every second of it.

At a knock on the door, she looked up to see Luca standing in the doorway, eyes trained on his phone. "Did you need something?"

He typed out a quick message before giving her his attention. "Lawyer's almost here."

"All right."

"Matteo wants you at the meeting."

Carina's brows shot up, but Luca disappeared from the door before she could ask any questions. She hadn't spent much time with Matteo since their confrontation at breakfast. When they'd passed each other in the hall a few times, he nodded politely but didn't initiate conversation. She didn't mind; she expected him to leave soon anyway. Meeting with the lawyer over the contents of the will was the last piece he needed to take care of before he could go. But she wasn't sure why he would want her there.

As a daughter in this world, she had little say in anything at all. Her father had certainly never asked for her opinion on anything or included her in business matters. What she knew about Bianchi interests, she knew secondhand. She hadn't even known about her father's plan to shove her back into Romano clutches until she overheard Alexei say it to her brother the other day.

She shivered at the idea. Laying still while one Romano grunted on top of her was bad enough. She couldn't imagine doing it a second time just so her father could hold on to whatever shred of power and security the alliance afforded him. Plus, Elio Romano was rumored to be even more heartless than his father was. If that was possible.

Carina would have slit her wrists before spending another second in Romano territory, closed up in that pretty house overlooking the sea that was more like a prison. If Matteo wanted her at that meeting so he could announce another Romano match, he'd be very disappointed with her reply.

Alexei wouldn't have to stop him; they'd be collecting her body from the base of the cliffs.

Pushing out of the chair and setting her book on a nearby table, she smoothed her skirt and made her way downstairs. Her father's study sat at the back of the house, tucked into a corner at the end of a long hallway. It's probably why no one heard the gunshot the morning he killed himself. A maid, checking to see if he wanted lunch, found him slumped over his desk in a pool of blood. Carina could still hear the maid's terrified screams.

Stopping in the doorway, she surveyed the room. It looked perfect, not a thing out of place, not a speck of blood in sight. The only noticeable difference was the Monet in place of the da Vinci on the wall behind the desk. Her mouth split into a wry grin. That must have been Matteo's choice, because her father hated French art.

Matteo was seated on one of the leather couches, sifting through a stack of papers in front of him, a glass of iced tea at his elbow. He glanced up when she cleared her throat and motioned for her to sit, but didn't speak. Sinking down into one of the leather armchairs, she watched him.

It was hard to remember what he was like before. So much time had passed. She remembered him being ambitious, constantly butting heads with their father over plans to grow their empire and their profits. He'd wanted to invest in more legitimate enterprises to cover their illegal dealings and create international connections, while her father wanted to stay rooted in Sicily, stick to the old ways that had always worked.

Matteo's push to make changes is why their father favored Dom. Dom was loyal and steady, ruthless in the ways their father appreciated. Dom policed the casinos with an iron fist, using Alexei and others to enforce deals and loans and discourage cheating the house. Matteo liked to plan. Dom liked to get his hands dirty.

Voices drifted in from the hall moments before Luca and Dom appeared, heads bent together, discussing casino business, no doubt. Dom handled the floor and enforcement, and Luca dealt with the business aspect. Luca was smarter than their father ever gave him credit for.

Matteo sat back against the couch, rubbing his eyes and pinching the bridge of his nose. He checked his watch. "Lawyer should be here any second."

Minutes later, the butler stepped into the doorway and announced the lawyer. He was a short, round man with a receding hairline and square glasses that looked about two decades out of fashion. He shook her brothers' hands and gave her a polite nod.

"Is everyone staying?" he asked, setting his briefcase on the table and casting Carina a sideways glance. She had to fight not to roll her eyes.

"Everyone stays," Matteo replied.

The man gave a quick nod and opened his briefcase with a pop, lifting the lid and pulling file folders out of its depths. Dom leaned one shoulder against the bookcase, eyes trained on the folders. Would their father go with tradition and name Matteo as heir, or did he give up on his oldest son and name Dom instead? They were all about to find out.

Flipping open the top folder, the man pulled out a piece of paper and began to read from it. "There are four properties in total. A villa in Marsala, an apartment in Naples, a townhouse in London, and the villa here in Palermo. There's a small collection of cars as well as the yacht. All of this is to be left to Matteo Bianchi in its entirety."

Dom shifted but didn't speak, and it was impossible to read what he was thinking, his face a blank mask. The lawyer cleared his throat, and when Carina turned to face him again, she noticed Alexei leaning against the opposite wall in the hallway, listening. He held a finger to his lips and grinned.

"Financial assets are to be divided as follows. Five million to Carina Bianchi Romano." Carina twitched at the use of her married name. If she could scrub that from existence, she would in a heartbeat. "Fifteen million each to Domenico and Luca Bianchi, with the remaining money going to Matteo Bianchi for the upkeep of the family properties and possessions."

Slipping another piece of paper out of the folder, the lawyer continued. "Then there is the matter of the family businesses. There are six casinos in the Palermo territory, and upon your father's death, once you are notified of the arrangement, 50 percent ownership transfers to Giuseppe Romano or his heir if he is no longer living."

"They what?" Matteo sat forward, elbows braced on his knees, and the lawyer shrank back from the look on his face. "What the fuck are you talking about?" Matteo twisted around to look at Dom and Luca. "Did you two know about this?"

"Of course not," Dom snarled. "You think I've worked this hard to bring profits up so we could split them with Elio fucking Romano?"

"I've been all over the offices at the casinos in the last few years," Luca said. "I don't remember ever seeing anything like this."

The lawyer mopped at the sweat beading on his brow and glanced at Carina. "This was part of your sister's marriage contract. Giuseppe Romano gave your father a sizable loan in exchange for Carina's hand in marriage and a 50 percent stake in the casinos."

"So he traded my body and our businesses," Carina spat, clenching her hands in her lap until they ached. "For cash."

The man flushed bright red. Matteo held his hand out for the paper, and the lawyer laid it in his palm. Eyes quickly scanning the page, Matteo made a guttural sound low in his throat. Carina's heart sank. There's no way they could be tied to the Romanos like this. They wouldn't survive it. Elio would destroy them.

"How do we get out of this?" Matteo demanded.

"The only way to avoid sharing ownership is to pay off the loan with interest in full."

"And how much is that?"

The man swallowed hard, accepting the paper from Matteo and placing it in the folder before responding. "One billion euros."

"Son of a fucking bitch." Matteo shoved off the couch to pace, raking a hand through his hair. "There must be a loop-hole, a weakness in the agreement we can exploit."

"Your father tried to get me to find one a few weeks before he died, but I couldn't. It's ironclad. Once I let the Romano lawyer know you've been notified, he'll confirm the deal with Elio, and it will be done."

He shoved the folders into his briefcase and closed it with a snap, quickly rising while Matteo continued to pace back and forth in front of the sofa. "You know where to reach me if you have any questions."

"How long?"

"I'm sorry?" the lawyer said, pausing to look back at Matteo from the door.

"If we decide to buy our way out, how long do we have to pay?"

"One month."

Matteo nodded in dismissal, and the man skirted Alexei in the hallway and disappeared. One month to come up with one billion euros in cash. It wasn't possible.

"This is insane. Neither of you knew about this?" Matteo whirled on Dom and Luca.

"That he pimped out our sister and sold off our

birthright?" Luca snorted. "It's safe to say that no, we had no fucking idea."

"And you." Matteo motioned Alexei forward. "You never heard a word of this from my father?"

"Your father didn't exactly keep me in his confidence. Most of our conversations consisted of who he wanted me to kill and for how much money." Alexei shrugged, but Carina could tell he didn't like this news any more than they did. "I knew he got something when he promised Carina to Giuseppe, but I had no idea he did this."

"You're not seriously considering paying Elio Romano one billion euros, are you?" Carina wondered.

"You'd rather share 50 percent of the casinos for the rest of our lives? Our children's and grandchildren's lives?"

"I'd rather do neither."

Dom snorted. "And how do you propose we manage that?"

"Refuse to pay and deal with the Romanos."

Luca straightened in his seat. "And by deal with, you mean…"

"Kill them."

The words were out of her mouth before she could stop them. But now that they existed, she had no intention of taking them back. She'd craved Romano blood from the first backhand to the face. And this shitty corner their father had backed them into presented the perfect opportunity. They could have what was theirs, and she could have her vengeance.

"Kill the Romanos," Matteo repeated, and she nodded. "That's a big ask."

"What other choice do we have?"

"She's right," Dom agreed. "When Varda gets wind of this, he'll descend in earnest. We've had to remove three Varda spies from the territory in the last three weeks."

"You're sure they were Varda men?"

"I'm sure," Alexei said.

She glanced up at Alexei across the room. He was leaning back against the wall, one foot pressed flat against the surface, but his eyes were alert. He dragged his thumb back and forth over his jaw while he watched her.

Sensing Matteo's hesitation, Carina changed tactics. "Transfers of power are messy, Matteo. You're Don now, but you've been gone for a long time. A show of force would go a long way in solidifying your place and earning respect. From all of Sicily."

"The agreement would only transfer from one heir to the next in perpetuity."

"People will agree to anything when you inflict enough pain on them," Alexei reminded him.

"A targeted attack until they back down." Matteo twisted his watch on his wrist while he considered. "We could spare some of them, I suppose."

"Those bastards have earned every scrap of violence they get." Shoving out of her chair, she gripped the back of it with white knuckles, anger racing along her skin. "Not a single one of them deserves to be spared."

When she looked at Alexei again, his mouth was set in a hard line, his eyes a storm. He studied her with a different kind of intensity now.

"Carina." Matteo's voice was soft, but his eyes were searching, calculating. "What did they do?"

For the first time in months, she let the memories she'd buried float to the surface. Let the pain and the fear and the anger hum along her skin. Let it fuel her. But she wasn't willing to share those details with her brother. Not yet.

"It doesn't matter." She crossed her arms over her chest. "Unless you want to sell off all our things, spend every penny we have, and weaken us in front of all of Sicily, breaking the Romanos before they break us is the only way forward."

Matteo didn't stop her when she turned for the door, but soft footsteps followed her down the hallway to the stairs. Only the hand that gripped her elbow and pulled her to a stop wasn't Matteo.

"What did they do to you?" Alexei's voice was a growl that had heat pooling in her core. The look in his eyes made her pulse pound.

Her chin ticked up. "If I'm not going to tell my brother, what makes you think I'll tell you?"

His smile was quick and wild, and she swallowed hard. He pressed forward until she felt the wall against her back, his body barely brushing hers. Like the other day when he'd almost kissed her, he smelled of warm spices, and she breathed it in.

"Because unlike your brother, I won't hesitate to make them pay." Alexei pressed the flat of his palm against the wall by her head and moved closer, dropping his head to whisper against her ear. "And I can make it as quick or as painful as you like."

She nearly groaned, both from the promise and the way his body dragged against hers. This was why he was so dangerous. Not because he would give her the violence she craved, the blood, the destruction. But because she would enjoy it.

"Whatever Matteo decides," Alexei whispered, his lips brushing the shell of her ear and sending shivers down her spine, "I'll make sure whoever hurt you pays a thousand times over."

He stepped away from her, and she suddenly hated the distance between them, hated the cold that swept over her skin now that he wasn't pressed against her.

"Alexei!" Matteo called from the study.

Alexei held her gaze for a long beat before turning and joining her brothers. When he was gone, she took a deep, shuddering breath. Maybe she should let Alexei coax out her own darkness. It would be a small price to pay to spill Romano blood and show all of Sicily what the Bianchis were capable of.

Chapter Six

Inhaling deep, Carina held her breath and dove under the surface of the water, angling toward the bottom and tracing her fingertips over her family's crest. The shield to represent strength, the knight's helmet to represent honor, the sun to represent glory. Kicking to the surface, she wiped water out of her eyes and floated on her back, staring up at the fat white clouds drifting past.

There was still no official word from Matteo on his plans for the family or the deal with the Romanos. He'd asked the lawyer to delay notifying the Romano attorney they'd been informed for a week so they could make plans. The lawyer had agreed, but Matteo only had two days left before Elio Romano knew his 50 percent stake in the company was activated—if he didn't know of his father's deal already.

The longer Matteo took to decide, the more restless she felt. She'd become singularly focused on getting her revenge since mentioning it to her brothers the week before. She knew Alexei would help her if it came to it. He'd already cornered her once in the hallway outside her room, demanding again to know who'd hurt her and what they'd done.

She was torn between giving him all the details and keeping it to herself. Not because she was embarrassed or ashamed, but because she knew how he would react, knew he would burst into Romano territory and dispatch them all brutally without an ounce of remorse. And as much as she wanted that to happen, she didn't want it to happen without her. She wasn't going to be an innocent bystander in this.

If they were going to die, she wanted to watch them writhe in pain first. She wanted to inflict it. The idea both thrilled and terrified her. She didn't know if she was capable of that kind of violence, but the more she thought about it, the more she wanted to find out. The more she wanted to ask Alexei to show her. It was its own kind of dangerous game. And she wanted to play it.

When a cloud eased across the sun and didn't relent, she swam to the edge of the pool and lifted herself out, drying herself with an oversized towel before the breeze had the chance to turn the water droplets on her skin to ice. The air might be warm and the pool heated, but the wind could still bite at this time of year.

Wringing out her hair, she twisted it into a quick braid to keep it off her neck and stretched out on one of the loungers, eyes fluttering closed. The cloud moved to free the sun, and a familiar prickling tingle washed over her skin. Alexei was watching her.

"Do you still paint?"

"Paint?" She looked up when his shadow fell across the lounger, shielding her eyes to see him more clearly.

He nodded toward the notebook at her feet. "I remember you used to paint when you came home from school. Your mother loved them."

She squeezed her eyes shut at the memory of her mother's delighted peal of laughter each time she was presented with a finished painting, her mouth tilting up in a sad smile. "No," she said softly. "I wasn't allowed to paint in Cefalù."

He studied her for a beat, the sun shining down on his dark blond hair and turning it gold, and then gave a curt nod. "Your brother called a meeting."

She leapt to her feet, ignoring the way his eyes raked down her body, lingering on her breasts. Ignoring how much she wanted to feel his hands and his mouth follow the path his eyes took. Wiping the last of the water from her skin, she slipped a thin cover-up dress over her head and belted it at the waist.

"Did he finally decide?"

"I assume so." He waited for her to scoop up her notebook and matched her pace inside. "Any idea which way he's leaning?"

"No." She slipped around him through the door when he held it open. "He's been holed up in the study most of the week with either Luca or Dom or both. I can't figure out if he's been selling off assets to pay back the loan or making plans to..."

"To do what you suggested?"

"Yeah." She blew out a breath. "What if he pays the loan?"

"Then he's an idiot, and I'll kill them myself."

She looked up at him, a small smile curving her lips. "I know. Alexei," she said when he moved to enter the study. "Thank you."

He reached for her, looping his arm around her waist and drawing her close. Cupping her jaw, he brushed the pad of his thumb across her cheek. Being this close to him had her heart pounding and desire skipping along her skin. She was finding it harder and harder to come up with reasons to stay away from him, to not give into this crushing need for him.

"Anything for you, Carina," he whispered.

He dipped his head to capture her lips, and she braced to let him, to drink him in, when the door opened behind them and Matteo pinned them both with a disapproving stare.

"I thought I told you to stay away from my sister."

"And I thought I told you it was none of your business."

With a roll of her eyes, Carina wriggled out of Alexei's grasp and poked her finger into her brother's chest. "And I'll remind you both I'm a grown woman, not a piece of property, and can make my own choices. You wanted a meeting?"

Matteo grumbled something unintelligible under his breath but ushered them both inside, where Dom and Luca were already waiting. She remained standing, too nervous to sit, and Alexei hovered close while Matteo leaned back against the edge of their father's desk. He drained the last of a glass of wine and set it on the wood with a delicate clink.

"I made a mistake."

"You'll have to be more specific," Carina said when he didn't continue, crossing her arms over her chest.

"Leaving Sicily, this family, was a mistake." He met Carina's gaze across the room. "One I won't be making again."

"You're staying?" She couldn't disguise the surprise edging her voice. She had to be careful not to expect too much from him. He'd let them all down before. "For how long?"

"*Finché morte,*" he replied. Until death was the family motto. You serve the Bianchi name until death and not before. "I've been going over the books and businesses with Dom and Luca all week, getting up to speed. Margins are good, profits are better."

Carina's heart sank, and she glanced at Alexei, who was shaking his head. He must be thinking the same thing she was. Matteo was going to pay.

"Which is why we won't be sharing any of them with the Romanos."

Her head whipped up, her hands tightening on her arms. "You're backing out of the deal?"

"I am. If I'd been here, I never would have let Father make that deal. I regret I wasn't and that you were the one who paid the highest price. So you'll get your revenge, we'll keep our casinos, and all of Sicily will understand the new Bianchi Don is not to be trifled with."

Carina took an eager step forward. "How?"

"I intend to make it very clear what this island can expect from me, starting with the Romanos."

She rubbed warmth into her arms while Matteo took them through his strategy. It wasn't just revenge or a show of force; it was a take down extending far beyond the Romano family and their territory. Matteo wanted to dominate all of Sicily.

These were the ambitious plans her father had always scoffed at, but she was ripe for them. It was time to shake things up, to pull the Bianchi name out of the shadows, and if they were going to do that, they might as well end up on top. A confrontation with the Romanos would no doubt filter down to the other families.

To the southwest, Varda had been pushing the border of their territories for years, always trying to goad their father into making a move. Now Matteo was making one—a very calculated one. And if Varda or anyone else decided to advance, they'd be playing right into Matteo's hands. It was brilliant.

"I'm going to meet with all of our capos tomorrow in Marsala. Make sure they understand I'm in this and want their support. We'll need them to be bought into this plan if we have a hope of succeeding."

"They will be," Alexei assured him.

Matteo nodded. "I'm hoping so. Still, I want the three of you there." He gestured at the men in the room. "The soldiers trust you. It'll be good for them to see you're on my side." His gaze shifted to Alexei. "Assuming you're on my side."

Alexei inclined his head, eyes flicking to Carina and back to Matteo. "I've defended Bianchi interests for over fifteen years. No need to stop now when it's going in the right direction."

"I want to help too," Carina said, chin ticking up when all eyes turned to her.

"Help how?" Luca wondered. "With what?"

"I want to have a hand in their destruction. I can give you whatever information you need about them. I won't be left out of this, Matteo."

"It's too dangerous." Matteo shook his head. "You'll be a target. I won't put you at risk like that."

"I don't care. I need to do this. For myself. You owe it to me," she finished.

When Matteo shifted his gaze to Alexei, she did as well. They studied each other for a long moment and whatever passed between them had Matteo reluctantly nodding his head. "Fine. But I decide if and when it gets too dangerous for you."

"But—"

"No buts. I won't risk you. You can help, but if I decide you need protection or to step back, you'll listen. It's my only offer. Take it or leave it."

She glanced at Alexei, who lifted a shoulder. Of course on this one thing they were agreed. "Okay. But whatever meeting you have with Elio, I want to be there."

"We'll see." Matteo held up his hand when Carina began to protest. "Once Elio knows of the deal, or knows that we know, in any case, I expect him to reach out. When he does, I'll set up a meeting under the guise of working out the details. If I think it's safe, you can go."

Carina huffed, but agreed. "Encourage him to meet somewhere public. He's unlikely to make a scene. He likes his image too much. Are you sure this will work?"

"Yes," Luca assured her. "He'll expect a reluctant partnership."

"And he'll get a war."

Chapter Seven

Alexei stood on the stone balcony overlooking the vineyards, neat rows of growing bushes stretching back as far as the eye could see. They rustled in the breeze off the water, their leaves stirring in a low symphony. The sound of car doors slamming and voices floated up from below, and after one last look, he headed inside.

He'd stayed up half the night with Matteo going over what Dom and Luca already knew. Matteo's plans for the onslaught were solid, and his orders for the men would instill loyalty and earn him more than a little respect.

Matteo wasn't going to hold them back. If they wanted to exercise old feuds on Romano men, hell, any men, they could so long as it furthered the end game. Matteo didn't want to topple the empire; he wanted to conquer it. And not a single capo or soldier would be opposed to that.

Staff scurried around, opening up the house for their last-minute arrival and quickly darting out of his way. He'd only been to this house once, when he was a boy. Marsala was their summer villa, and Alexei wasn't family.

The only time they'd ever brought him on holiday was

right after Lorenzo scooped him up off the streets and brought him back to the villa in Palermo. It was only a few days before they were set to leave for Marsala, and the wound on his face was still healing, angry and in constant need of cleaning and changing.

He'd been off on an errand, running something to a club or a soldier. He couldn't quite remember. When he got back and sought out Lorenzo for his next task, he heard arguing. Lorenzo's gruff voice, a woman's softer one, and a girl. A defiant, stubborn girl.

He has to come, Father, she'd said. *He's hurt, and we need to look after him until he's better.*

It was one of the only times in his life when someone wasn't fighting to leave him behind. He'd still spent most of his time working, running errands and fetching papers. It's not like Palermo and Marsala were far.

But Carina had spent the entire summer slipping him cakes and candy and his favorite fruit from the kitchens when no one was looking. He hadn't been back since, but it would forever remind him of her, of the only person who'd never expected something in return for their kindness.

Jogging down the stairs, he turned toward the front of the house and made his way out to the courtyard, where a large round table and chairs had been arranged. There were seven steadfastly loyal Bianchi capos left since Lorenzo never replaced Andrea DiMarco after he went to America and got himself killed for his trouble. DiMarco might have been a favored Bianchi capo once, but he'd wanted more than he could get for himself in Sicily. Turns out he hadn't been able to find it in America either.

Alexei knew from Berto and some of his own conversations the men were wary, but Matteo needed them on his side if this was going to work. His father had always been good at inspiring his soldiers. Hopefully Matteo had a hell of a speech planned. Alexei didn't doubt they would recognize Matteo as the new Don, but they'd go a lot farther if they actually respected him.

The men nodded in his direction, but no one approached. Alexei held an odd place in the Bianchi organization. Not a capo, but not quite a soldier. Since he was thirteen, he'd essentially operated as Lorenzo's personal errand boy until he graduated to assassin when Lorenzo learned of his unique skill.

Alexei had killed so many people in the last decade he'd lost track. His body count and his proximity to the Don had afforded him respect and trust, but he still didn't belong. He was a Russian boy who'd been dumped at an orphanage in Naples. He was left there to wither until, by some miracle, he was unearthed and transported to Sicily and given a purpose.

It might not be the life he would have chosen for himself, but he'd always been destined for violence. And if not for Lorenzo, he'd never have met Carina.

Matteo stepped into the courtyard, interrupting Alexei's thoughts, and the chatter died. He was dressed down today, opting for white slacks and a light green button-down instead of his usual dark suit and tie. He looked...relatable, Alexei mused. And it worked, the men visibly relaxing before taking their seats.

"Thank you for coming." Matteo moved to the head of the table. "My father's death was sudden, and unfortunately, we'll never really know why he did what he did. But his desire for me to take over the family was made clear in his will."

Matteo gestured toward where his brothers sat on either side of the head of the table. "I've spoken with both of my brothers, and I know everything you've done to keep this territory going, keep profits up, and protect Bianchi interests in my absence, and I thank you."

A rumble of appreciation went around the table before dying down again. "I have neglected my birthright for far too long, but I'm back to take my place. Until death," he added.

"Until death," a few of the men intoned.

"You're staying for good then, is what you're saying," Abela piped up.

"Yes. I'm staying for good. I have big plans for us."

"Like what?" someone demanded. Alexei couldn't see who.

Matteo flashed a grin. "I know Bianchi influence has been declining. It was tenuous when I was here. Not enough to be challenged, at least not outright, but enough to spread us thin and siphon off some of our profits."

"Yeah," Carlozzi said. "Like the bigger casinos that keep popping up in Antonetti hotels."

Matteo's jaw clenched, then relaxed again. "I have plans for Antonetti, but first, we're going after the Romanos."

Matteo took them through the deal his father made, and Alexei could tell it surprised some but not others. He'd have to dig more into that later. If their men knew the deal was happening, why didn't any of them reach out to Dom or Luca or even him to stop it? Or maybe they weren't surprised Lorenzo would sell his soul for whatever he needed that cash infusion for.

He remembered the casinos being in a rough spot in those months, but he'd never really known why. And once Carina was promised to Giuseppe, he'd been too consumed with that to question why things seemed to turn around almost overnight. Looking back, he felt like a fool for missing what was obviously right in front of him.

"So when this is all over," Abela said, "Elio Romano will be..."

"Dead," Alexei replied, drawing everyone's attention.

"You're taking out the Romano Don?"

A murmur went up around the table, and Matteo glared at Alexei over his shoulder, who only shrugged. No point in lying to them. No matter what went down, Elio Romano wouldn't walk away from this.

"He has other crimes to answer for. So yes, I'm taking out the Romano Don. He doesn't have any sons to step into the role, so I plan to choose a successor. One who will be pliable, easy to manipulate."

"All you have to do is distract any of them with big tits, and you can do whatever you want," Rossi added, and the table burst into laughter, voices overlapping.

None of them would make it out of this alive. Alexei planned to take out the entire Romano line. But no sense in interrupting Matteo again and earning another irritated scowl.

"The point is," Matteo continued, refocusing everyone's attention, "my goal here is to bring the Romanos in line. To remind them the Bianchi organization is not to be trifled with."

"To bend the knee," Luca added, and the men pounded the table with their fists in agreement.

"And you think this is possible?"

The question rang out over the noise, but it wasn't directed at Matteo. Abela was looking directly at Alexei. Matteo turned, eyebrows raised, and the rest of the men quieted, waiting expectantly.

"This move has been a long time coming. Lorenzo backed us into a corner with this deal, and none of us want to watch our money land in Romano pockets. Hell, most of us would prefer it be the other way around."

"Damn right."

"Hear, hear."

"Matteo's plan is solid." Alexei met Matteo's gaze. "He'll do right by Bianchi interests."

Matteo inclined his head and turned back toward the men. "I plan on earning your trust every day. This is a new era for the Bianchi organization. There are drinks and food set up on the north lawn if you'd like to eat before you head home."

The men filed out, slapping each other on the back, their voices fading as they rounded the side of the house. Alexei moved to stand next to Matteo as Luca and Dom pushed to their feet.

"You really mean all that shit you just said?"

Alexei's mouth quirked up in a wry smile. "You really think you can pull off all that shit you just said?"

Matteo blew out a breath. "We'll see. Thank you," he added. "The men need you in this all the way. I need you in this."

"I'm in it," Alexei assured him.

"I still don't want you to touch my sister."

Alexei pinned him with a dry stare, and Matteo rolled his eyes. "Right. Whatever you want to think, it *is* my damn business. I'll hold my tongue on it for now. But if you hurt her or get her hurt, I will kill you."

"I would expect nothing less."

Chapter Eight

Carina stood outside one of her father's casinos—her brother's casino now—clutching a worn piece of paper. She'd folded and unfolded it so many times over the past few days it was in danger of falling apart. Their timer had run out.

Elio knew of the deal, and the meet was scheduled for tonight at a Romano strip club. Dom would have preferred somewhere neutral along the border, but Matteo wanted to let Elio think he had the upper hand in this. Cocky, overconfident men said stupid, arrogant things. But before that happened, Carina needed to secure a promise.

She eyed Alexei's Aston Martin parked near the employee entrance. She'd driven to three other casinos looking for him before finally spotting his car here. It had taken her most of the day, looping all around the territory, and she'd almost given up.

But her mind was made up, and she wanted to make sure she got what she needed when this was all said and done. If her instincts were right, the only person who would keep the promise she was after was Alexei. Luca would try to talk her out of it, Dom was unpredictable at best, and Matteo would flat out refuse. Alexei was the only one who would give her what she craved.

Steeling herself, she crossed the parking lot on shaky legs, shivering at the blast of air conditioning that hit her when she walked through the automatic doors. The sound of beeping machines and competing voices crashed over her like a wave, and she wondered how anyone could stand to be in here for more than a few seconds without going crazy.

She scanned the floor, paper clutched tight in her hand, but didn't see anyone she recognized. Fuck. She hadn't thought this part through. How to actually find him in the sprawling building once she found the right one. He could be anywhere. On the floor, in one of the high-stakes poker lounges, in the labyrinth of hallways marked only for employees.

Doing her best to drown out the noise, she approached the window where people exchanged cash for chips to play poker or blackjack and waited in line. When it was her turn, she stepped up to the window, the blonde behind the counter giving her a curious stare.

"Do you know where I can find Alexei Sokolov? I'm—"

"I know who you are." She held up a finger, reaching for the phone at her elbow and dialing a short number. "I've got Carina Bianchi for Alexei." A brief pause. "Of course."

The woman hung up the phone and smiled politely. "Alexei is busy, but if you wait by the slot machines on the left side of the floor, someone will come to take you back to his office."

Carina glanced over her shoulder, wrinkling her nose at the machines that strobed and screamed every time someone pulled the lever. She offered the woman a thin smile. "Thank you."

Other employees paused to stare and gesture, whispering

behind their hands as she made her way across the space and waited. She'd never been inside a Bianchi casino before. Why would she? But she didn't understand why her presence now would cause such a stir.

The staff dispersed when a tall, lanky man with legs too long for his body approached from the back of the casino. He gave her a curt nod before stopping in front of her.

"Signora," he said, and her eyebrows winged up.

While technically a widow after being married for five years, it still felt odd to be addressed so formally. At least he hadn't called her Romano.

"My name is Berto. Alexei should be finished with his… meeting soon. You can follow me this way."

He shortened his strides, but not enough to prevent her from having to jog to keep up. He led them past poker and roulette and blackjack tables, past a bar filled with patrons sipping everything from brightly colored cocktails to wine to hard spirits, and through a door marked Private.

When the noise immediately disappeared, she breathed a sigh of relief. The only sound now was the click of her heels against the concrete floor. They turned down first one hallway and then another, and when Berto made a third turn, she began to wonder how the hell she was going to get out of here again without an escort.

At the end of the final hallway, Berto unlocked a door and waved her inside. "He shouldn't be long. Do you need anything?"

"No. Thank you."

He closed the door behind her with a snap, and she turned to study the space. It was small and plain, with a single desk under a pair of long shelves attached to the wall. A large metal filing cabinet was pushed into one corner and in the opposite corner was a wide, deep safe with a biometric lock.

The narrow space between the desk and the door wasn't even big enough for an extra chair. Whatever business Alexei did in this room, he did it alone.

The few papers on the desk were arranged in a ruthlessly straight stack, a cup of pens placed just so at the corner. And the leather-bound books and ledgers on his shelf were arranged first by size and then by date.

There was nothing on the walls. No photos, no art, no mementos. They were stark, bare, mysterious. Like the man who used this office and these things. It fit him, in a way. Coldly efficient while not giving away much about who he was at his core.

She'd known Alexei for a long time, but she didn't know much about him. About where he'd come from or who he was before her father brought him home with that cut on his face. About who he wanted to be before he became her father's killing machine. The problem was, she wanted to know more about him. She wanted to know everything about him.

At the sound of the knob rattling, she pivoted toward the door. It swung in on Alexei, barely missing the corner of the desk before tapping against the wall. He made her mouth water. Chiseled like a Greek god from head to toe, with blond hair that turned to gold in the sunshine and smoky gray eyes that darkened with anger and desire.

The scar trailed a white line down the side of his face from the corner of his eyebrow to the edge of his jaw. Somehow it only made him more appealing, like it was announcing how dangerous and damaged he was for all the world to see.

"To what do I owe the pleasure?"

This was it. She fingered the paper in her hand. "I need a favor."

He stepped into the office and closed the door, but he

didn't round the desk like she expected him to, leaving their bodies close enough that she could smell the soap on his skin.

He leaned back against the edge of the desk, legs extended in front of him and brushing against her thigh. "What kind of favor?"

"Before the meeting tonight with Elio and his men, I need your word on something." He nodded for her to continue. "On this piece of paper are three names."

His eyes drifted to the paper she held up between her fingers. "Okay."

She huffed out a breath and wet her lips. "Before this is all said and done, I want all of them dead." When he reached for the paper, she pivoted to keep it out of reach, which angled her body closer to his. Focus. "I want to watch them die. I want to have a hand in it."

His eyes bored into hers, and she wondered if he could see into her soul, into her dreams, into all the horrible things she'd imagined doing to the people on the list in her hand.

"You want to help kill those people?"

"Yes."

"Why are you asking me?"

Something in his voice had changed. It was deeper, huskier, and she took a step toward him before she realized what she was doing.

"You're the only one who will say yes and mean it."

He held his hand out for the paper, and she laid it in his palm, electricity sparking where their skin touched. He unfolded it slowly, carefully, eyes finally dragging from hers to read the three names she'd written in her neat, looping cursive.

Elio Romano
Giovanni Romano
Vincenzo Romano

He must have read them at least three times before meeting her eyes again. "Why these men?"

She swallowed hard and his eyes dropped to her throat, lingering there before meeting her gaze again. "Does it matter?"

"It does." He trailed his fingertips up her arm to her neck, pulling her close to whisper against her cheek. "Tell me why you want to help me kill these men."

"Because they deserve it," she whispered back, bracing her hand on his shoulder, fingers curling into the fabric of his t-shirt. "That can be enough for now. Will you help me?"

He wrapped his free hand around her waist, shifting her body until she was standing in front of him and straddling his outstretched thigh. Their faces were nearly level in this position, though he still had a few inches on her. He dragged his thumb from the back of her jaw to her chin, slowly tilting her head up until she was looking him in the eye.

His fingers tightened ever so slightly on the column of her throat, and she dragged her lower lip between her teeth with a sharp intake of breath. This time when his lips descended on hers, there was no one to interrupt them.

His mouth was rough, demanding, when it crashed into hers. His tongue traced across her lower lip until she parted them, and it slipped inside. His hand tightened on her throat again, increasing the pressure until she groaned softly against his mouth.

She felt his lips curve into a smile, his hand tightening on her waist and pulling her down flush against his thigh. Her hips rocked instinctively, and it was his turn to groan, lifting his thigh to increase the pressure.

Skimming her hands across his shoulders and down the roped muscles of his arms, she delighted in the feel of his warm skin against hers. She nipped at his bottom lip, and he hissed, his fingers digging into her hip until her shirt rode up to reveal the bare skin of her stomach.

His fingers explored there, caressing, squeezing, scratching. He slid one hand up her torso to capture her breast, palming it roughly, his thumb and forefinger immediately finding her nipple and giving it a tug through the fabric. Her breath caught in the back of her throat, and she arched against the pain, silently begging for more, needing more from him.

He rocked her hips against his thigh again, and pleasure shot through her, quick and bright, and she gasped. "Alexei," she pleaded, shoving her hands under his shirt and dragging her fingernails over the defined muscles of his abs. Christ, he felt perfect. Every fucking inch of him.

When he shifted to press kisses from her lips to her jaw to her earlobe, sucking it between his teeth and biting it gently, she tilted her head, groaning as he sent shivers down her spine and shockwaves through her core.

"You're going to make me come if you keep doing that," she said, breath hitching when he ground his thigh up against her pussy through her shorts.

He chuckled against her neck, flicking his tongue against her skin. "Do you want me to stop?"

"No," she whispered, voice hoarse.

He slid his hand down to her ass, squeezing it while he increased the speed, the pressure, shifting the angle of her body against his thigh. His lips nipped her throat, and his fingers expertly worked her nipple until she was vibrating against him, her nails digging into the skin of his hips as he worked her closer and closer to release.

"Carina," he crooned against her ear. "Come for me. Now."

"Yes," she hissed, arching her back with one final, violent

twist of her nipple, her orgasm consuming her until she could feel only where their bodies touched.

She slumped against him, burying her face in the crook of his neck. She'd had plenty of sex at her husband's insistence, but never like that. "I didn't..." she panted, still trying to catch her breath while he stroked his fingers lazily up and down her back under her shirt.

"You didn't what?"

"Nothing." She shook her head. She was too embarrassed to tell him she didn't know it could be like that. "I only came here for a favor."

He chuckled, lifting his thigh against her pussy and making her shudder. "You have your favor. How could I deny you? But if you change your mind, if your heart or your stomach aren't in it, just tell me."

"I won't. You're going to the meeting tonight, right?"

"I am. Matteo asked me this morning."

She nodded. "Good."

"Hopefully your brother's plan actually works." He nuzzled her jaw and then nipped at her skin. "As much as I want to peel off every piece of clothing you're wearing and bend you over this desk, I regretfully have to go see a man about some money. Dom is going to text me any minute."

His phone dinged a scant second later, and she laughed. "I guess I'll just have to come back for another favor."

Without warning, he tightened his fingers in her hair and pulled her in for another kiss, this one hungry, urgent, sinking his teeth into her lower lip until it stung. He released her just as quickly, shifting her off his leg and pushing to his feet.

"I have to go, or I might never leave this room," he said, voice thick. "Try and behave yourself until I can get my hands on you again."

"I can't make any promises," she replied, grinning at the

look on his face and dropping back against the desk with a heavy sigh.

Alexei's lips on hers, his command in her ear, his teeth and tongue and fingers on her skin weren't why she came here, but now that she'd had a taste, she knew she wanted more. Already she craved him like a drug, all the things he might be able to show and teach and awaken in her.

She wanted every bit of ruin he might bring. She'd happily bask in it until he pulled her under.

Chapter Nine

Carina stood in front of the wide, tall mirror propped against the wall in the corner of her room and tugged at the hem of her dress. She'd bought this specifically for tonight, for this meeting. It made her feel powerful, in control, confident. It was exactly the kind of thing her husband would have ripped from the hanger and tossed into the fire or torn to shreds.

Giuseppe had dressed her like a doll in conservative clothes that were perfectly tailored but revealed nothing. Not too short, not too low cut, not too tight. Only whores showed off their bodies, and he would never marry a whore.

He'd examined her entire wardrobe the morning after their wedding and confiscated almost all of it, assuring her how lucky she was to have married a man who could show her how a woman was supposed to dress and carry herself and behave. He was forever instructing her.

Elio treated his wife much the same way. Dictating the clothes she wore and the people she spent time with and the way she spoke. Carina considered her plan to kill Elio a public service to the women of the world. When she was finished with him, no woman would ever be subjected to his cruelty again. Elio would hate this dress. And that's precisely why she wanted to wear it.

Matteo hadn't included her in the meeting tonight, purposely scheduling it without her input. But he'd made a promise to her. She was in this, and that meant all the way. She might not have Luca's head for business or Matteo's thirst for power, but she wasn't stupid. And she knew Elio better than all of them.

"That's quite the dress for laying around the house all night."

Carina raised a brow and met Alexei's gaze in the mirror, reaching up to tighten a pin in her hair and swallowing a grin at the way his eyes dipped down to her legs when the hem rode up at the movement.

"It would be if I were staying home."

"You're not going. And definitely not dressed like that."

She adjusted the long sleeves of her dress, smoothing the fabric and running a fingertip over the pendant necklace hanging from a long chain. The dress's deep V cutout slashed almost to her belly button, exposing her chest and the sides of her breasts.

"I am absolutely going, and I'll wear what I please. Giving me one orgasm in your cramped office doesn't make you the boss of me. Or my keeper."

He stepped into the bedroom, closing the door behind him and crossing the room in quick strides. He wrapped an arm around her waist and yanked her back against his chest. Dropping his head, he traced his nose along the line of her jaw, inhaling her perfume.

"How many orgasms would that take?"

She looped an arm around his neck, digging her fingers into the hair at the base of his skull. "More than you can give me."

He flashed her a wicked grin, his hand snaking up to trace the underside of her breast, fingers inching dangerously close to exposed skin. "You sure about that? Maybe I should take you now so you can feel me between your thighs all night long."

He dropped his free hand to her leg, eyes never leaving hers, and dug his fingers into the skin. Dragging his hand up, he captured the hem of her dress and inched it higher. Her breath caught in her throat when she realized he was dangerously close to discovering she wasn't wearing anything underneath.

He stilled when someone knocked on the door but didn't release her.

"Carina!" Matteo shouted. "Meet me downstairs. I'd like to talk to you before we go."

"You sure you won't change your mind on this?"

"I'm going," she insisted.

He sighed, dragging his thumb roughly across her nipple and smiling when she shivered under his fingers. "How am I supposed to sit in the same room with you all night with you dressed like this and not think about fucking you?"

"I'm sure you'll manage," she said, a little breathless.

"Are you?" Alexei met her eyes in the mirror again, one hand splayed possessively over her stomach while the other drew circles around her nipple without touching it. "No one takes this dress off but me. Understand?"

She nodded, shuddering out a deep breath when he stepped away and following him to the door.

"Your brother's going to hate everything about this," he murmured when they reached the bottom of the stairs.

Matteo eyed her dress with a disapproving frown. "Where the hell do you think you're going?"

"To the meeting." She smoothed a nervous hand over her hair.

"Absolutely not," Matteo replied. "We're meeting deep in Romano territory. It's not safe for you."

"You left me to fend for myself in Romano territory for five years. All of you," she added, pinning each of them with a hard stare, and guilt flashed in Alexei's eyes. "I think I'll be fine for a few hours with the four of you there."

"We're going to a strip club," Dom said.

Carina rolled her eyes. "I'm not sure if you've realized this, but I know what a woman looks like naked. Considering I am one."

"No, Carina. I—"

"You promised me, Matteo," she snapped. "When you said I could have a hand in this, were you telling the truth or were you lying to me to get me to shut up?"

He rubbed his forehead. "Of course I wasn't lying. But this—"

"I know Elio better than any of you. You want him to slip up tonight? To get past his perfect act? I know exactly which buttons to push."

Matteo shared a look with Alexei, who lifted a shoulder, studying her face before finally relenting. "Fine. You can come. But Alexei doesn't leave your side, and if I think you need to leave, you will."

"Fine."

A pair of black SUVs waited in the drive for them, one already filled with their men who would provide escort during tonight's meeting. Matteo might want to meet on Elio's turf to give him the illusion of control, but that didn't mean he wanted to go in unprotected.

"Does he know what to expect?" Alexei asked once they were in the SUV and pulling out of the drive.

"I only told him I was willing to meet to discuss details. I didn't give him any more info than that."

"It'll be interesting to see what he chooses," Luca said, and Carina turned to study her brothers.

"You want him to make the choice?"

"Yes," Luca said with a nod. "Whether he wants a stake in the casinos or the payout will tell us a lot. It'll give us an angle to exploit."

"Just remember," Matteo said, "the plan is to agree with whatever he says. To a point. If he suspects we're bluffing or being insincere, he gets the upper hand." He pinned Dom with a hard stare. "So make sure you keep yourselves in check."

"Why the fuck are you looking at me?"

"Because you're terrible at poker."

Dom scoffed, and the car fell silent, the lights and sounds of Palermo whizzing by as they followed the coast into Romano territory to one of their premiere strip clubs. The white stone was uplit with blue and purple lights, making it glow in the darkness. A long line of people, mostly men but some women, curled around the side of the building, waiting to get inside.

This was Giuseppe's pride and joy. Whenever she had a night of reprieve from him, she knew it was because he was here, forcing some other woman to pretend to enjoy it while he rutted and grunted on top of her. At least they got paid.

The man who came out to lead them inside looked familiar, and when the lights illuminated his face, her heart hammered in her chest. Giuseppe's personal bodyguard must now be Elio's. Lepera was as terrifying as he was sadistic. A name she might need to add to her list.

Music pulsed through the club, but she could barely hear it over the blood rushing through her ears. They were led through the main floor with women twirling themselves around on poles, gripping the thin tubes with strong thighs and hanging upside down topless. She snuck a glance at

Alexei. He seemed wholly uninterested, and she brushed away the satisfaction that gave her.

They climbed to the second floor and turned down a long hallway, the music fading into thudding bass. Elio was already inside the private room waiting for them, and her steps faltered at the sight of his uncle and cousins flanking him, fear punching into her throat until she could hardly breathe from it.

"They're dead men walking," Alexei whispered into her ear, resting his hand against her lower back to steady her. "They will never touch you again."

She lifted her chin and squared her shoulders, satisfied when Elio's lip curled in disgust at the sight of her. "If I'd known it would be that kind of meeting, I'd have brought my wife."

"I'm sure she's happier at home without you," Carina replied, lowering herself onto a small leather sofa and crossing her legs. Alexei perched on the arm next to her, his presence steadying.

Elio sucked his teeth before reclaiming his seat. "Quite the entourage, Bianchi. A woman and your lap dog. Interesting way to do business."

"And how I conduct mine is none of yours." Matteo claimed an empty chair across from Elio, smiling at the scantily clad waitress who came in with a tray of drinks. "Well," he said once the door closed behind the woman, "you wanted to talk. Talk."

Elio shared a look with his uncle, who gave a curt nod. "I imagine you were as pissed off to learn about this ridiculous contract as I was."

Carina's eyebrows shot up, and she glanced around the room at her brothers, who looked as surprised as she was by Elio's admission.

"You didn't know about this?" Matteo asked, his tone level but his gaze sharp.

"Of course not," Elio replied, as if the idea offended him. "That much money for some casinos and a willing cunt?" He sneered at Carina, and Alexei tensed. "Hardly a good deal."

"I'm sure your wife thinks much the same when you leave her unsatisfied," Carina said smoothly.

Angered burned hot in Elio's eyes and the cruel twist of his mouth. "You little bitch." He jerked forward, stopped short by his uncle's hand on his shoulder, forcing him to keep his seat.

Alexei's body was rigid beside her, and she leaned against his thigh as much to soothe him as to soothe herself, to quiet the rapid beat of her heart at the rage in Elio's eyes she knew all too well. Elio raked a hand through his hair, and his voice was harder when he spoke.

"I'll be quick. I couldn't care less about your pathetic collection of casinos." He flashed a malicious grin when Luca growled low in his throat. "I have neither the time nor the patience to bring them up to Romano standards. The only thing I want from you is my money back."

"You mean daddy's money," Dom said.

"I mean Romano money," Elio said through gritted teeth. "Had I known about this deal in the first place, I never would have let it go through."

"And if we would prefer to share ownership?" Matteo wondered.

Elio tossed back the drink in his hand and set the empty glass on the low table between them with a heavy thunk. "Then I will take what I am owed by force."

Dom shot off his seat, and Matteo and Luca bolted up to block him. "Easy," Matteo said, shoving Dom down by his shoulder before turning to face the Romano men. "I'll remind you, Elio, you have no fucking idea what I'm capable of. It would be wise not to threaten me. Lucky for both of us, I want nothing to do with you either. I'll meet the terms. One billion euros due in thirty days."

"And you're able to get the money together that quickly?"

Desperation shown in Elio's eyes until his uncle cleared his throat, and then it was gone again, replaced by his smug sneer. That was interesting. If the Romanos were hurting for cash, all they had to do was find out why and increase the pressure.

"We'll settle the terms of the agreement to everyone's satisfaction," Matteo assured him, rising to his feet. "I have to make some arrangements. I'll wire you the money in thirty days."

"No," Elio said as they turned for the door. "We do the exchange in person. I want to watch you transfer it to make sure you're not fucking with me."

Luca's lip curled, and Dom snorted his irritation, but Matteo nodded. "Fine. We'll meet on our turf next time."

"We can meet wherever you like as long as you have my money and leave your whore and your pet at home."

Carina gripped Alexei's arm when he lunged toward Elio, her fingernails digging into the skin of his forearm. Elio's eyes sparkled as he leaned back in his chair, and Carina couldn't help the laugh that escaped her. There was something deliciously satisfying knowing he thought he had the upper hand but wouldn't live to see his next birthday.

"What the fuck is so funny?" Elio snarled.

Alexei shifted to press against her back, one hand resting possessively on her hip. Elio didn't seem to notice, but his uncle did, his eyes darkening with an anger she would never let scare her again.

"Just remembering something your father used to say about you. He was quite the talker when he was...relaxed." Alexei's grip tightened, his fingers digging into her skin.

"Little Elio, always content to follow and never to lead. He wasn't sure you had what it takes." She cocked her head. "Maybe he was right."

When Elio surged to his feet, Alexei shoved her behind him, and each of her brothers took a step forward. He started to speak, but his uncle gripped his arm and lifted a brow in warning. Alexei moved quickly, using his body to shield her from Elio's view and his rage. Luca reached for the door, unsealing the barrier between their meeting and the club, filling the room with music.

"I am ten times the man my father was," Elio spat, unable to hold his tongue, and she bit back a grin. "I sure as fuck wouldn't have penned my name on these deals."

Deals. Multiple. Carina knew Matteo and Alexei heard it too by the look they shared.

"Excellent work, little sister," Matteo whispered in her ear as they joined Dom and Luca in the hall.

She smiled as they descended the stairs, winding back the way they'd come. Alexei's hand rode low on her back, his fingertips brushing the top of her ass, and she turned to offer him a teasing grin, brows knitting together when she saw him staring at a stripper instead.

"Been here before?" she wondered, something ugly and foreign in her tone.

He shrugged but increased the pressure on her back, propelling her forward. It was too late, though. The woman had already spotted him, and when she did, she made her way over.

"Back again so soon? And you brought a friend," she purred, eyes shifting to Carina as she ran her fingernails up and down Alexei's arm.

Alexei caught the woman's hand, squeezing until her eyes widened. "Just here on business," he explained.

She massaged her fingers when he released them, that

sultry pout fixing itself to her mouth again. "That's what they all say. Enjoy this one, honey," she said to Carina. "He's very generous."

Carina watched the woman walk away, then looked up at Alexei, who was studying her carefully. What was that viscous, slithering sensation behind her sternum? It couldn't be jealousy. He wasn't hers to be jealous over. Just like she'd told him earlier, one orgasm between them—with both of them fully clothed, no less—meant nothing. He was free to fuck whoever he wanted whenever he wanted.

Even if the thought made her want to rip the woman's eyeballs out.

She pivoted quickly toward the door, weaving between the patrons and strippers. She heard irritated grunts and exclamations from people behind her as Alexei shoved his way through the crowd to keep up with her.

"Carina," he said, gripping her elbow and pulling her to a stop in the parking lot. "That isn't—"

"It's fine, Alexei. It's really none of my business."

"Y—"

"Will you two hurry the fuck up?" Matteo shouted, head sticking out the rear window of the SUV. "I don't exactly want to stay here all night."

Carina glanced up at Alexei's face again, but it was unreadable. When he said nothing, disappointment wound its way through her, and that only served to piss her off.

She'd always known getting involved with Alexei was a bad idea. At least now she could stop it before it really began.

Chapter Ten

Alexei watched Carina closely on the drive home, but she refused to meet his gaze, staring intently out the window, her hands clutched tight in her lap. Not that he could say much of anything to her with her brothers in the car. Something stirred inside him at the thought she might be jealous he'd been with someone else. Her jealousy only fueled his need for her.

He let the conversation and speculation about Elio and his mysterious deals drift around him. Fact finding and strategy weren't his job. He was the tip of the sword. He'd leave the Bianchis to their digging, and when they had a target, he could get to work doing what he did best. Getting whatever information he wanted out of an unwilling victim.

The car pulled into the driveway, and as soon as it rolled to a stop, Carina jumped out, her heels clicking across the stone pathway. He raced after her, catching her around the waist and hauling her into the shadows at the side of the house for some privacy.

"Get the fuck off me." She pinched and scratched his arm,

shoving at his chest when he set her on her feet. "What are you doing?"

"I want to talk to you, and since you—"

"We don't have anything to talk about. I told you it doesn't matter."

His arm tightened around her waist when she tried to leave, and he hauled her up against him. He could barely make out her features in the dark, but her body was tense, angry.

"I didn—"

"Just drop it. So you screwed a stripper. Who cares? It's none of my business and—"

"Goddamn it, woman."

Intent on a fucking minute of silence, he gripped her chin roughly in his free hand and tilted her head up for his lips. He wasn't gentle about it; his anger and irritation were simmering too close to the surface for that. He took from her instead. Using his teeth on her lower lip, lashing his tongue against hers until she groaned, her body softening under his touch.

He slid his hand down to her ass, tugging her sharply against him and grinding his growing cock against her stomach. She gasped against his lips, her hands sliding up to fist in the fabric of his shirt, gripping it tightly as he sucked her bottom lip, then teased it with his teeth.

When she shoved him away, he let her but didn't release his hold, dragging his thumb over her swollen lips, cupping her ass and squeezing. Her breathing was ragged against his finger, and that only made him harder.

"I did not have sex with that stripper."

"Not that stripper." Fuck, that jealous streak of hers was going to undo him. "But others."

"Yes, I've fucked other women. And I'm sure you had plenty of lovers before me."

"We're not lovers." Her mouth turned to a pout under his thumb, turning him on even more. "And I haven't."

He slid his hand down to the hem of her dress, dragging it up her thighs, smiling when she squirmed to help instead of stopping him. "Haven't what?"

"Nothing," she said quickly.

He jerked her chin up so her eyes met his. "Haven't what?"

Her eyes darted away, then back to his face. "Haven't had plenty of lovers," she mumbled, clearly embarrassed.

The admission made his cock twitch, and he shoved her roughly against the wall, tugging her dress up to her waist. "Good," he said, slipping his hand down to squeeze her ass again and finding it bare. "Fuck, Carina. You haven't been wearing panties all night?"

"No."

He heard the smile in her voice, and he slid his fingers down the crack of her ass, rubbing his fingertips roughly over her pussy lips and making her gasp and rock against him.

He leaned in and pressed a kiss against her lips, increasing the pressure of his fingers. "I've been thinking about being inside you since I first saw you in this dress. And your pussy is nice and wet for me."

"Yes," she whispered, hands drifting down to the button of his slacks and undoing them with shaking fingers.

He hissed when her fingertips grazed him through his boxers, and she hesitated, rocking hard into his fingers when he slid one between her lips and teased along her slit. Fuck, he needed to be inside her.

She whimpered when he pulled his hand away, and the sound was music to his ears. Sliding his damp fingers around her hip and down her pelvis, he found her clit and pressed two fingers against it, loving the way she shuddered against him at the pressure.

He rubbed it roughly, dragging another delicious moan from between her lips before sliding his fingers down and plunging them both inside her. One arm moving up to wrap around his neck, she raked her fingernails across his skin while the other freed his cock, squeezing and pumping it in her fist. He rocked against her hand while he curled his fingers forward to drag across that sensitive spot inside her.

Leaning in to capture her moans with his lips, he used his thumb to rub circles over her clit, pushing her closer and closer to release with his fingers. He needed her to come so he could take her. He wanted to feel her come apart in his hands before he put his mark on her and claimed her completely.

She tore her mouth from his on a sharp intake of breath, nails biting into his skin until it stung. Suddenly, her bucking hips went still, and he cinched his arm around her waist to hold her upright while she squeezed his fingers with her orgasm. She was going to feel so good around his cock.

Gripping the backs of her thighs, he lifted her off the ground, groaning when she instantly wrapped her legs around his waist and his cock brushed the length of her warm, wet slit.

"Alexei," she panted, dropping her head back against the wall, each rapid rise and fall of her chest exposing more of her breasts to his eyes.

He reached up with one hand and tugged her dress off her shoulders as much as the long sleeves would allow, nudging the fabric away from her breasts until they were bared to him. Leaning down, he wrapped his lips around her nipple, hardened by the breeze and her desperate arousal. The same arousal that had her grinding her hips against his rock-hard length, sliding him between her lips, coating him with her wetness.

Still feasting on her nipple, sinking his teeth into it until her breath hitched, he supported her with one hand and used the other to align the head of his cock with her entrance. He bit down on her nipple again, her back arching to get away from the pain at the same time he surged inside her. She cried out, loud enough for anyone still outside to hear, but he was past the point of caring.

"Fuck, baby, you feel so good," he panted, tonguing her nipple before turning his attention to the other one.

Her pussy tightened around his cock at the praise, and he filed that away for later, grinding into her with each upward thrust. He could tell when he hit her clit just right in the way she groaned for him low in her throat.

Trailing kisses up her breasts to her shoulders, nipping her collarbone with his teeth, he kept up his steady, grinding thrusts as he nibbled along the column of her throat and across her jaw. She shuddered and groaned, her breath hot against his cheek each time her breasts dragged against his chest in time with his thrusts.

"Are you going to come on my cock?"

She nodded, and he grazed her earlobe with his teeth, her arms wrapped tightly around his shoulders, holding on as he fucked her relentlessly. "Tell me." When she didn't immediately respond to his command, he pulled nearly all the way out of her, grinning at the way she squeaked in surprise.

"What are you doing?" she panted.

"Waiting for you to answer my question," he replied, pressing a kiss to her chin.

Carina tightened her legs around his waist, trying to pull him back inside of her and grunting in frustration when he wouldn't budge. "Alexei, please. I need to…I want to…"

"Mhmm." He molded his lips to the pulse fluttering in her throat. "Say it, Carina."

"I want to come on your cock."

As soon as she rewarded him with those words, he slammed inside her again, hips resuming a brutal pace while she writhed and bucked against him. Rough, urgent thrusts inside her, against her clit, his lips and teeth on her skin, his fingers twisting and pinching her nipple, left her vibrating against him, and he could feel her orgasm approaching by the way her entire body tightened around him.

When she finally, blissfully, tumbled over the edge, he followed her, emptying himself inside her with one final, brutal thrust. He buried his face against her neck while her hands roamed into his hair, gripping it tight in her fingers.

"You are so much more than I ever imagined you would be," he confessed, pressing a kiss to the side of her neck before pulling back to look at her face.

"What now?" she wondered, her voice going small and unsure again.

He grinned and ground his cock inside her until her breath hitched and her pussy tightened around him again. "Your room or mine?"

Chapter Eleven

Carina paced the floor in front of the dark fireplace in her mother's old sitting room, muttering to herself. For days they'd been trying to uncover the thread they would need to tug to unravel whatever Elio had meant when he said he wouldn't have signed the deals his father had. They were no closer now than they had been the night they left the club.

And everyone just went about their business around her, not noticing or not caring that she was crawling out of her skin with impatience. Seeing Elio, Giovanni, and Vincenzo the other night brought it all flooding back, spilling the memories she'd so carefully packed away since Giuseppe's death.

Her brothers might be okay with simply bringing down the Romano empire, reducing it to nothing. But she didn't want to just destroy their livelihoods. She wanted to end them. She'd wipe the entire goddamn family from existence if she thought she could get away with it. And all her brothers cared about was getting their hands on Romano strip clubs and absorbing their drug trade and its profits.

The only distraction she had from her vendetta was when Alexei would slip into her room once the rest of the house was asleep. Doing incredible things to her body in the dark, whispering words into her ear that made her writhe with need, pushing her to the punishing brink and then swallowing her cries with his lips.

In the morning, she would be sore and sated and alone. They'd yet to wake up together, which was just as well. There were too many things about her body, her life before all this, that she wasn't ready to explain yet. Besides, no matter what he whispered to her with his cock or his fingers buried inside her, she couldn't let herself get attached.

Alexei was intoxicating. A drug she'd never be able to get enough of if she let herself lose control. As much as she wanted him, as much as he called to her, she had to be careful not to skim too far below the surface of this thing between them. She couldn't risk falling so deep she became trapped and unable to get out again.

She would not end up a pawn or a plaything to a man ever again. Even if she had to leave Sicily to be free. Maybe she could do what Matteo did and disappear to make her own way, see the world. She had her inheritance and her widow's estate. She could go and experience life on her own terms without a man dictating her every move. It might be nice.

But not until Elio Romano and the rest of them were dead, their blood staining her hands. She couldn't even think of leaving until that was done. Which meant as impatient as she was to get on with it, she'd have to play by her brother's rules a little longer. Once Matteo had his financial information, she could push him to do what came next. Push him to do the only thing she really cared about.

Dropping onto the overstuffed sofa with a sigh, she forced her mind to wander back to her years spent closed up in

Cefalù. Giuseppe really did talk too much after sex. Every filter in his head shut off once his cock was satisfied. She shuddered to think what the strippers and whores he liked at his clubs knew about his business dealings.

His usual routine was to come to her rooms shortly after dinner. He wouldn't knock—she had no privacy in that house, really—just barge in and take his clothes off. Then he'd watch her strip, his lecherous, greedy eyes taking in every inch of her body.

But he didn't look at her the way Alexei did, like a treat to be savored, like an object of desire. He looked at her like a thing, a toy, a warm body for him to use to get himself off. Nothing about her marriage had been what she expected it to be.

Shaking those thoughts from her head, she searched her memories for the one that had been poking at the edge of her consciousness since leaving the club. Well, since the morning after, anyway. That night her head had been too full of thoughts of Alexei and the way he moved inside of her, giving her exactly what she'd needed for years, to waste thoughts on Elio Romano or his dead father.

But now that she was ready for it, she couldn't grasp it. Every time she tried, it darted out of reach before returning to prod its dull edges at the recesses of her mind. There was a reason she'd said those words to Elio to get a rise out of him, even if her brain couldn't consciously remember.

Chewing her bottom lip, she dropped her head into her hands. When Giuseppe first started coming to her rooms after dinner, she would pretend to enjoy it, certain in all her naïveté it would get better. Eventually she learned to just lay there until he was done. On the nights he didn't come to her, he stayed at one of his clubs. Those nights were her favorite.

But on rare occasion, especially toward the end of their marriage, he would wake her up out of sleep late at night, crawling into her bed. There was always something different about him on those nights. He was slower, more affectionate —as much affection as he was capable of, anyway—kissing her while he moved inside her. She'd learned to block him out by then, wordlessly going through the motions, sighing and moaning at the right moments to encourage him to finish.

One night he came in so late the sky had already started to shade lighter, going from black to a deep blue, a thin line of gray skimming the horizon. *It might all be falling apart around us, but at least I have you to entertain me*, he'd said, not realizing she was already awake and bracing herself for his touch.

She hadn't understood it then, but maybe this was what he was talking about. Making multiple deals behind Elio's back. Deals that were souring. He'd climbed onto the bed, the mattress dipping under his weight, and shifted her onto her back. He hadn't even waited to make sure she was awake before jabbing into her.

He wasn't gentle, but it didn't take long, and soon he was rolling off her, staring up at the dark red velvet canopy that covered her bed. *I don't know if Elio has what it takes to build the empire back up*, he'd said, but she didn't respond, certain he wasn't actually speaking to her.

He peeked over at her, but she'd kept her eyes squeezed tight, pretending to be asleep again, and he grunted in something that sounded like pride. Shifting off the bed, he'd stood there staring at her before leaning over to squeeze her breast roughly and run a hand down the flat plane of her stomach.

Too bad I haven't bred you yet. Another son to raise and put in Elio's place would be better. Aroldo is going to eat Elio alive after I'm dead.

Then he was gone, the door snicking softly closed behind him. She'd been too repulsed by the idea of carrying his child to think about much else. But now she could zero in on the rest of it. Aroldo. The Varda Don. Why would he eat Elio alive?

Shooting to her feet, she raced down the stairs and to the back of the house, calling out an apology to a maid she nearly knocked over in her mad dash to the study. Bursting through the door, she sucked in a deep breath, adrenaline pounding through her veins.

Matteo was seated behind the desk, papers splayed out in front of him, with Luca seated in one of the overstuffed chairs that faced it and Dom sprawled out on the couch. She had no idea where Alexei was. He hadn't even come to her room last night, and when she'd peeked out the windows at his cottage, the lights were off.

"Aroldo Varda," she said, all but panting.

"What about him?" Dom wanted to know.

Matteo gestured her forward with the crook of his fingers, and she closed the door behind her, moving into the center of the room.

"What I told Elio at the club. About his father being worried about him."

"It was brilliant," Luca said with a grin, and she smiled back.

"It was, but I didn't make it up. Giuseppe said it to me once. I just couldn't remember the details of it." She wrapped her arms around her middle and squeezed, looking up to see Matteo watching her intently.

"But now you do?"

She nodded. "He was talking about getting another heir. Out of me." Luca's lip curled, and Matteo's brows drew together. Even Dom looked angry. "A new heir to replace Elio because he didn't think Elio could stand against Aroldo Varda."

Dom jerked upright, and Luca's head spun around to

meet Matteo's gaze. "You think he borrowed Varda capital?" Luca said.

Matteo tapped his fingers against the leather blotter on top of the desk. "If he did, no wonder Elio's feeling the pressure. Varda sharks are ruthless once they smell blood in the water."

"And loans come due in full upon death," Dom added. "A new policy he added a few years ago when people started killing themselves to get out of repaying."

Leaning back in his chair, Matteo chuckled. "What's the best way to find out how much he owes?"

"Find his best enforcers," Dom said. "And let Alexei handle the rest."

She felt a quick stab of jealousy that Alexei would get to bloody his own hands while she remained pristine and cooped up in this house, but she brushed it away. She had to have patience.

"How long will it take you to find them?" Matteo wondered.

"A couple days, without interruptions. They have a few places they like to hang out, but we can't exactly be obvious about it. No need to fight a war on two fronts by stirring up trouble with Varda. Yet," Dom added, a gleam in his eye, and Carina wondered what other plans her brothers were already laying for the rest of Sicily.

"Use as many men and resources as you need to find someone who can give us reliable information as quickly as possible. I don't want to ride too close to Elio's deadline."

Dom pushed to his feet. "Done. I'll let you know when I have something."

"Nice one," her brother said as he breezed by her on his way out the door. It was the most conversation they'd had in years.

"We've got that meeting about the renovations in an hour," Luca reminded Matteo, glancing at his watch.

"Right," he said, shifting his gaze from Luca to Carina. "I'll meet you in the car."

The dismissal clear in Matteo's tone, Luca rose, giving Carina's shoulder a squeeze before he left. She wasn't entirely sure why Matteo was staring at her like that, his gaze deep and searching as he pushed to his feet.

"I'll admit, you're more of an asset than I thought you'd be."

Carina's eyebrows shot up, and she dropped her hands to her hips. "I'm full of surprises, Matteo."

His smile was quick and genuine, so much like the boy she remembered. "Yes. You always have been. I'll have to keep you more in the loop," he said simply, skirting the desk and moving to the door. "We all have the same goal, Carina."

She wasn't so sure of that. Matteo wanted to absorb the Romano empire into his own, or what was left of it. She wanted to obliterate it. Maybe he thought she would change her mind and be content with the money and the power and the influence. But she wouldn't be. Elio Romano and his uncle and cousins had committed far too many sins to be let off so lightly.

But there was time to get Matteo to see reason. She'd let him dig into the Romano connection to Varda and move his chess pieces to conquer Romano interests. But this would end in blood. No one, not even Matteo, would deny her that.

Chapter Twelve

The distant shriek of gulls winging out over the water roused him from sleep. The balcony doors were flung open to the breeze, the curtains dancing in it as the cool air washed over his skin. Alexei felt the heat of Carina's back against his chest, and he tightened his arm around her waist, fitting her snugly against him.

He hadn't been able to take nearly as much time with her as he wanted since that first night, forced to be content with stolen moments with her in the dark between late nights and early mornings cleaning up Bianchi messes. She was addicting. The more he had of her, the more he wanted, like he would never be able to satisfy his deep hunger for her.

The sun was just peeking over the horizon, sparkling off the water, and a slow smile curved his lips at the idea of slipping inside her while she was still half asleep, feeling her squirm against him before she came fully awake and moved with him.

He reached up to cup her breast, squeezing it while he dragged his thumb across her nipple. Once, twice, a third time until she was rocking against him, pushing her ass back against the hard length of his cock.

Nuzzling the back of her neck, he pressed kisses there, smiling when she sighed. Skimming his fingers across her hip and wrapping them around her thigh to position her for his cock, he groaned in frustration when his phone rang and jolted her out of sleep.

With one more nibbling kiss to her shoulder, he rolled away from her and leaned over the side of the bed to fish his phone out of the pocket of his jeans. He was absolutely going to murder whoever the fuck this was.

He felt her scramble on the bed behind him as he glanced at the screen. Dom. Why did it seem like every Bianchi except the one he wanted was always commanding his attention?

Clearing the sleep from his voice, he accepted the call and pressed the phone to his ear. "I sincerely hope this is important. If not, I'm hanging up."

"I'm in need of your skill set."

Alexei sat up, leaning back against the headboard and frowning when he realized Carina was no longer beside him. "Which skill set would that be?"

"We're on our way back with one of Varda's men. When we get there, I'll need answers from him."

His eyes found the sliver of light under the bathroom door, and his mind drifted to taking Carina in the shower, the hot water beating down on them both while he pressed her up against the cool tile. His hand around her throat, holding her steady while he pounded her from behind. The thought made his cock twitch, and he sighed. These assholes really had the worst timing.

"How badly have you beaten him already?"

Dom hesitated. "He's still breathing."

Alexei cast his eyes to the ceiling. "I know you like using

your fists, Dom, but there's a time and a place for it. If you want answers, you have to use finesse."

"Yeah, yeah. Are you saying you can't do it then?"

"Of course I can do it. But it might take longer now. How far away are you?"

A pause. "About twenty minutes."

Alexei glanced at the clock on the nightstand. "Okay. I'll meet you at the casino closest to the house. Put him in my workroom and leave him in there blindfolded with the lights off until I get there. And Dom? Don't fucking touch him again."

The line went dead without a response, and he tossed the phone into the middle of the bed. Carina emerged a second later, a robe belted over silk pajamas she had definitely not been wearing when she got out of bed.

"Who was that?" she asked, running her fingers through her hair.

"Dom." He held a hand out to her and waited until she came to him, climbing onto the bed and sitting back on her heels next to his thigh. He tucked a strand of hair behind her ear, his thumb tracing the line of her jaw. "He found one of Varda's men."

"And now he wants answers?"

He smiled. "Yes. Now he wants answers."

She drew her bottom lip between her teeth while his fingers continued to stroke down the side of her neck, tracing the outline of her collarbone.

"Can I come?" His gaze snapped to hers, and her earnestness sent lust coursing through him. "Just to…to watch."

"You want to watch me torture a man?"

He moved his fingers lower, slipping them inside her robe and closing his fingers around her nipple through the soft material of her tank top but not squeezing. She nodded, and his fingers slowly increased the pressure until she sucked in a shaky breath between her full lips, leaning toward his teasing fingers to ease the sting.

He thought her bloodlust for the Romano men came from her need for revenge for whatever things had been done to her while she was trapped there. Things she still wouldn't share with him. But maybe it wasn't only that. Maybe it was more. Maybe his sweet little Carina was as fascinated by blood and death as he was.

"Soon," he promised, releasing her nipple and leaning in to press a slow, deep kiss against her lips. "But not today. I'll make sure you're there for every Romano death with a blade in your hand. My word on that."

She sighed when he slid out of bed. "If Matteo hasn't changed his mind. He seems less and less interested in keeping the promise he made to me. All he cares about is the money and the power."

Alexei hopped into his jeans and slipped on his shirt, gripping her robe by the belt and pulling her onto her knees, urging her forward until her body was flush with his. "I don't give a fuck what Matteo wants. If you want them dead, you'll have it."

"When?" she whispered.

"As soon as Matteo has the control he needs. As much as I hate to make you wait." He smiled, wrapping his fingers loosely around her throat and using his thumb under her chin to tilt her head back. "As much as I will love watching you get exactly what you want, however you want, I understand the sense in making sure Matteo has them where he needs them first. There's all of Sicily to consider."

"And if my brother sways you with money? What should I do then?" she asked, eyes wary.

"He won't." He pressed a kiss to her lips before she could reply. "He won't, Carina. Do you trust me?"

She tilted her head, studying him, and he didn't realize how much he needed her to say yes in that moment. "I do."

"Then trust me on this. Your brother might talk like he'll do business with Elio in the future, and I'm happy to let him think that for now. But you and I both know otherwise."

"You promise?" she asked, wrapping her arms around his neck and pressing against him.

"I promise."

She offered her mouth to him, and he drank her in, his hands skimming down her back to her ass and pulling her in tighter against him. Leaving her every morning was becoming more and more difficult. He wanted to stay and sate them both, make her writhe and beg for him. Soon. He'd make it a priority to take his time with her.

Stepping out of her embrace, he gave her ass a light smack, smiling when she squeaked in surprise and left as the sun crested the horizon and threw rough shadows against the wall. They'd better get some good information out of this Varda prick, or Dom was going to pay for the interruption.

When he arrived at the casino, the parking lot was scattered with cars. It always amazed him people would be out gambling at this hour, sitting bleary-eyed in front of the ringing slot machines or making bad bets on shitty hands at the card tables. Still, it paid well, and that's all he really cared about.

He let himself in the side entrance closest to the basement where he liked to work and took the stairs down into the damp. The lights were on in the main area, and he heard the low rumble of voices as he descended. Dom spotted him first and waved him over.

"He's in there," he said, nodding toward the largest room. "Lights off, blindfold on."

"Good. You can go." He reached for the knob, pausing

when nobody moved. "I don't need an audience, and I don't want him to hear anything but me."

There was a slight hesitation, but eventually he heard the shuffle of feet across the concrete and the thump of footsteps on the wooden stairs. He waited until the upper door closed and the quiet settled heavily around him before pushing the door in.

The room was pristine. Not a drop of blood from Eduardo Cappelletti remained. It was as if he'd never existed at all. The man in front of him now didn't look like a typical Varda enforcer. He was tall and thin, with a round bald spot shining at the back of his head. His knuckles weren't scarred, and he strained weakly against the bindings on his wrists and ankles holding him to the chair.

This might be more intriguing than he thought. Less bravado to slice through than he would with one of Varda's typical men. Alexei stepped into the room, and the man turned his head at the sound, though he could see nothing through the blindfold wrapped around his face. Flipping on the single overhead bulb, he closed the door and leaned back against it.

"Who's there?" the man rasped, and Alexei could see the bruises on his throat.

"What's your name?" Alexei asked, and the man jerked at the sound.

"Like I'm going to fucking tell you."

Alexei grinned. He liked when they had spirit. "You can tell me, or I can cut it out of you. That will be the only choice you get today."

After moving a small table into the center of the room, Alexei unfolded a chair propped in the corner and sat. He laid his tool kit across the tabletop, slowly undoing the ties that held it together. He'd spent years studying how to inflict maximum pain without killing a man. Some men lasted longer than others before spilling their secrets. But they always did. He wondered how long this one would hold out.

Unrolling the kit on the table's surface, he ran a fingertip over the instruments and selected a simple, thin blade about three inches long. It was light in his hand, perfectly balanced and dangerously sharp. He sat back in his chair, flipping the knife in his fingers.

"Tell me your name."

"Fuck you."

"An unfortunate name, really. Is that what your mother was always shouting at you?" Alexei trailed the tip of the knife down the man's thigh, making him jump. "Last chance."

The man bared his teeth, but Alexei could read the anxiety in his features. "I'm not telling you shit."

"Very well." Lifting his fist, Alexei sunk the length of the blade into the man's thigh in a single thrust, holding it tight to the skin while the man thrashed against his bindings. "We have so many more questions to go."

"Paolo," the man gasped. "It's Paolo."

"Paolo," Alexei said, wrenching the knife from his flesh and watching the blood soak through his jeans. "And who do you work for?"

"You brought me all the way here, and you don't know who the fuck I work for?"

Alexei tsked, slamming the blade down into a second spot on Paolo's thigh and giving it a subtle twist. Paolo shrieked in pain, trying and failing to scoot away.

"Varda. I work for Aroldo Varda," Paolo panted.

"Very good. And what do you do for him?" Alexei left the blade embedded in the man's thigh and reached for a scalpel.

"I'm one of his accountants."

Alexei's eyebrows lifted. Forget enforcers; Dom had gone right for the source. "And you know about Varda loans."

"Yes," Paolo confirmed. "Most of them."

Drawing the scalpel's dull edge lightly along Paolo's forearm, Alexei watched goosebumps rise over his skin. "What can you tell me about Varda's business with the Romanos?"

"Why do you want to know about that?"

Alexei pressed the scalpel into the skin until Paolo yelped, carving a jagged line down to Paolo's wrist. "That's none of your concern. All I need from you are details about Romano dealings with Aroldo Varda."

"I don't know about any Romano deals," Paolo said, but he hesitated a fraction of a second too long, and Alexei knew it for a lie. He'd been doing this too long not to know the signs.

Gripping the man's hand, Alexei wrenched it until his palm was facing upward, shoving the bindings higher on his forearm to expose his wrist.

"Did you know most people don't slash their wrists correctly when trying to commit suicide?" He nicked the skin, coaxing a drop of blood to the surface. "They make horizontal cuts." He drew a shallow cut across the skin of Paolo's wrist. "And then they bleed out too slowly, someone happening on their body before they're dead."

Paolo whimpered, squeezing his hand into a fist and forcing more blood out of the cut. Alexei drew a second line under the first. "It can take hours to die, your body slowly weakening as the blood seeps out of your arm. Imagine how much pain I can give you in the course of a few hours, Paolo."

When Alexei repositioned the scalpel to draw a third line, Paolo shuddered, his whole body shaking from adrenaline and fear. "Wait!" he yelled when Alexei's blade bit into the skin.

"The Romanos do have some loans on Varda books. Big ones."

"How much?"

"I don't know." Alexei slashed Paolo's skin, making him cry out. "At least seven hundred fifty million euros, but I don't know if that's all of it. I swear I don't know," Paolo said on a shuddering sob.

"Has Romano paid?"

"I don't think so." Paolo sniffled. "I haven't seen those ledgers in a while, so if he made payments, I don't know about them."

"I thought payments were due immediately upon death these days."

"They are," Paolo assured him. "Elio made some kind of arrangement with Aroldo to buy him more time."

That was intriguing. "What deal was that?"

"I don't know." Paolo hung his head as if expecting another painful blow, but Alexei believed him.

"Very good, Paolo." He reached up to remove the blindfold, and Paolo blinked rapidly against the unexpected light. "Now, tell me, do you want to die quickly or slowly?"

Paolo let out a moaning wail. "Please. I won't tell anyone what happened. I swear."

"We both know that isn't true." He used Paolo's shirt to clean the scalpel and slid it back into his kit. He'd have to clean it properly later. "Normally, I like to take my time with liars, but since you were so helpful, I'll make it quick."

Yanking the knife out of Paolo's thigh, Alexei moved it an inch to the left and plunged it in again. This time when he pulled the blade free, blood poured from the wound, pooling on the seat of the chair and dripping onto the floor. Femoral artery wounds bled out fast.

Paolo was already slumped in the chair, unconscious, by the time Alexei cleaned the worst of the blood off his knife and slid it back into its spot in his kit. By the time he crested the stairs and found Dom in the next room, Paolo was dead.

"Well?" Dom asked, pushing to his feet when he spotted Alexei in the doorway.

"Said his name was Paolo, and he worked as an accountant for Varda."

Dom nodded. "One of them."

Good. Alexei preferred to know nothing about his targets. If they were willing to answer his easier questions truthfully, they were more likely to answer the others the same way. Even if it took a little persuading.

"He said Romano got them in deep for about three-quarters of a billion." A triumphant grin spread across Dom's face. "Apparently Elio's made some kind of arrangement with Varda to delay payment, but he didn't know the details."

"You're sure?"

Alexei shrugged. "Didn't feel like he was lying to me."

"Okay. Matteo can decide what he wants to do with that information, but at least now we know how deep Elio is with Varda. And how desperate he is to fix it."

"Should make it easier to bring him to his knees."

Dom flashed a sinister grin. "Exactly."

Chapter Thirteen

Carina sat at a little wrought iron table at the edge of the backyard, the breeze fluttering the pages of the sketchpad in front of her. It was late in the afternoon, the sunlight beginning to fade through the branches of the shade tree overhead, the soothing sounds of the water lapping against the side of the pool at her back.

Aside from her mother's sitting room, this was one of Carina's favorite spots on the entire estate. Her father had built a seating area at the edge of the grass, perched on top of a cliff, for their mother when she received her first cancer diagnosis.

Men had worked for weeks laying stone, building a pretty iron railing, and planting big trees. Plants in copper urns with bright flowers spearing up out of the dirt were brought in. Her mother would tend them diligently, naming each one until she was too tired to stand long enough to do it.

After she died, Carina wouldn't let anyone touch the flowers for weeks, determined to keep them alive herself. They'd withered shortly after Matteo walked out. At some point in the last five years, though, someone had planted new ones and made them thrive. Her mother would have been able to name the vivid blooms hanging heavy from their stems, but Carina could only admire them.

A gull called, and she turned her attention to the horizon dotted with small boats, their sails unfurled and fat with wind. It was the same view she had in Cefalù, but far less constricting. Here in Palermo, there was no heavy weight around her shoulders, no tiptoeing waiting for the other shoe to drop. Especially with her father gone.

When she'd arrived on the doorstep after Giuseppe's funeral, her modest bags in hand, her father's welcome had hardly been warm. He'd looked at her, lip curled, and asked if the Romanos were too cheap to put her up in a widow's apartment.

She'd nearly laughed. As if the Romanos cared enough to see that she was comfortable. Whether they could afford it or not. She was surprised she'd made it out with the widow's inheritance promised to her in the will.

It wasn't much compared to their supposed fortune, a couple million euros, but it was enough to keep her comfortable if her father turned her away. He hadn't, though, and she wondered how much of that was Alexei's doing. Alexei had always been good at planting ideas in her father's head as if they were his own.

With Giuseppe's money sitting somewhere Elio couldn't reach and her piece of her father's estate, she could get far away from here when it was all said and done. There wasn't much for her here anymore. Not with her mother gone.

Matteo would likely be glad to be rid of her, and she and Dom had never been close. Luca she would miss, but not enough to stay. Then there was Alexei. There was so much history between them, and so much of him was still a mystery. It was probably better that way.

They didn't talk in the dark of the night, and that was just as well. There would be questions he had she didn't want to answer. She was happy to let him use her body. He made her feel things she didn't know were possible, and that was enough. Getting any closer than that was a recipe for disaster.

The sound of a door slamming jerked her out of her thoughts. Were they home from their little strategy meeting, or was that the wind blowing through the house? At the sound of a second car door, she leapt out of her seat, leaving her sketchpad forgotten on the table, and rounded the edge of the pool.

Matteo had been dragging his feet on taking decisive action for almost a week now. Just over five days had passed since Alexei left her to get answers from one of Varda's men, and Matteo seemed no closer to making any sort of moves that didn't involve him sitting behind a desk counting stacks of cash.

She could see the wisdom in bringing pieces of the Romano empire under their control, weakening them to the point where no one could rise up once Elio and the rest were eliminated. But the longer Matteo hesitated, the more she doubted that was still his plan.

She'd hoped Alexei's persistent absence from her bed meant Matteo was gathering the right kind of intel, but last night Alexei had told her he'd been busy collecting debts for the casinos, not drawing out more information on Romano businesses. Carina wanted Matteo to look her in the eye and give her a straight fucking answer. She was tired of his games and half-truths.

Letting herself into the great room through the sliding doors, she spotted Matteo, followed closely by Dom and Luca, stepping in through the front door at the same time she entered the hall. A look of irritation passed over Matteo's face when he saw her before disappearing. He'd been hoping to avoid her. The asshole.

"I trust everything went well?"

"It did," Matteo said, sweeping past her toward the study. Dom and Luca flanked him, and she hurried to keep up.

"What are you going to do next?"

"We've set some plans in motion that we'll be executing over the next few days."

She followed Matteo into the study, surprised to see Alexei already inside waiting for them. "And then?"

Matteo crossed to the desk and dropped into the chair, busying himself looking through the drawers to avoid meeting her gaze. "And then we'll take the next steps."

She had to fight hard to keep the exasperation from her voice. "And what next steps are those?"

He looked up at her, a deep crease between his brows. "I'm handling it, Carina. Don't you trust me?"

"No, Matteo. I don't." She clasped her hands in front of her when he scowled. "You walked out on this family seven years ago, and then you waltzed back in like nothing happened. I suggested taking a run at the Romanos. All I asked for was your help in making them answer for their offenses against me. You said you would give that to me."

"And I will," he bit off.

She shook her head. "I don't believe you."

"I don't know what you want me to say. I can't give you any more assurances than I already have."

"I don't want assurances, Matteo!" She threw her hands in the air. "I want action! Dates, plans, something, anything other than you keeping me out of the loop and treating me like a nuisance every time I ask for even the slightest scrap of information."

Matteo shoved to his feet, planting his hands on the edge of the desk and glaring at her from across the room. "I'm doing what's best for this family."

"No! You're doing what's best for you!" She hurled the

accusation at him, not caring how deep it sliced. "You have always and only ever done what was best for you. You think running away after my mother died was in the best interest of the family? You think leaving us all here with that son of a bitch who fathered us was in the best interest of the family?"

Matteo flinched, but she couldn't hold the words in any longer. They poured out of her like a dam finally broken.

"You think me being sold off to the highest fucking bidder was in the best interest of the family? You are as selfish now as you've always been. Family is supposed to mean something, and it means nothing to you."

"It isn't nothing," Matteo spat. "I made mistakes, and I'm here now trying to fix them."

"You're here trying to line your own pockets and pad your own ego," she scoffed.

"You want me to take up your petty revenge fantasies so you can feel better about having to play house for a few years? I don't care what I promised. I'm not going to do it if it's not what's best for the family. Get over it, Carina. Giuseppe's dead."

She noticed Alexei shift toward her out of the corner of her eye, but she was too angry to worry about what he might do, too worried he might stop her. Rage bubbled along her skin. It felt like knives stabbing her all over from the inside out.

"Playing house," she repeated, her voice strained and hoarse to her own ears. "Is that what you think I was doing?"

Matteo held his hands out to his sides and let them fall. Without thinking, she reached down and gripped the hem of her shirt, ripping it off over her head. She watched Matteo's eyes dip down to her torso, to the scars there, and then snap up to meet her gaze again.

"Was I playing house here?" she wondered, running her finger over a jagged scar to the left of her belly button. "When

Giuseppe came home drunk and accused me of cheating on him even though I hadn't been allowed to leave my rooms in weeks?"

She moved her hand to a large puckered circle under her left breast. "What about here? Was I just playing house when Giovanni Romano burned me with a cigar by the pool for talking back to him?"

Turning to the side, she dragged her finger over a series of cuts dotting her ribcage. "Maybe it was these. From the time Vincenzo threw broken bottles at me while my husband and Elio laughed. I guess we were just playing fucking house."

She blinked back the tears burning her eyes. She would not cry in front of her brother. She wouldn't give him the satisfaction.

"That was me doing *my* best. For family." She sneered the word. "You left, Matteo. And you have no idea the price that was paid—that *I* paid—for your selfishness."

She didn't wait for him to speak. She couldn't bear whatever empty words he might offer her anyway. Instead she turned on her heel and fled the room, needing the fresh air and the wind on her face.

Tears spilled over her cheeks and slid down her neck while she struggled to make sense of her shirt so she could tug it back on, abandoning it in favor of shoving her way through the door and into the evening air. She gulped in greedy lungfuls, the breeze cooling and drying the hot tears on her skin.

She sank onto the edge of a pool lounger, wrapping her arms around her waist and doubling over with shame and grief. Shame for ever letting anyone treat her that way, grief for the woman she might have been if her life had gone differently.

There was no sense crying about it now; it was over and done with. But she couldn't seem to stop.

Chapter Fourteen

Alexei stepped onto the pool deck and noted the way Carina immediately tensed. She looked up and met his eyes, swiping at her cheeks and springing to her feet. Her hands frantically worked over the fabric of her t-shirt, trying to pull it back on, and he crossed to her, gripping her wrist before she could cover herself again.

"Get off me," she said, her voice thick with tears, her face streaked with them.

He stepped closer, wrapping his hand around her ribs and dragging his thumb over the circular scar. A cigar. It was the right size and shape for it. His blood burned white hot at the idea of Giovanni fucking Romano pressing a cigar into her perfect skin hard and long enough to leave this kind of permanent mark.

He'd heard the screams of people being burned; he'd inflicted them himself often enough. Already he was making a list of all the ways Giovanni could die. Fire was right at the top. In his car, maybe, where he'd be trapped, his body slowly consumed by flames while he screamed.

"Let go, Alexei," she said, and the defeat in her voice had him dropping his hands and stepping back.

As he watched her slide her shirt back into place, he thought about the morning he'd woken up beside her with the gray light of early dawn filtering into the room. The way she'd bolted out of bed when his phone rang and covered herself up.

"You've been hiding those from me."

She glanced down at herself even though she was already covered, crossing her arms over her chest. "Not hiding. You take what you want from my body when you come to my room in the dark. Exploring every inch of me under a microscope doesn't seem to be quite what you're after."

He took a step closer, forcing her to look up at him. "You should have told me."

"Why? So you can look at me with pity like my brother did in the study? Poor little Carina." She shifted, her gaze sweeping out to the water beyond the cliffs. "No thank you."

"Is that what you feel when you look at me?" he wondered, gripping her chin to turn her to face him and tilting his head to display his scar. "Pity for the boy who was so horribly disfigured?"

"Of course not. I have never said that."

It's true, she hadn't. She was probably the only woman he'd ever known, certainly the only one he'd ever had in his bed, who didn't stare at it or run their fingers over it in morbid fascination, wondering how he got it but too afraid to ask.

"Then why do you think I'd feel pity for you?"

She shook her head and took a step back, his hand falling from her chin. "It's different. I just..." Her breath caught, and she took several deep breaths before continuing. "I've had so little say in my life. I wanted a say in this. I thought Matteo was giving me a say in it. But like everyone else, he only cares about himself. He says one thing to your face and does another behind your back."

Scrubbing her hands over her face, she shoved them through her hair, holding them against her neck. "Maybe I shouldn't wait."

"Wait for what?"

"To leave."

Something constricted around his chest, stealing his breath at the thought of her leaving. His hands balled into fists at his sides. "Leave?" She nodded. "And go where?"

She was quiet for a long moment, and when she spoke again, her voice was sad. "Anywhere but here. Matteo is never going to give me Elio or the others. I'll let him stay and do what's right for the family, and it'll be my turn to go."

"I'll kill them whether you're here or not." Her head slowly turned, her gaze meeting his, her eyes skeptical. "They touched you." He took a step closer. "They hurt you." He snaked an arm around her waist, his voice thick with rage. "They marked you. They will pay for that. Painfully. Excruciatingly so."

Her eyes searched his, her palm pressed flat to his chest. "You really mean that."

Alexei dipped his head, pausing with his lips a hair's breadth from hers. "I really mean that," he whispered before taking her mouth.

Her arms came around his neck in an instant, her body pressing against his. He lifted her off her feet, and she wrapped her legs around his waist. Gripping her ass, he rocked her against him while his tongue swept along hers, and she nipped it with a needy moan.

He captured her bottom lip between his teeth, pulling back and letting it slip through. He loved to see her lips swollen from his kiss as much as he loved to see them wrapped around his cock while she sucked him. The strong, sudden desire to see all of her, to study and memorize every inch of her body, swept through him. But he had to deal with Matteo first.

He set her on her feet, smiling when she huffed in protest and wrapped her hands around the back of his neck, dragging him down for another kiss. He gave in to her and let her take what she needed from him. He'd get every bit of what he wanted from her later.

"I want to see you, Carina. All of you. I want to take my time."

"Why?" Her voice was thin and whisper quiet.

"Because I want to mark every inch of you as mine." He watched her eyes darken, felt the subtle press of her body against his. "And I want to make sure you know pity is the last thing on my mind when I see you, when I touch you." He pressed a quick kiss to her lips and took a step back. "Come to my cottage tonight. I have some late business, but I should be home by midnight."

He turned on his heel and crossed to the door without waiting for her to respond. If she didn't come to him, then he would seek her out. Either way, the night would end with her underneath him, coming on his cock and his fingers and his tongue. He would make sure of it.

Matteo was alone in the study when Alexei stepped into the doorway. The hopeful look in his eyes when he glanced up made Alexei wonder if he'd been expecting Carina. The look quickly shifted to one of annoyance.

"I suspect you spoke to my sister when you left here," he said, voice clipped.

"I did."

"Did you know?" It was clear Matteo meant only one thing.

The unpleasant sensation of guilt rippled through him. "I didn't."

"How's that possible? Fucking her with your clothes on?"

Alexei's grin was feral. "If you want a detailed list of all the ways I've fucked your sister, you'll be waiting quite a long time."

"Please spare me," Matteo said with a wave. "I'd rather pretend you're leaving her alone like I told you to."

"Let's not go there again. We both know you won't get your way. If we're going to talk about Carina, we have more important matters to discuss."

Matteo sighed. "It's not that I don't want to give her what she wants—"

"Yes, it is. That's exactly it. I've heard your talks with Dom and Luca. You lean more toward partnering with Elio than eliminating him. I'm here to tell you that's not going to happen."

Matteo's eyes narrowed on Alexei's face. "Meaning what exactly?"

"Meaning, whether you approve or not, Elio, his uncle, his cousin, and anyone else who laid a hand on her will pay by mine. You're not the only one who failed her in the last five years. You're just the only one not willing to fix it in the way she deserves."

Leaning back in the chair, Matteo swiveled to look out the window at the trees swaying in the breeze and the stretch of blue beyond. "If I'd known that would be her life…I'd do it over a thousand times."

Alexei couldn't say he disagreed with the sentiment, but it still wasn't a solution. "I'm sure that's true for any of us. But Elio is done, Matteo. You need to make other plans."

He turned back to face Alexei, brow raised in challenge. "And if I don't?"

"Then don't." Alexei lifted a shoulder. "But you have two weeks, and then those Romano fucks are going to start disappearing. You get to decide how prepared you are for that eventuality."

"Four weeks."

"Three," Alexei countered. "That's my final offer."

Matteo tapped a pen against the blotter on the desk, lips pressed into a thin line. Even from this distance, Alexei could tell he was calculating the changes to his plan, moving the chess pieces, rearranging the outcome. Ultimately he nodded, meeting Alexei's gaze.

"Three weeks," he agreed.

Chapter Fifteen

Carina stood in the kitchen, peering through a window overlooking the back of the estate. It was late, a few minutes after midnight, and the room was empty, quiet, only the low hum of the refrigerator for company.

She told herself she'd come down to make some tea, something to help her sleep. But from this vantage point, she had an unobstructed view of the row of small cottages nestled at the back of the property for their live-in staff.

Alexei had moved into one of those cottages when he was about eighteen, right before she left for her first year of boarding school. It was the first time she remembered him having a space of his own. She'd asked him about it once, if he liked living there, but her father had interrupted them, a violent look in his eye. He'd sent Alexei off on an errand and chastised her for being alone with him.

A black figure moving down the path caught her eye. She'd recognize the long, lean lines of him anywhere. He stopped at the door of the last cottage, and then a light came on, his dark silhouette moving across the faint yellow glow.

He paused in the front window, his broad shoulders tapering down to a narrow waist and what she knew to be powerful hips and thighs. She loved everything he did to her, and she wanted more. She'd been wondering all day what might happen if she actually went to him tonight. That heady promise of wanting to see all of her, wanting to mark her as his.

Did she want to be his? Something funny fluttered in her stomach, and she pressed her hands against it. She'd belonged to someone before. And look how well that had worked out for her. But there was something about Alexei; there always had been. An invisible force drawing her to him.

But would the reality live up to his fantasy? Would it live up to hers? Maybe it didn't matter. This was a temporary fix to a problem she would never be able to solve. She'd long since given up on the fantastical notion of love and other silly childhood fantasies. This thing with Alexei, it wasn't about love. It was about need. And that was enough.

Turning for the back door, she tugged it open, picking her way over the damp grass in her bare feet. The closer she drew to his cottage, the more urgently her heart thudded against her rib cage. Once she reached it, she followed the stone path connecting the cottages to one another and to the courtyard.

Pausing on the shallow stoop, she wrung her hands. She didn't know what Alexei meant when he said he wanted to mark every inch of her. She shouldn't want to know. She should turn around, run back to her room, and insist they carry on as they had been. Stolen moments in the dark where he used her body as much as she used his. But God help her, she wanted to find out.

She raised her fist to knock, the door swinging open before she could. With the light at his back, she could barely make out his features, but she saw the slow grin spread across his lips. He stepped back silently, and she followed him inside.

"You came faster than I thought you would."

He closed the door with a soft click, and her eyes took in the small space while she collected herself and willed her heartbeat to slow. Like his office, it was sparsely furnished. A single couch was pressed up against the longest wall, a low coffee table in front of it. He didn't have a TV, and for some reason that struck her as odd. Didn't men love to watch sports? Even her father had liked to yell at a game of soccer every now and again.

The living room transitioned into an eat-in kitchen with a small table and two chairs. The fridge was a third the size of the commercial-grade appliance in the villa, and for the first time, she realized how different their lives had always been. It seemed a stupid thing to notice just now after all this time.

He moved further into the room, and she turned in time to watch him set a leather roll on the kitchen table. She'd seen him carry it around before. He called it his tool kit, and she had the sudden urge to look at whatever tools he kept inside. To run her fingers over them, feel the weight of them in her hands.

"Soon," he said, noticing the path of her gaze.

He held out a hand to her, and she went to him, pushing up onto her tiptoes when he leaned down to brush his lips against hers. She sank into the kiss by degrees, sliding her hands up to fist in his hair and holding him close while his lips and tongue worked magic against hers.

His hands came up to her waist, fingertips exploring under the fabric of her pajama top, and she flinched. This kind of intimate moment is exactly what she'd been trying to avoid. He started to push her top up over her stomach, but she stopped him with a hand on his arm.

"I won't be answering any questions about whatever you

see. I don't want to think about that, about them. Not tonight." Her eyes traced the line of his scar. "If you don't ask me about mine, I won't ask you about yours."

"For now," he agreed, pulling her shirt off and filling his hands with her naked breasts.

His fingers circled her nipples, slowly tracing the sensitive skin around them but refusing to touch them. His eyes trailed down her body while he teased her, his gaze lingering on her stomach and her side. Being on display for him was intoxicating, despite how vulnerable it made her feel.

Sinking down into one of the kitchen chairs, he pulled her between his thighs and flicked his tongue against her nipple before dragging the flat of his tongue across it. It shot pleasure straight to her core, and she bowed her back, desperate for him to do it again.

He switched to her other nipple instead, flicking then tonguing it. He moved back and forth between them until both were painfully hard and wanting more than his soft, teasing licks. She much preferred his roughness to his lover's caress.

Shifting his hands down her hips to the waistband of her pajama pants, he pressed kisses across her stomach, lingering over the burn scar he'd been transfixed with this afternoon. She ran her fingers through his hair while he nibbled her skin, trailing kisses down to her belly button.

Hooking his thumbs in the waistband of her pants, he slid them down over her hips, groaning low in his throat when he realized she wasn't wearing any panties underneath. He shoved at the material until it pooled at her feet and then quickly lifted her to sit on the edge of the table.

"Lean back and grip the opposite edge," he said, pushing her thighs wide as she did so.

His breath was cool against her skin, making her ache with need for him. Reaching out with a single finger, he traced the tip down her slit. Not pushing, not applying any pressure, just a long, light line that made her thigh twitch against his palm.

He grinned, using two fingers to spread her lips and expose her clit. A breath hissed from her lungs, and he looked up at her. He'd barely touched her, and already her breathing was ragged, needy.

Leaning down, he paused, his mouth close enough to her clit that she could feel his breath against it when he said, "Eyes on me, Carina. And don't come until I give you permission."

She groaned, long and low, when his tongue darted out to flick against her clit and then wrap around it, suckling it gently. His fingers held her open, and she tried to buck her hips to get him to move them, slip them inside her, something.

He grinned, continuing his lazy assault on her clit with his tongue, and used his other hand to wrap around her hip and hold her flat against the table. Slowly he increased the pressure and speed of his tongue, but each time her hips would jerk involuntarily against his grip, he'd ease off, denying her the orgasm she was panting for.

Finally, blissfully he slipped one finger, then two, inside her, holding them deep while his lips wrapped around her clit and he curled them up against just the right spot.

"Fuck," she gasped, pussy clenching around his fingers.

"Not yet, Carina," he said, easing the pressure inside her and drawing his fingers out.

"Alexei," she panted, wanting to feel him fill her again, needing him to push her over the edge and release the tension coiled tight inside her.

"Hmm?" he murmured, dragging the flat of his tongue down her slit and then back up. "Did you want something?"

"I hate you."

He chuckled, shoving two fingers back inside her and pumping them in and out slowly. "Do you? Doesn't seem like you hate this to me."

The muscles in her thighs shook, her fingers gripping the edge of the table so hard they hurt while he wrapped his lips around her clit again. His fingers picked up speed, thrusting frantically and grazing just the right spot with each thrust.

"You're so close. Almost there." He replaced his tongue with the pad of his thumb and looked up at her, blue eyes sharp and piercing. "I want to watch you come for me. Not yet." He pumped her faster, his thumb dragging brutal circles on her clit, her body vibrating with the effort of waiting for his command. She wanted to wait for it, but she…

"Please, Alexei," she sobbed.

"Now," he barked, surging to his feet and gripping the back of her neck to bring her lips against his while his fingers drove in and out of her. He bit her lip, twisting her nipple roughly and murmuring praise in her ear while she shattered in his hands. "That was good. So good," he said, pressing a kiss to her ear, her jaw, her neck.

He lifted her off the table and carried her through a door in the kitchen to a small bedroom dominated by an enormous bed. Laying her down, he smiled when she relaxed bonelessly against the pillows.

"You look so beautiful when you come for me," he said, undoing his jeans and shoving them down his legs.

She slid her hands down her stomach to her thighs, trailing them lightly over her skin. His eyes tracked her movements while he toed off his shoes and stepped out of his jeans. Tugging his shirt off over his head, he palmed his cock, giving it a rough stroke, and she licked her lips.

"Not yet," he said with a grin. "I need your pussy first."

Carina sat up when he knelt on the bed, groaning softly when his hands gripped her hips and flipped her onto her stomach. He slid his body over hers, his weight pressing her into the bed, her sensitive nipples dragging against the duvet.

His hands traveled from her shoulders to her waist, lingering over scars she knew were there. He pressed a kiss to her shoulder where an array of them looked like a starburst from the time Vincenzo shoved her into a mirror when she was wearing only a towel.

Lips trailing lower, his hands moved down to squeeze her ass and then around to the back of her thighs, positioning her on her knees. She pushed up onto her hands, rocking back against him when she felt his fingertips trail across her pussy, but he used his other hand to push her shoulders back toward the bed.

She felt the smooth head of his cock trace up and down her slit, and she sighed, groaning when he eased his full length inside her. He reached down to tap against her clit with his fingers, holding his cock deep while she squeezed around him.

He tapped harder, making her jerk as he drew his cock out and slid back in again, not fast, but hard, jolting her body forward and scraping against her g-spot. Each thrust was measured and deep, sending tingles through her nerve endings until she sparked.

"Alexei." Her voice was thin, breathy, while he continued to pound against her, his hips slapping against her ass and dragging needy moans from her lips.

He kept one hand on her hip, the other sliding up her back to grip her shoulder for leverage. Each pump of his cock thrust her closer and closer to the edge, and when he leaned down again to rub at her clit, she fisted her hands in the duvet, shoving her ass back against him while she raced to the peak of her orgasm, crying out as stars exploded across her vision.

Alexei's cock stilled inside her, and he leaned over her back to whisper in her ear. "Do you want more, Carina?"

"Yes," she whispered. She might never get enough of him and the things he did to her.

She groaned when he rolled them onto their sides, keeping his cock buried inside her. Sliding his hand around to cup her breast, squeezing gently, he moved it lower and positioned her leg. Stroking his long fingers over her inner thigh, he gave it a gentle squeeze, pulling nearly all the way out and thrusting in deep again.

Reaching behind her, she wrapped her arm around his neck while his hand slid around to play with her nipple, rolling it between his fingers and tugging it sharply away from her body. She dug her fingernails into the back of his neck, holding on as he thrust inside her.

She was already so sensitive, and he was demanding more. Or, more accurately, giving her exactly what she wanted. His breath was harsh in her ear, his fingers tight and unrelenting on her nipple.

"You take my cock so good, baby."

"Yes," she whimpered, rocking her hips against him.

"Make yourself come. I want to watch you again."

She snaked her hand down her stomach, stopping just before her clit. "I want—" He thrust into her hard, stealing her breath.

"You want what?" he asked, dragging his teeth over her earlobe.

"I want you to come with me."

"Do you?" He rammed his cock in deep and ground his hips against her ass.

"Yes," she groaned, fingers inching closer to her aching clit.

"Good, baby. Make yourself come, and I will."

Her fingertips connected with the sensitive bud, rubbing it

in tight, frantic circles while his hand slid up from her breast to wrap around her throat. He squeezed, but not enough to cut off her air, while his cock slammed into her over and over.

"Alexei."

"I know, baby. Come for me."

At his hoarse command in her ear, she let the orgasm overtake her. Her pussy spasming around his cock, her back bowing, her toes curling. And with a few more wild thrusts, he emptied himself inside her.

"You are…incredible."

"Me?" She fought to catch her breath. "I thought that was you?"

He chuckled, nuzzling the back of her neck and releasing her thigh. She groaned softly as his cock shifted inside her at the movement. One of his hands still rested lightly on her throat, the other at her hip, and she knew she'd be content to lie here like this with him all night.

His arm settled around her waist, and he hugged her tight against him. "You still want my cock in your mouth?" he whispered.

"Yes," she said without hesitation, and she felt his lips curve into a grin against her ear.

"Good." She stifled a yawn. "But later. Right now you should sleep."

He positioned her body under the covers and lay on his back next to her, pulling her up against his side and sliding his hand down to squeeze her ass. She was right about one thing when it came to Alexei. He was going to ruin her. And in all the best ways.

Chapter Sixteen

The steady beat of Alexei's heart thumped under her ear, his fingers combing through her hair, pulling her out of sleep. Bright light from the high window behind the bed slashed across the opposite wall, and she grumbled her displeasure. She didn't want to be awake yet. She wanted to slip back into her dream where Elio Romano lay bloody and broken at her feet.

Alexei's hand traveled down her back and over her ass, squeezing it before giving it a light slap and making her grunt softly. "Stop that," she said, voice still thick with sleep.

"Stop what?"

His hand skimmed further south, shifting to brush his fingers against her pussy where she was spread open with her leg draped over his thigh.

"It's too early, Alexei," she said, squirming away from him.

He twisted under her to check the clock on the little side table. "It's almost noon."

He slid strong hands around her hips, lifting her over him until she straddled his waist. She swallowed a groan when his already hard length brushed against her core, still tender from the night before. Leaning down, she brushed her lips against his while his fingers stroked the backs of her thighs.

"You just want another orgasm out of me before you have to go."

He grinned, rocking his hips up against her. "Of course I do. You do it so well."

She let him slide his cock against her, sucking in a sharp breath when he lifted his hips and made contact with her clit. "You've had me on every single surface in this entire house over the last two days. How could you possibly need more?"

He captured her lips, hungrier this time, his fingers tightening on her thighs to hold her in place for his cock still moving against her. "If you have to ask the question, you're not paying attention. Sit up."

She shivered at his demand but did as he asked, sitting back on his thighs. She hated being told what to do. So why did Alexei's gruff commands make her pulse with need and eager to obey?

"Slide down on my cock." His hands trailed up from the backs of her thighs, over her ass to her hips, resting gently as he watched her.

Reaching down between them, she wrapped her fingers around his cock and stroked him from root to tip, twisting her wrist as she reached the head and making his hips jerk. She grinned. It was nice knowing she could make him just as needy for her when she wanted to.

She rubbed his head against her clit and down to her entrance, holding him in place while she slowly sank down, rocking her hips with a groan. She wanted to lean down and kiss him, but she knew what he wanted, so instead she braced her hands on his stomach and lifted herself off his cock, only to slide back down slowly. He wouldn't control her movements. Yet. So she had at least a little time to tease him.

He slid one hand up to cup her breast, dragging his thumb over her nipple while she rode him at a languid pace, rocking and grinding her hips with each downward thrust.

"Carina," he growled in warning, roughly tweaking her nipple.

"Mmm?" she hummed, arching against his fingers and squeezing his shaft inside her.

"You're going to get fucked if you don't pick up the pace."

She grinned, pulling slowly up and then sliding down just as slowly. She could feel every inch of him, and when she leaned forward slightly to grind her clit against his pelvis, she shuddered. "I fail to see the problem."

He growled again, and she felt it in every cell of her body. "Come here."

Leaning down, she sighed when her sensitive nipples scraped against his skin. She pressed a lazy kiss to his lips, and he deepened it immediately, his fingers digging almost painfully into the tops of her thighs, which somehow only managed to make her want him more.

"Do you want to get fucked?" he demanded, his breath hot on her lips.

"Yes," she whispered urgently.

He repositioned his hands on her ass, lifting her slightly off his cock and slamming his hips up against her in one hard thrust, drawing a low groan from deep in her throat. He pulled back and gave her one more hard, deep fucking.

"Are you sure? Because once I start, I'm not going to stop until I come inside you."

She groaned, nibbling his bottom lip, shifting to wriggle against his grip. "I'm sure."

"Good girl," he said, gripping her ass so tight he was sure to leave bruises and pummeling his cock inside her.

She braced her hands on either side of his head while he pounded her, her nipples too sensitive to drag against his chest anymore, but he tilted his head up to suck one into his mouth, tonguing it roughly before wrapping his lips tight and sucking it hard. She whimpered, barely able to hold herself up as electricity raced over her skin and her body trembled.

She could feel every inch of him sinking inside her, and still she craved more. She didn't know she could want someone this much, and it scared her. But the fear was its own kind of thrill. And when he pushed her to the brink, she wanted to take whatever he would give her and be greedy about it.

His thrusts became harder, faster, more urgent, and she knew he was close. She loved to make him lose control, loved to know she was the one who was responsible for it. And when he slammed inside her with his release, her own orgasm burned hot and bright until she screamed his name.

He pulled her down tight against him, his face buried in her neck, his lips pressing hot wet kisses against her skin as he rocked her hips against him, sending shockwaves through her body.

"Do you really have to go?" she asked, her voice muffled against his shoulder.

"I do." He ran a hand down her hair and across her back. "I've been ignoring Matteo long enough."

She huffed at the sound of her brother's name and flopped onto her back, lifting her arms over her head to stretch out her sore muscles and smiling when Alexei rolled onto his side to look at her.

"I told you he agreed to my deal," he said, laying his hand flat against her belly, his fingertips circling the burn scar under her breast. It seemed to be the only one he couldn't overlook.

"I know you did. But I don't trust him."

He leaned down to give her a quick kiss before rolling out of bed and crossing to the small bathroom. "You don't need to trust him. Only me." He looked back at her over his shoulder, one eyebrow raised, and the corner of his mouth tilted up in a grin. "Want to join me in the shower?"

She laughed. "Absolutely not. It's too small. One minute I'll be washing my hair, and the next I'll have your cock inside me again."

He tilted his head and grinned. "You say that like it's a bad thing."

"No," she said quickly, shaking her head when he turned from the door. "If you want to have sex in the shower, we'll do it in mine. It's bigger. With massaging jets. And a little bench."

His eyes darkened at that, and he nodded. "We're trying out your shower very soon."

She waited until the water squeaked on and pummeled against the shower walls before slipping out of bed and pulling on the pajama bottoms and top she'd arrived in. It was the first time she'd put clothes on since showing up on his doorstep. She didn't know where he found the two days to devote to her, but she wasn't complaining. Her muscles might be, but she certainly wasn't.

Pulling coffee beans down from the cabinet, she added some to a grinder and pulsed them into a coarse powder. She missed her morning cappuccino. Regular coffee with a bit of milk wasn't the same. Adding hot water to the bottom of the moka, she dropped in the little cup of coffee grounds and carefully added the pot on top, setting it on the small countertop burner.

It was finishing its hissing and bubbling when Alexei appeared from the bedroom, his hair still damp from the shower. He was shirtless, a pair of jeans riding low on his hips but unbuttoned. Her mouth watered, and she considered how easy it would be for him to talk her into another round if he wanted to.

He stepped up behind her, wrapping an arm around her waist and leaning down to nuzzle her neck, nipping the skin while she reached into the cabinet for two mugs.

"You're getting very good at that," he said, still holding her while she poured the dark liquid into the cups.

He reached behind her and opened the fridge, pulling out a small carton of milk and setting it on the counter in front of her. He didn't release her until she added milk for both of them—him just a splash—and handed it to him. It was all terrifyingly domestic. She tried not to think about it.

"You think I can sneak back to the house in pajamas at this hour?" she wondered, studying him over the rim of her mug.

"Why do you need to sneak? You think the entire house doesn't know what we've been up to these last couple days?"

The thought had heat rising to her cheeks, and she ducked behind her mug to hide it while he chuckled. "I have no interest in getting some sort of lecture from Matteo over it."

"Just do what I do," Alexei said, turning at a soft knock on the door. "Tell him to go fuck himself."

She laughed, and he pulled the door open on Giulia, whose eyes widened at the sight of Alexei without a shirt on and Carina in her pajamas. Giulia had started working at the villa after her wedding, and Carina had only known the older woman for a few months. She was competent but always worried about what was proper and easily scandalized. The look on her face made Carina want to laugh, but she swallowed it down.

"Did you need something, Giulia?"

"*Il Signore*"—Carina sighed at the title—"would like to see you in his office. As soon as possible," she added, her eyes sweeping down over Carina's clothes.

What the hell did Matteo want? She shared a look with Alexei over his shoulder and nodded at the maid. "Tell him

I'll be there in ten minutes. No sneaking for me, I guess," she muttered as Alexei closed the door and crossed to her.

He laid his hands on her shoulders. "Remember. It doesn't matter what he says. They're dead either way."

She nodded. She trusted Alexei would keep his word; it was one of the few things she felt steady in right now, but that didn't mean Matteo would be happy about it, that he wouldn't retaliate if he felt like it. And that possibility had nerves twisting her stomach into knots.

"Coming back tonight?"

"What?" She dragged herself out of her thoughts and back to the moment.

"To the cottage. Coming back?"

"Oh. Actually, I thought you could come to my room. We can use my shower."

He grinned, cupping the back of her neck and hauling her up onto her toes. "You'll have to be quieter than you usually are."

The corner of her mouth lifted into a wry grin. "So will you."

He kissed her quick and easy before releasing her, and she squared her shoulders and set off for Matteo's office. Whatever empty words her brother wanted to placate her with, she hoped he finished it quickly. She could use a shower and something to eat.

His head was bent over the papers he was studying, his lips moving as he read whatever was on the page. He looked so much like their father, dressed in a suit with the jacket tossed over the back of his chair instead of hung on the coat rack in the corner.

His hair was tousled, like he'd been running his hands through it, and the sleeves of his shirt were rolled up to the elbows, exposing tattoos along his forearms. Did he have those before he left? She honestly couldn't remember.

She stepped into the room and cleared her throat, biting her cheek to keep from grinning when his eyebrows shot up at her appearance. "Late morning?"

"Something like that."

Pushing away from the desk, he indicated she should sit and took the seat opposite her when she perched on the edge of the long leather couch. "About the other day. I was unfair to you."

"Yes," she agreed, refusing to give him any more than that. She was done placating men to protect their feelings.

"You're right, Carina. I've been away for a long time. There are things I don't know. Things that happened while I was gone that I should have been here to stop. Things that happened to you." He was silent for a beat. "I'm sorry."

His apology caught her off guard, but she wasn't willing to let him down so easily. "Sorry for what?"

"For leaving you, for not being here to protect you. For not trusting your word when you said they deserved to die."

"Thank you." She still wasn't sure she trusted him, not all the way. But it was a start. "Is that it?"

"No, actually." He got up and paced back to the desk, returning with the stack of papers he was reading when she arrived. "I've spent the last two days reworking my plan. An offense against one of us is an offense against all of us, and the Romanos will pay for what was done to you."

She shifted to the edge of her seat, gripping her hands in her lap and glancing down at the papers in his hand. "Okay."

"But I do have strategy to consider. We wipe them out without sufficiently weakening their financial strongholds and connections, and all we do is leave the door open for someone else to take their place. When this is done, I want the Romanos or whoever's left to be beholden to me and only me."

"And then you'll move on to someone else."

"Yes, exactly."

She narrowed her eyes. "Why are you telling me this? You've refused to include me in any of your plans since the start."

"You're right, and that was my mistake. We've already started taking direct hits at their illegal dealings. Drugs, mostly. Sometimes they smuggle girls into their strip clubs, but not often."

"You want to weaken his income stream, to twist the screws."

He flashed a quick smile. "Exactly."

"I can't imagine you're going to let me help with that."

"No." He handed her a paper from the top of the stack.

A list of legal Romano holdings. They weren't completely aboveboard. She knew the Romanos laundered money through their strip clubs the same way they did through their casinos. Covering their drug trade with clean cash from a legitimate business. But she had even less knowledge of Romano assets than she did Bianchi ones.

"I don't know what I'm supposed to do with this."

"I need better financial information about Giuseppe's businesses, and I think you might be able to get it for me."

She barked out a laugh. "And how do you propose I do that? Ask Elio nicely?" She handed the paper back to him. "I think there's a flaw in your plan."

"Not Elio. The bank. We want to know how deep underwater he might be on his remaining properties. All the strip clubs and his three homes."

"Why? How would that help?"

"I need to know exactly how desperate Elio is so I can push the right buttons. If it's as bad as I think it is, he's probably not paying his bills, and if he's not paying his bills, that means disgruntled employees and soldiers."

"And disgruntled men are easy to turn into spies and traitors." He nodded. "What can I do? Giuseppe is dead."

"Right." Matteo flipped through the stack and moved a paper to the top. "But you're his widow. A banker would be allowed to give you information on the accounts. Especially if you were sufficiently…persuasive."

She raised a brow. "You want me to fuck a banker so you can get financial information on Elio Romano?"

"What? Jesus. No. I want you to go there for a meeting and ask the right questions. Say you're trying to find out more information about his properties so you can plan for your future. Hint you're pregnant, say you want to sell, expand. Whatever the fuck you have to do to get your hands on a comprehensive list of the financial health of as many Romano businesses as possible."

She chewed the pad of her thumb, eyes darting from the paper in his hand to his face. "You really think I'm capable of doing that without fucking something up?"

"I do. I also think you're the only person who can do this for us. So…are you in?"

She looked up at him, eyes bright with challenge, and a slow smile spread across her lips. "I'm in."

Chapter Seventeen

"And if you want to stay this side of breathing, you'll keep the fuck out of Bianchi establishments."

Alexei wrenched open the steel door that led from the casino to the parking lot and shoved the man so hard he stumbled and nearly fell. He watched the guy bob and weave on unsteady legs through the rows of parked cars until he climbed into a beat-up Fiat and drove away.

Clenching and unclenching his fist, Alexei glanced down at his raw, red knuckles. He might have volunteered to beat down the guy who'd been caught counting cards at one of their poker tables, but that didn't mean it wouldn't hurt like a son of a bitch later. He much preferred the effortless sweep of a blade through flesh to using his fists.

But he had to get his frustrations out somehow. The days on Matteo's deadline were ticking down too slowly, and he hadn't been able to talk Carina out of their insane plan of going into Romano territory to try and get these financials for Matteo. It was too dangerous.

She was supposed to go in a few days, and even though

he'd already insisted on going as her driver and bodyguard, he didn't like the idea of releasing her into the lion's den and hoping it all worked out. If the plan backfired, she could get hurt. Then Alexei would be adding another Don to his hit list.

Turning to go back inside, he noticed Berto's bright blue convertible pull into the lot and screech through the rows of cars before angling across two spaces. Berto jumped over the side without bothering to open the door and ate up the distance between them with long strides.

"Is that…" Alexei inclined his head toward the envelope Berto shuffled out of his jacket pocket.

"Another Cappelletti installment?" Berto slapped the envelope into Alexei's outstretched palm with a grin. "Yes it is."

"How many fingers does he have left?"

"Eight. Turns out he's easily persuaded."

Alexei snorted and stepped back into the casino. Following the narrow hallway onto the floor with its beeping machines and swirling lights whenever someone hit a jackpot on the slots, he weaved through the ignorant tourists and old men playing grab-ass with girls young enough to be their daughters.

He signaled to Dom, who stood at the corner of one of the poker tables, a bottle blonde in a too-tight dress pressed against his side with her tongue in his ear. Dom nodded, wrapping his arm around the blonde's waist and leaning down to say something that made her flush bright red and then walk away from the table with him.

"How the fuck does he do it?" Berto demanded, trailing Alexei into another back hallway toward the casino's offices.

"He's got more money than you." He paused with his hand on the doorknob. "And probably a bigger dick."

"Fuck off," Berto growled, shoving at Alexei's shoulder and following him into the office.

Alexei chuckled, pulling down a ledger and dumping out the stack of bills to count it. Cappelletti decided to pay extra today. No doubt eager to keep the rest of his fingers. Marking down the amount and calculating the remaining balance, he shook his head. The kid was going to be making payments for a while at this rate. Not that Alexei cared, as long as the funds found their way back into Bianchi coffers.

Replacing the ledger on the shelf, he opened the safe with his thumbprint and unique numeric code and placed the envelope inside. They were expecting at least two dozen more payments this week, all from men too stupid to realize their limits when they were losing at blackjack or couldn't pick the right number on a roulette wheel or wanted to try just one more hand at poker to win their chips back.

He closed the safe and pressed the button to lock it with a buzz as his phone signaled in his pocket. He dug it out and swiped the pad of his thumb across the screen to unlock it. Carina.

Confirmed appointment Friday at one. Are you available, or should I ask Luca?

Like hell anyone but him would go with her to that goddamn meeting. *You don't have to do this for him.*

She ignored him like she had every other time he'd said something about her not taking the risk, and he grit his teeth. He scowled when her response flashed on the screen.

I'll ask Luca then.

Fuck Luca. I'll take you.

He tossed his phone on the desk with a sharp crack, and Berto looked up, eyebrow raised. "Everything okay?"

Alexei pinned him with a hard stare. "Why do you ask?"

"You've been awful moody lately. Worse than usual," Berto added, undeterred by Alexei's menacing frown.

"I'm fine."

Except he wasn't. He was bewitched by the most stubborn

woman he'd ever met. The woman who was insisting on going deep into Romano territory to attempt to get the financial documents Matteo needed to make sense of his world domination plans.

Not that Alexei would mind the Bianchis sitting on Sicily's throne. Salvatore Antonetti deserved to be taken down a peg or two. But that didn't mean Alexei wanted to throw Carina into the deep end to do it.

He raked a hand through his hair. He needed to get out of this place for a few hours, do something that felt productive. Matteo had seventeen days left before his deadline was up, and then Alexei was going to start dropping bodies.

He'd already begun to formulate a plan for each Romano man. Fire for Giovanni, death by a thousand cuts for Vincenzo. Davide, Giovanni's younger son, wasn't on Carina's list, so he could make it quick, merciful. He hadn't decided on Elio yet. Whatever it was, it wouldn't be pleasant. Alexei intended to make the son pay for the father's crimes too.

All he needed now was to know where to find them when he was ready. Since he couldn't run surveillance and tail them to log their patterns—too risky spending that much time in Romano territory—he'd need a source. And who knew the comings and goings of powerful men better than their side pieces.

"What do you know about Romano mistresses?"

Berto looked up from his phone in surprise at Alexei's off-the-wall question. "Only that they're not very discreet about it. If you're going to pull a stripper out of the gutter and dress her up, the least you could do is hide it better from your wife."

Alexei snorted. Lorenzo hadn't exactly been quiet about his affairs, and he didn't bother with strippers. But Alexei seemed to recall Elio liked to keep his mistresses working. If he did, that would make for easy access.

"Elio have a mistress right now?"

Berto wrinkled his brow. "Don't think so. Last one I saw him in the papers with was some redhead. Think she works at their club on the west side now."

Alexei grinned, skirting the desk and reaching for the door, an idea forming in his brain.

"Where are you going?"

"Suddenly I'm feeling in need of a lap dance."

"Fuck yeah." Berto followed him into the hall and matched his pace to the employee entrance. "One of their clubs sits on the border of the territories. It's not far from here."

"I was thinking the west side," Alexei said. "I need to find the redhead."

Berto stopped short, the door nearly smacking him in the face before he recovered and jogged to catch up. "You want to casually stroll into Romano territory? Now? With everything going on?"

"I do." Alexei pressed the remote start for his car, and it growled to life. "We're only going for a little entertainment. It's not like we're going there to make trouble." Not unless they started it. "Stay here if you're that worried about it."

Climbing behind the wheel, Alexei grinned when Berto jumped into the seat next to him. It might be risky showing up in Romano territory, but Alexei needed information. And he was willing to pay or threaten whoever he needed to in order to get it.

It was dark by the time they pulled up to the club. This one wasn't as nice as the one they met Elio in, but it wasn't their worst either. Whoever the redhead had been to Elio, she had clearly fallen out of favor. They liked to keep their best girls at their high-end property, smack in the middle of the territory. Romanos were well known for enjoying their own product, whether it was a line or two of coke or a willing mouth.

Berto wolf whistled over the music, and Alexei shook his head. At least Berto's enthusiasm would cover his own fact-finding motives. They claimed a seat on a low crescent moon sofa in front of the main stage.

The dancer caught his eye as she rotated around the pole and sent him a cheeky wink. Not her. She was blonde and didn't really strike him as Elio's type, more angular than curvy with small breasts and large nipples. Berto looked taken, though, balling up singles and tossing them at the stage.

When the waitress came to take their drink order, he made a big show of removing a wad of cash from his pocket and giving her a generous tip, following her gaze when she shared a look with a woman dressed in a very low-cut but very expensive sheath dress. A redhead. Bingo.

The redhead smiled, extracting herself from the lap she was perched on and leaning down to whisper something into the guy's ear. Not ten seconds after she walked away, another dancer was there to take her place.

He sprawled on the sofa, one arm draped over the back of it while he watched her approach. Each time she was stopped by another patron, she made a polite excuse, and then her eyes found his again. She wasn't really his type, but she looked exactly like the kind of woman Elio might go for—stacked and a little plastic. Alexei had no doubts she was a treasure trove of information.

"I hope you two are having fun," she purred, sitting down without waiting for an invitation.

Alexei nodded at Berto, who barely glanced their way, his eyes transfixed on the dancer who was cupping her breasts as she dropped to her knees. "He is. I'm not sure I've found what entertains me yet."

She pouted a pair of full lips painted bright pink and scooted closer, her hand gripping high on his thigh. "Well, I hope I can help with that."

Grinning, he leaned forward, circling her waist with his arm and giving it a squeeze. "I'm sure you can. But maybe there's somewhere more private we can go first."

"What about your friend?"

He shifted closer, sliding his hand up to brush his fingers against the side of her breast. "I don't like to share."

A slow smile spread across her lips, and she gave his thigh a squeeze. "I know just the spot we can go, and you can tell me what you do like."

Alexei followed her out of the booth, watching her hair sway over her shoulders and down her back, brushing the top of her round ass. She led him down a short hallway to the last door, opening it to a room furnished with black leather couches and dark teal velvet walls. Lights were secured in ornate sconces and gave an ethereal feeling to the space.

There was a minibar in one corner and a giant mirror affixed to the long wall. Even as the woman backed him onto one of the couches, all he could think about was pressing Carina up against that mirror and fucking her from behind until she begged to come.

"You're in luck tonight..." She paused, prompting him for a name with a lift of her brows.

"Angelo," he lied while she settled herself across his lap. "And why is that?"

"Because in this room"—she leaned down to nibble his earlobe—"anything goes."

"Anything?"

"Anything," she assured him, pressing her lips against his jaw and rocking her ass against his cock. "For a price."

"And what if I just wanted to talk?"

She giggled. "That doesn't feel like what you want to me." Her hand snaked its way up his thigh, but before she could grip him through his pants, his arm shot out to grab her wrist, twisting it enough that her eyes went wide.

"Let's have a conversation."

Her demeanor changed the moment he lifted her off his lap and dumped her on the couch, huffing out an irritated breath and crossing her arms over her chest. "I thought you were really going to be a good time."

"How long have you been fucking Elio Romano?"

Her spine straightened, and her eyes narrowed. "Who says I've ever spread my legs for Elio Romano?"

Alexei shot her a dubious look and reached into his pocket, slapping two two-hundred-euro banknotes on the cushion between them. Snatching them up, she folded them carefully into her bra before replying.

"We fucked for about two years before he moved on to someone else. He was very generous."

"That make up for all the times he hit you?"

She shifted in her seat and wouldn't meet his gaze. "He's a very passionate person."

Alexei raised a brow. "Did he put you up somewhere while you were together? An apartment or a house?"

"He did." When she didn't continue, he slapped another banknote onto the leather. "A nice condo overlooking the Tyrhennian," she said, plucking up the bill and tucking it away with the others. "He treats all his girls well."

"Financially," Alexei said, and her mouth thinned. "Where else does he spend most of his time?"

"He keeps an office in the city. When he gets tired of his frigid wife, he comes here. Or he used to." She twirled a large emerald ring around on her index finger. "Now he's got some VIP bitch."

He bit back a grin. Jealousy was an emotion he could press. "Maybe she's a better lay."

She snorted, crossing her arms over her chest. "You don't seem interested in finding out how good of a lay I am. What do you want to know about Elio for anyway? Hoping to sneak your way into his bed yourself? I think you'll be disappointed."

"Careful."

She slid away from him a fraction at the venom in his tone. "Elio dropped me when his father died. Said he had to focus. But all he did was focus on another slut closer to home."

"You haven't seen him in three months?"

She shrugged. "More like a few weeks. He came here late one night, maybe two weeks ago, all pissed off. He likes it rough when he's pissed off." Now that Alexei could understand. "I like it rough even when he's not," she said, her grin transforming into a pout when he pushed her foot out of his lap.

Elio probably stopped by to work out his frustrations after their meeting over the agreement. "And you haven't seen him since."

"No." She sighed, clearly disappointed by that fact. "I haven't."

He peeled two five-hundred-euro notes off the stack and held them up in front of her face, jerking them out of reach when she grabbed for them. "If I wanted to find Elio right now, where would he be?"

She bit her lip, eyeing the cash. "What time is it?" She reached for his wrist, turning it over to read the hour on his watch. "He's either at the office or the club. Like his father, he prefers to fuck his wife after dinner and then find something better to do."

Alexei clenched his jaw, letting her have the cash and stuff it into her bra. He shoved off the couch, leaning down to grip her hair and wrench her head back hard enough that she cried out. He brought his lips a scant millimeter from hers.

"I need you to remember one thing about our little chat. I don't give a fuck about you. If I find out you told anyone, even your goddamn cat, I did anything in this room other than gag you on my cock, you won't live to dance another day. Understand?"

Her eyes welled up with tears, but she nodded as frantically as his grip would allow. Releasing her, he strode from the room and signaled to Berto, who was being dry humped by the girl from the main stage. Berto groaned, copping a feel of the girl's breasts when he shoved some money down her top and slid her off his lap. He adjusted himself before following Alexei outside.

"Couldn't you let a guy finish what he started?"

Alexei gunned the engine while Berto climbed in. "If you wanted to fuck her, you should have taken her into a private room while I was busy."

"Yeah, yeah," Berto grumbled. "Some of us like to take our time."

They drove back to the casino in silence, Alexei's fingers tapping a fast rhythm on the steering wheel. Seventeen days. And then Alexei was going to make plans of his own. Bloody ones.

Chapter Eighteen

Alexei was waiting for her at the bottom of the stairs, brows pinched together in disapproval. He might not want her to go on this fact-finding mission today, but that didn't stop his eyes from roving over her from head to toe.

She'd gone for a relatively conservative dress in soft blue, with capped sleeves and a sweetheart neckline. It hugged her breasts and then flared out to swish around her knees. She'd completed the outfit with pumps in deep navy rather than the stilettos she preferred.

"Are you going to be able to run in those things if you have to?" Alexei asked, eyes tracing the line of her legs and ending at her feet.

"Yes." He raised a brow in disbelief. "Would you like to chase me for a demonstration?"

The corner of his mouth quirked up into a grin before thinning out again. "I still don't approve," he said, keeping pace with her when she moved around him toward the door.

"Lucky for me, I don't need your approval."

Before she could open the door, he pressed her back

against it, using his arms to cage her in. Irritation warred with desire as he pressed his body against hers, and she met his eyes with a hard stare.

"I know what you need," he murmured, his breath hot against her lips. "And I'd rather stay here and give it to you than put you in danger."

She laid her hand against his shoulder, intending to push him away so they could go. Instead she gripped the fabric of his shirt and pulled him closer, fusing her mouth to his and darting her tongue against his lower lip, then nibbling it with her teeth. One of his hands dropped to her waist, pulling her against him, and he ground his hardening cock against her.

Groaning against his mouth, she slid her hand up into his hair, gripping it tightly in her fingers. She gave his lip one last rough bite before pulling away. The look in his eyes, the feel of him against her, already hard and wanting, made his offer more than tempting. But she had to do this. She didn't just want Elio dead anymore. She wanted to watch him lose everything first.

"You can give it to me later," she said, leaning forward to nip his chin and wriggling out of his grasp. "Right now I have an appointment to get to."

He hung his head between his shoulders and took several deep breaths before pushing away from the door and reaching for the knob. Matteo insisted they take a black SUV. Something plain, nondescript. He didn't want them to be made as soon as they drove across the border.

Alexei opened the door for her, sliding his hand over her ass and giving it a squeeze before helping her inside. She couldn't help but notice the backseat was big enough for him to finish what he'd started inside. But after. Once she had the documents in her hand.

He climbed into the front seat and, after a quick peek at her in the rearview mirror, put the car in drive and pulled around the fountain. They traveled in silence, which was just as well. Her adrenaline was pumping too fast to be able to focus much on conversation. Or on more of his insistent nagging to change her mind.

Once they crossed the border into Romano territory, she felt Alexei's eyes on her at every possible moment. Ignoring him, she focused instead on her plan. First she'd muddle her way through pleasantries with the banker who'd danced with her at her wedding and spent time at the villa in Cefalù with his wife. He had several grandchildren now and one on the way, if she remembered correctly.

He'd be most sympathetic with a baby involved, and that's exactly the tactic she planned on using. If all went well, she anticipated being in and out in less than an hour with the papers in hand. She just hoped he didn't mention her little visit to Elio any time soon.

The car lurched to a stop, and Carina glanced out the window at the towering glass and stone structure of the bank. The soaring arches and spires had always reminded her of a cathedral rather than a financial institution. Though Giuseppe had always worshipped money.

Reaching for the handle, she heard Alexei's slow inhale and shook her head. "I'm not going to argue with you about this again."

He slid out of the front seat and opened her door, offering his hand to help her down. She gave it a hard squeeze, smiling softly when he squeezed back. Taking a deep breath, she squared her shoulders and darted across the street.

"You really can run in heels," he said, and she laughed.

Voices echoed in the atrium, and her heels clicked over the tile floors as she crossed to an ornate reception desk. The woman behind it looked to be in her mid-fifties with graying hair and bifocals perched at the end of her nose while she studied the computer in front of her. She looked up at Carina, her eyes shifting to study Alexei over her shoulder.

"Good afternoon. I have an appointment with Signore Fusco."

"Name?" the woman asked, fingers poised over the keyboard.

"Carina Romano." She felt Alexei shift behind her, and she glanced at him over her shoulder. She didn't like using the name any more than he liked hearing it.

"Ah, yes. Here you are. Signore Fusco is expecting you. You will need to take the middle elevator up to the third floor and turn left. His secretary will show you to his office."

Carina smiled. "Thank you so much."

She crossed the atrium to the elevators and pressed the button, gripping her wrist to steady herself. The rapid pulse under her fingers did nothing to ease her anxiety. This couldn't go wrong. If she didn't get what Matteo needed and Elio found out, their plan would be dead in the water.

"Relax," Alexei said softly once the elevator doors closed behind them. "You pretended with these people for five years. You can pretend for another hour."

Carina nodded, blowing out a slow breath as the doors opened. The hallway was busy, and she didn't have much time to think before people stepped into the car and she stepped off. The woman at this desk was much younger, and unlike like the woman downstairs, the look she sent Alexei was one of interest rather than interrogation.

Tamping down the flutter of jealousy, she cleared her throat. "Carina Romano for Signore Fusco, please."

"Of course," the woman said, pushing to her feet, eyes traveling over Alexei again. "Right this way."

Alexei's grin was wide when she peeked over her shoulder at him, and her eyes narrowed. He enjoyed seeing her jealous entirely too much. Maybe she wouldn't ask him to make use of the backseat of the SUV after all. Purely on principle.

The woman stopped at a hand-carved door and pushed into a richly decorated office. An empty, richly decorated office. "Signore Fusco should be along any moment. Can I get you anything to drink?"

"Some tea, please," Carina said, just to give the woman something to do so she'd stop looking at Alexei like that.

When Alexei moved to follow her into the office, the woman put a hand on his arm to stop him. "Oh, I'm sorry. Signore Fusco insists on meeting with clients alone. I'm afraid staff must be stuck with me at the front." Alexei frowned and looked past her to the office. "Not to worry. Your charge is safe here."

Carina cleared her throat and grappled for her haughtiest voice. "Don't go far. I shouldn't be long."

Alexei inclined his head and let the woman lead him away. Carina dug her fingernails into her palm as the woman ran a hand down the back of his arm and gave his bicep a flirtatious squeeze. Focus. She needed to focus. She couldn't let herself get distracted by images of shoving that woman down the nearest flight of stairs.

Perching on the edge of an antique leather chair, she sat with her back ramrod straight, legs crossed at the ankles, and waited. It didn't take long before Fusco swept in, closing the door behind him with a snap. He was all smiles when he stepped up beside her, leaning down to press quick kisses to each cheek.

"Carina, you're looking lovely as ever. I was so sorry to hear what happened to Giuseppe. You must be devastated." He settled into the chair behind the imposing desk and fixed her with a pained expression.

Carina dropped her eyes to her hands and forced a note of

grief into her voice. "I've hardly known what to do with myself these last few months."

"Of course not. To lose a husband so young and without any children to fulfill you. Tragic."

This was going to be too easy. "Well, that's why I'm here." She pressed a hand to her belly, smiling softly while she caressed it with her fingers. "Life is a funny thing."

He was beaming when she looked up at him again. Perfect. "Are you…?"

"I am." She nodded. "I didn't realize at first. I was so upset when I lost him. I wasn't…" Her voice broke, and she cleared her throat before continuing. "I wasn't sure I could ever be happy again. And now…"

"That's wonderful news! Is there anything you need?"

"I think you might be the only one who can help me with something."

"Of course, my dear, anything."

She scooted closer, dropping her voice as if keeping him in confidence. "I haven't known very long, and I haven't told Elio yet. I've been afraid…afraid he would be upset. Especially if it was a boy." She moved her hands to her stomach to shield it. "I don't want anything to happen to my baby."

"I see." His bushy white brows drew together. "Things can get messy when two potential heirs are involved. And Giuseppe did mention to me once that he wished you two had children so he could name a different successor."

"He said the same to me. I wish he could be here to…" She muffled a soft sob with the back of her hand, barely hiding a grin when he slid a box of tissues toward her across the desk. She plucked one out and dabbed at the corner of her eyes. "Thank you. I'm not really sure what I need. I only want to make sure my son is well provided for. That he has what he's entitled to as a Romano heir and that Elio doesn't steal it out from under him."

Fusco tapped thick fingers on the edge of his desk while he studied her. "It would be difficult to challenge Elio in court. He could put up a lengthy battle, force a paternity test."

"I know. But my son is worth it. And you yourself said Giuseppe would have wanted the best for him."

"Without a doubt. You were a treasure to him."

Carina's smile was sharp, but Fusco didn't seem to notice. She'd been a possession and nothing more. "I don't really know what I need, what would help." She sniffled and wiped her nose. "But my husband considered you a true friend. And since Elio turned me out of the villa in Cefalù before I even had time to grieve, I didn't know where else to go."

He puffed up at her lie about Giuseppe considering him a friend. She'd never once heard Giuseppe say anything about Fusco at all. Except that his wife had great tits. Fusco turned toward the computer on the corner of his desk.

"If I was Elio," he said, fingers flying over the keyboard while a printer hummed to life on the credenza behind him, "I would make sure you got as little money as possible by hiding assets. But he can't do that if you know about all the assets, can he?"

She smiled softly. "I suppose not."

When the printer stopped whirring, he swiveled in his chair and collected a stack, shuffling them into a plain envelope and sealing the top. "Now, I'm sure these things will be confusing to you. There are quite a few loans against some of the more successful businesses, but that does not diminish their worth to the right buyer."

"Oh, Signore." Carina shot to her feet and reached across the desk to grip his hand. "You don't know what a relief this is to me. That you would help me, help us"—she pressed a hand to her stomach again—"make things right. For Giuseppe."

He stood and rounded the desk, placing a hand on her back and guiding her to the door. "Of course, my dear. Elio Romano is a ticking time bomb. I'm sure the territory would prosper far better under a man raised by your lovely hand."

He bent to kiss her knuckles after he opened the door, and she heard Alexei clear his throat from the hallway. "Thank you so much, Signore. How will I ever be able to repay your kindness?"

Fusco offered her the folder and gave a cheeky wink. "Well, Nunzio is a beautiful name for a little boy."

Carina ducked her head to pretend to hide a blush, and Fusco laughed. Alexei was standing in front of a small bench opposite the office door, one eyebrow raised. His hands were tucked into his pockets, but she read the tension in his body.

She turned to go and then stopped herself. "Oh, I nearly forgot. I would appreciate if we could keep our meeting between us. I don't want Elio to know about any of this until I've had someone look over these papers, and I know for sure it's a boy."

With a smile, Fusco gave her arm a squeeze. "Your secret is safe with me, Carina. Now, I'm glad you brought a guard with you. You must be careful." He nodded toward her belly. "Protect the future."

Fusco stepped back into his office and shut the door, and Alexei followed her down the hall to the elevator. They both ignored the cheerful goodbye from the secretary as the doors slid open, and they stepped inside the empty car.

"Protect the future?"

"Nunzio Fusco has a thing for babies." She grinned and held up the envelope. "He gave me a full list of Romano assets in case I have to fight Elio in court for an inheritance for my son." Alexei's eyes dropped to her stomach, and his lip curled back over his teeth, making her laugh. "My imaginary son."

"Damn well better be imaginary. Since the only son you'll be having is mine."

The doors opened with a ding, and Alexei immediately stepped into the lobby, but she was too stunned by his statement to move.

Chapter Nineteen

lexei took two paces away from the elevators before realizing Carina hadn't followed him out. Turning on his heel, he shot his arm out to catch the door before it slid closed again. She was rooted in place in the middle of the car, envelope still aloft, staring at the opposite wall. A moment frozen in time.

He blocked the entrance with his body so people wouldn't be able to get on and watched her. He wanted to know what she was thinking, but her face was half hidden behind the envelope in her hand.

When the elevator began buzzing angrily to announce the open door, she jumped, crushing the papers she held before loosening her grip. Without making eye contact, she darted around him and bolted for the lobby doors. He chased after her, cursing under his breath.

He didn't know why he'd said it. But the idea of her being pregnant with that bastard's baby, with anyone's baby but his, tore open a feral place inside him. A place that wanted to clearly mark her as his, to make sure the world knew exactly who she belonged to.

Children had never really crossed his mind before. He couldn't honestly say they were crossing his mind now. Though picturing Carina swollen with his child was becoming more enticing by the minute. Knowing she'd be his. Forever. He didn't hate the idea. Carina, however, seemed to be of a different opinion on the matter. And it was starting to piss him off.

Gritting his teeth, he followed her through the gaudy gold doors onto the street, eyes quickly darting over their surroundings to make sure no one was following them. That was his purpose here today, after all. He didn't see anyone who looked out of place or watched them a little too long.

By the time he refocused on her, she was already halfway across the street, expertly weaving through the rush of traffic on those damned heels. The same heels that did things to her calves and her ass that made him want to fuck her wearing nothing else.

When she moved to wrench open the car door, he slapped a hand against it to keep it closed. For the first time, she looked up at him, and the look in her eyes surprised him. He'd expected anger, maybe outrage, but it was something else entirely. Fear? No. It couldn't be that. Why the hell would the idea of being a mother to his child make her afraid?

"Are you going to say something?"

"I have absolutely nothing to say to your absurd outburst." Her mouth thinned into a hard line, and she crossed her arms over her chest.

"Absurd," he repeated, rolling the word around on his tongue and angling his body closer to hers.

"I hardly think now is the time to talk about it," she said when he opened his mouth to speak. "Unless you want to stand out in the open, in the middle of Romano territory, trying to explain to me the perfectly rational reason you had for casually discussing your desire to breed me like a bitch in heat."

"That is not what I said."

She cocked an eyebrow. "If you have a better explanation, I'm all ears. Hopefully one of Elio's men doesn't recognize us while you think it through."

He glanced over his shoulder to check the street again. He still didn't see anyone, but she was right. They shouldn't linger. "Get in," he gritted out, pulling the door open and waiting for her to scramble inside.

He claimed his seat behind the wheel, slamming the door behind him with a satisfying crack. After a failed attempt to catch her eye in the rearview mirror, he threw the car into drive and peeled away from the curb.

"You're being ridiculous," he growled once they'd pulled onto the highway, unable to stand the silence any longer. "Childish."

"I'm being ridiculous? What the hell kind of thing was that to say to me? You manage to finally shove your way into my bed, and the first thing you want to do is trap me with children?"

His hands gripped the steering wheel so hard the car jerked to the left before he righted it again. "Seriously? Shove my way in? It's not as if I had to pry your legs open and beg you, Carina. It's not as if you don't let me fill you up every chance you get."

"They make pills for that now, you asshole." She pounded her fist against his headrest, and he scowled at her in the mirror. "I might have been willing to spread my legs for you, but that hardly makes me willing for all the rest."

"Forgive me," he spat. "I didn't realize my genes were so undesirable. Maybe you should have tried harder to get a Romano brat in your belly after all."

The barb landed too well, and she winced, her body

deflating as the fight went out of her. Alexei kicked himself. Why the fuck was he even arguing about this? It's not as if he'd spent a single solitary second thinking about children, with or without Carina. His life didn't exactly allow for it. What would he do, raise a kid in a two-room cottage on someone else's land?

But he hadn't been able to stem the visceral, overwhelming desire to make sure no other man could ever claim her in such a way. If he was going to picture that kind of life with someone, who else would it be besides Carina?

He doubted anyone else could come close to her. He still had so much of her to unwrap and discover, and even now, he knew no other woman could hold a candle to her.

"Carina—"

"It'll be better if you don't," she said. "You might say something else you mean and wish you hadn't."

"I didn't mean that. You know I didn't."

"So you said it just to hurt me?" She scoffed. "That hardly makes it better."

Fuck. He ran a hand through his hair, gripping it at the roots before releasing it. "I don't know why I said it. Any of it."

"Okay."

When she said nothing else, he let her have the silence. She'd calm down eventually. And when she did, she'd see that what he'd said meant nothing. That it wasn't what he wanted. That this thing between them was…something else. Something that didn't end in children or commitments.

He had no intention of letting her leave Sicily, of letting her stray that far from him. But he'd never considered what came after this was over. After she didn't need him for her revenge anymore. The thought that she might be using him as a means to her own end had him jerking the car off the road and angling it behind a dense patch of trees.

"What are you doing?" she demanded as he climbed out of the SUV and yanked open her door.

He pulled her out of her seat and shoved her back against the side of the car, his hand darting out to grab her hip and hold her in place. "We're finishing it, Carina. So say what you need to fucking say."

"The minute the doctor pronounced Giuseppe dead, I was free!" She drilled a finger into his chest, anger sparking in her eyes. "I will not be anyone's pawn or toy or plaything ever again."

"I never said I wanted that."

"No. Only that you wanted me pregnant and tied to you. Forever. I wouldn't do that for my husband, and I sure as hell won't be doing it for someone like you."

"Someone like me." He clenched his fingers into a fist by her head, shoving away from her before he did something he'd regret. "I apologize," he said, letting his cool mask slide into place. "I almost forgot I serve at the pleasure of whatever Bianchi has me by the balls. First your father, who molded me into what I am and told me to be grateful. He used me to settle all kinds of scores. Then you. Begging for my help with your revenge."

Her chin ticked up, but the fire had gone out of her eyes. "I never begged."

His laugh was bitter. "No. I suppose you didn't. But it's what you want to use me for all the same. I guess you and Lorenzo aren't that different after all."

She flinched like he'd slapped her, but he was too angry to care.

"Where are you going?" she demanded when he turned for the tree's edge.

"I need some fucking air."

Without a backward glance, he stalked away from the car and disappeared into the green.

Chapter Twenty

Carina watched the trees rustle as he passed, and then he was gone. How the fuck had this become her fault? He was the one who'd started this whole damn thing in the first place. Whatever the hell this thing even was.

She didn't want children. She might have once, before her father sold her off and ruined her, but not anymore. And she had no intention of apologizing for it. She'd spent years carefully and painstakingly hiding her use of birth control from her husband after her first pregnancy scare. If Giuseppe had ever found out what she was doing, the consequences would have been extreme.

There was no way in hell she'd ever put herself in a position to be owned and controlled by a man ever again. Especially not with a child. And if that hurt his feelings, then he'd just have to get the fuck over it.

If that's what Alexei really wanted, he could go find it with someone else. That thought sent jealousy and disappointment rippling through her, and she ruthlessly stamped it out. He would not break her. Not on this. The stupid, impulsive, arrogant, sexy asshole.

She paced away from the car toward the trees, but the ground was soft and spongy under her feet, and she had no idea how far he'd wandered. It was probably best to just wait in the car for him to walk off his mood. Then they could be on their way and do their best to avoid each other for a while.

Turning to reach for the handle, she noticed the man too late, his body a blur as he darted forward and wrapped one arm around her waist and the other around her shoulders. She opened her mouth to scream for Alexei, and he clamped a hand over it.

"Look what I found," he murmured against her ear. "A lonely little slut on the side of the highway."

She froze, instantly recognizing the sound of his voice. Lepera. Elio's bodyguard. The hand around her waist inched its way down across her stomach, cupping her between her legs, and she shuddered. Shoving her elbow back into his abdomen, she thrashed against his hold, but he barely registered the move, gripping her tighter and rubbing his cock against her ass.

"You teased me for five years. I think I deserve a taste before I kill you and your little bodyguard. Don't you?"

"He'll be back any second," she said when he moved his hand away from her mouth to grope her breasts, nausea rolling in her belly. "And he'll kill you."

"I don't know." His hand moved under the hem of her dress, pushing it up until his palm was pressed against her pussy through the fabric of her panties. "He looked pretty pissed. He'll probably be a while. And it won't take me long to get what I want from you."

She inhaled sharply to scream again, but he was faster, his hand slapping against her mouth so hard it stung. When she kicked and flailed, screaming uselessly against his palm, he pinched her nose with his fingers, cutting off her air until her lungs burned and her vision blurred.

"That's right, you little bitch," he said when she went slack against him. "Stop pretending you're not going to enjoy what I'm about to give you." He yanked down her panties, forcing her to step out of them when they fell to her ankles. "Pick them up. And if you scream or try to run, I'll make it hurt ten times worse."

When she bent to pick them up, a wave of dizziness washed over her, and she squeezed her eyes against it. She balled up her panties in a fist, eyes darting around for something, anything she could use against him as a weapon.

She spotted a rock, but it was too far. He'd have her on the ground before she could reach it. She stood and turned, taking a step away from him and lifting her chin defiantly.

"Yeah, you always did have such a stubborn streak," Lepera said with a nasty chuckle. "Giuseppe hated it, but thinking about breaking you made my dick hard." He grabbed his crotch, and her blood went ice cold, her heart beating erratically against her rib cage.

He held his hand out for her panties, and she laid them in his palm, careful not to touch him as she took another step back. She was not going to let this man rape her. Either he died today or she did.

"You really don't want to do that," he warned her when he noticed her eyes dart toward the trees in search of Alexei.

"Fuck you," she spat, backing away another step.

He grinned and surged forward, gripping her by the waist. "That's my job." He shoved her panties into her mouth before she could reply. "Now be quiet. I know you're going to enjoy this. Cunts like you always do."

He spun her around, shoving her down to her hands and knees, and she winced when the rocks bit into her bare skin. The sound of displaced gravel signaled his position behind her moments before she felt his hands groping her breasts. The rock was close enough; all she had to do was stretch forward a bit.

When his hands left her body and she heard the clink of his belt buckle, she sucked in a deep breath through her nose and dove forward, closing her fingers around the rock and yanking it free from the damp earth. Her movement threw him off, and as he jerked behind her, she rolled onto her back, using her free hand to rip the panties out of her mouth.

He pinned her with a leering stare, his pants halfway undone and his cock straining against them. "If you want it on your back, I'm fine with that."

She tensed as he laid his body over hers, his lips wet against her skin. Her stomach lurched, and her fingers twitched on the rock in her hand. The rock he hadn't noticed. When he focused on freeing his cock again, she brought the rock down against his skull as hard as she could and felt something warm and wet splatter her face.

He wobbled a bit and shook his head to clear it, sending more droplets of blood flying onto her skin. But she didn't want to give him any more time to react. She smashed the rock into his face at the same time she brought her knee up into his groin.

He collapsed on his side with a strangled grunt, and she felt her adrenaline kick in, pumping warmth and strength through her body with a buzzing electricity. Scrambling to her feet, she kicked him hard in the side, and when he reached for her, she brought the heel of her shoe down hard against his crotch, satisfied with his pained howl.

He grabbed her ankle and twisted until she landed on top of him, knocking the breath out of her. But he had blood dripping into his eyes, and she was still holding onto the rock. Gripping it with two hands, she raised it over her head and brought it down onto his face again and again.

Blood rushed from his nose, but he didn't scream, the only sound from his lips an incoherent gurgle. He still twitched under her, and she wanted to ensure he never moved again. She slammed the rock into his face and head and neck until her arms ached with it and she could barely catch her breath.

With every blow, she remembered the maids she'd seen in Cefalù who'd scurried away from him with fear in their eyes and bruises on their bodies, remembered every time he'd stood too close or followed her like a jailer or locked her in her rooms. He deserved to die. The bastard had it coming.

Strong hands gripped her arms, and she fought against them, screaming and thrashing until Alexei's voice finally penetrated her rage.

"Carina, stop. Stop! He's dead."

She held the rock aloft, preparing another blow, breath coming in shallow pants, and realized Lepera wasn't moving. His face was unrecognizable, partially caved in from her blows and covered with blood. The rock fell from her hands on a sob, and she looked down at her arms, her dress, her legs. All of it covered in blood. Lepera's blood.

She reached up to touch her face, and she felt it under her fingers. The coppery scent filled her nose, and she let Alexei pull her to her feet and wrap her in his arms.

"What the fuck happened?" He stiffened, and she followed his gaze to her discarded panties. "Did he rape you?" His voice vibrated with rage.

"He tried."

Alexei jerked her back and looked into her eyes, stripping off his t-shirt and using it to wipe the blood from her face as best he could. "He tried, and you killed him." She nodded, though he already knew the answer. The evidence lay at their feet. "Good. That's good, baby."

"Where were you?" she whispered, suddenly exhausted.

Crushing her to him, he ran his hands down her hair and

pressed his cheek against the top of her head. "I'm sorry. I'm so sorry, Carina."

"What are we going to do?" She tried to turn to look at the body, but Alexei wouldn't let her. "We can't leave him here."

Alexei released her long enough to find Lepera's cell phone, using the dead man's thumbprint to unlock it. Then his arms were around her again. He quickly swiped his finger across the screen, looking for…whatever the hell he was looking for.

"It doesn't look like he called or texted anyone, so no one should know he was following us. But we can't leave him here for someone to find. Hold this." He shoved the man's phone into her hand and dug out his own, dialing a number.

"Berto. I need you to bring three guys to the location I'm about to ping you. There's a body that needs hiding." He listened to Berto's answer. "How long? Good."

He disconnected the call and wrapped his arms around her again, his hand cradling the back of her head. She pressed her cheek against the warmth of his bare chest and let herself get lost in the steady sound of his heartbeat in her ear.

She was supposed to be mad at him for acting like an asshole, for accusing her of using him, for abandoning her. But she'd be mad later. Right now she never wanted to leave the safety of his arms.

When tires crunched over gravel, she jumped, but Alexei immediately whispered soothing words into her ear, running his hands down her back. "It's okay. It's Berto and the guys."

"What the fuck happened?" Berto demanded, joining them behind the SUV that shielded them and the body from the road. His eyes traveled from a shirtless Alexei, his chest and face smeared with blood, to Carina's bloodstained dress and drenched arms and face.

"He tried to rape me." She nodded her chin at the man on the ground. "So I killed him."

"No shit," Berto whistled.

"Get rid of him," Alexei barked. "Elio will miss him eventually, but I'd prefer they never find a body."

"What about his car?" one of their men wondered.

"There's a chop shop you can take it to. Owned by loyal men. Berto knows the one."

Berto nodded, motioning to one of the guys with him to grab shovels out of the trunk of their SUV while the other two moved forward to heft the body off the ground.

"I'm taking her home," Alexei said, already pulling her toward the car. "Text me when it's done."

Berto grunted his agreement, and she let Alexei help her into the front seat of the SUV. At eye level, he gripped her face in his hands and pressed a long kiss against her forehead before releasing her and closing the door. He jogged around the hood and climbed behind the wheel, reaching for her hand before maneuvering back onto the road.

When they pulled into the driveway, her head was clearer, the buzzing in her ears fading. But each time she moved, she felt the thick layer of dried blood on her body, and she wanted to be rid of it. To wash it out of her hair and off her skin and banish it forever. She didn't regret killing him. She'd do it again if she had to.

If anything, now she had more proof she could stomach death, that she could be the cause of it, however bloody, and not turn away from it. Maybe even enjoy it a little. She gave Alexei's hand a squeeze before he got out of the car and moved to open her door. They'd have to talk about what happened between them earlier, but not now. She needed something different from him than words now.

He dragged her across the driveway and through the courtyard. They managed to avoid people until they rounded the corner toward her room, and she heard a gasp. Giulia was frozen in the middle of the hallway, the towels she'd been carrying in an untidy pile at her feet.

"Signora! Are you all right?"

"I'm fine," Carina said, voice steadier than she expected. "Don't tell my brother about this, please. I'll tell him when I'm ready."

She barely caught the older woman's nod before Alexei yanked her into her bedroom and slammed the door, flipping the lock. Rough hands reached behind her and tugged down the zipper of her dress, shoving it off her shoulders until it pooled at her feet.

When she stepped out of it, he grabbed it from the floor and stalked to the fireplace, throwing it inside and using the matches from the mantle to set it aflame. She frowned. She liked that dress.

He stared into the flames so long she crossed her arms over her chest in an attempt to chase away the goosebumps pebbling her skin. She wasn't going to stand here covered in blood and freeze to death while he worked through his mood.

Leaving him to his thoughts, she turned and headed for the bathroom. She needed punishingly hot water and lots of fucking soap.

Chapter Twenty-One

Alexei glanced over his shoulder at the sound of the shower turning on to find the spot where he'd left Carina empty. Tiny smears of blood from her dress and shoes trailed a path to the bathroom. His jaw clenched at the sight of it.

He'd failed her. Again. He'd gotten so caught up in his own stupid bullshit, his own stupid imaginary bullshit, that he'd left her alone on the side of the road when she needed him most. He shuddered to think what might have happened if she hadn't gotten the better of Lepera with a fucking rock.

The water muffled, and he moved to the door she'd left open to watch her tilt her head back under the spray. The water ran bright red, then muddy brown, until it was clear. She squeezed shampoo into her hands and lathered it with her fingers, scrubbing ferociously at her scalp. She might have been taking a shower on any normal day if he couldn't see the faint red flow as it slid down her body.

She shifted again to rinse out the shampoo and saw him standing there. Her eyes locked on his, and he straightened. He should go. Take his own shower and give her some privacy and some space. He imagined she'd want plenty of that from him after today.

Then her lips moved, beckoning him forward with a question he couldn't understand over the steady beat of the water. "What?"

"I said why are you so angry at me? Is it because I told you I don't want kids?"

His eyebrows drew together, and he took another step closer. "I told you I didn't mean what I said. It was stupid. And I'm not angry at you."

She finished rinsing the last of the bubbles from her hair and slicked it back from her forehead. "You seem very angry."

He watched her hold her arms under the spray, scrubbing her fingertips over her skin until the blood was gone.

"I am." She jerked, pinning him with wide, dark eyes, and he softened his tone. "But not at you. I'm angry at that bastard for touching you. And I'm angry at myself for leaving you alone so he could. I'll go so you can finish."

"Wait." Her voice, soft and pleading, stopped him in his tracks. "I don't want you to go. Come here," she said when he still didn't turn around.

He braced himself, pivoting to face her, but didn't come any closer. She tilted her head and pressed her palm flat against the glass door, easing it open. Her skin was pink from the heat of the water, and some blood still dotted her shoulders and stomach where it had soaked through her dress.

"Please, Alexei. I don't want Lepera to be the last man who touched me."

His gaze snapped to her face, and he knew he couldn't deny her, knew he didn't want to. He toed off his boots and socks, then stripped out of his jeans as he crossed the room. She made room for him, backing up until she was almost against the wall.

He braced a hand on one side of her head and leaned down to capture her lips, deepening the kiss with a sweep of his tongue. He tilted his head and nibbled across her jaw and down the column of her throat.

When she sighed, he eased back, reaching for the soap that smelled like her and lathering it into a cloth. He turned her, pulling her back against his chest, and gently smoothed the suds over her shoulders and down each arm. He washed each finger just for an excuse to touch her in as many ways as possible.

Massaging her breasts, he gave in to the temptation to give her nipples a light squeeze, smiling when she rewarded him with a breathy moan and slid her hand up to wrap around his neck, her fingers playing in his hair. He washed the blood from her stomach and the tops of her thighs, but he carefully avoided her core. He would touch her, but she wouldn't get more unless she asked for it.

Sinking to his knees, he ran the cloth over her inner thighs and down her calves, scrubbing away each drop of blood until she was perfect again. He felt her watching him, and the fact that she was so steady after what happened to her made his cock twitch. His Carina was a warrior. A natural with blood and death.

Using his hands, he slicked away the bubbles with fresh water, leaning in to press a kiss to her thigh and smiling when her hips jerked. When he stood, she turned and wrapped her arms around his neck, pulling his mouth down for a searing kiss that sent heat and need coursing through him.

Backing her against the wall, he drank deeply from her lips, tasting her with his tongue and savoring every moan and whimper. She ran her hands down his arms and over his chest, gently massaging away the blood on his skin.

When her arms circled his waist, he felt her fingers

tremble against his back, and he pulled away. "Carina," he murmured. "I don't want to—"

She pushed onto her toes, sighing as her breasts dragged against his chest, and demanded his lips again, dragging her teeth over his upper lip until he groaned.

"Are you—"

"I need you to touch me. Please. I need to forget. Make me forget," she whispered, fingernails digging into the flesh of his hips.

Without hesitation, he moved his hand down the flat plane of her stomach and dragged his finger against her clit, eliciting a groan. Sliding a finger inside her, he bent to suck her nipple into his mouth, circling his tongue around it as he applied pressure to her clit.

If she wanted to forget, he was happy to oblige. He wanted to sear himself into her memory so the only touch she thought about was his. The only hands on her body, lips on her skin, cock moving inside her would be his. He intended to keep her. Forever. Even if she didn't realize it yet.

He released her nipple, pressing a gentle kiss to it. "Put your foot on the bench."

She shivered but obeyed, shifting to prop her foot on the low bench to her right and spreading herself open for him. He plunged a second finger inside her, grinding his thumb against her clit while she gripped his shoulder for support.

He reached up to circle his fingers around her nipple, pinching it between two fingers and groaning softly when he felt her pussy clench on his fingers. "Not yet, baby."

"Alexei," she panted, almost pleading.

"I know," he crooned, speeding up his thrusting fingers and pinching her nipple harder. "Don't come yet. Not until I say."

He drove her to the brink of orgasm, and knowing the only thing that kept her from falling over the edge was his command made him ache to be inside her. But he wanted to push her a little further, to increase the intensity of her release until the pleasure only he could give her was all she could think about.

When her nails bit into his skin and her body vibrated under his touch, he leaned down to nibble her earlobe and whisper against her ear. "Now, baby. Come for me."

Instantly her whole body tensed, her back bowing against the shower wall while she screamed his name. He shoved his fingers deep, massaging lazy circles over her clit until she relaxed, panting as she looked up at him.

"I don't know why I like that so much."

"Like what? Coming?"

"Letting you boss me around like that."

He grinned, moving her foot from the bench and sliding his hands around to grip her ass and lift her into his arms. "I told you before. I know what you need."

She wrapped her legs around his waist when he pressed her back against the wall, and he groaned, dropping his head and dragging his teeth along her jaw to her earlobe. He nipped it roughly before tracing the shell of her ear with the tip of his tongue.

He reached between them to notch himself at her entrance and slid slowly inside her, grinding himself against her until she shuddered in his arms. Her legs tightened around his waist, holding him close, and he contented himself with rocking his hips against hers, delighting in her sharp intakes of breath each time his pelvis ground against her overly sensitive clit.

She slid her hands into his hair, arching against him as she gripped it in her fingers, and he let her guide his mouth to her breast, tonguing her nipple in the way he knew she loved. Whatever she wanted from him, she could have. He would happily give it a thousand times over.

"Alexei," she whispered, voice hoarse as he swirled his tongue around her nipple, teasing it with his teeth.

"Yes, baby." He peppered kisses across her chest to her other breast, lavishing it with the same attention. "Tell me."

"I want you to fuck me."

He ground his hips into her roughly, making her gasp. "You want it? Or you need it?"

"Need," she panted. "I need it."

He drew his cock out slowly, biting down on her nipple when he slammed home again. She arched against his mouth, and he obliged the offering with another testing bite of his teeth, grinning against her skin when he dragged a needy moan from her lips.

He pounded her with a steady rhythm, the water beating hot on his back while he pushed her closer and closer to the edge, her pussy clenching around him as he drove into her.

He reached up to wrap his hand around her throat, and her eyes shot open to meet his. She dragged her tongue over her lower lip, and he leaned in to take a taste, squeezing lightly as he did and groaning when her pussy fluttered around him in response.

"Are you going to come for me again, baby?" He kept his thumb under her chin to keep her head tilted back, her eyes on his as he fucked her.

"Yes," she whimpered, writhing and grinding against him.

"Good." He bit roughly into her bottom lip and dragged it away, only to let it snap back against her teeth. "That's so good, baby. Come for me."

He thrust into her with long, deep strokes, the pulse at her throat fluttering rapidly under his fingers. Then her body spasmed. Her fingernails dug into the skin of his scalp, and she sobbed his name like a prayer as her orgasm overtook her.

He fucked her through it, hand on her throat, fingers gripping her ass as he pounded into her slick heat until she rewarded him with another shuddering orgasm. And when she begged for him, he emptied himself inside her.

Before he fell over, or worse, dropped her, he shifted to sit on the bench at the back of the shower, groaning when she dropped her knees to either side of his hips. She sat back to look at him, and he ran his hands over her hair, then cupped her face.

"I'm sorry, Carina." He'd never be able to say it enough.

She cupped his face in her hands, rubbing her thumb over his bottom lip. "I don't need you to save me, Alexei. I think today proved I'm quite capable of saving myself."

He studied her, nipping at her thumb with his teeth. "I'd say so."

The smile slowly faded from her lips, her expression sobering. "But I'm tired of waiting for Matteo's chess pieces. I want them to pay."

Nodding in agreement, he slid his hands up her sides, fingertips brushing the underside of her breasts. "I've been thinking about that. Your brother will want those documents if he doesn't have them already. Then I'll press him to make a move."

"Who first?" she asked softly, eyes intent on his.

"Giovanni." His fingers traced over the burn scar under her breast. "I know exactly how I want him to pay."

"What if Matteo says no?"

"Is this what you need, Carina?"

She nodded slowly, swallowing hard. "This is what I need."

"Then I'll make sure you get it."

Chapter Twenty-Two

It was dark when she opened her eyes, the balcony doors left open to the breeze, curtains fluttering in the wind. She rolled onto her back in search of Alexei, but the bed was empty, and she sighed. He hadn't left her side often in recent days, no matter how many times she told him or her brothers she was fine.

And, even if they didn't believe her, she *was* fine. It was her life or Lepera's on the side of the road that day, and she was damn glad she was still alive to tell the tale. If anything, his death had whetted her appetite.

She didn't need them tiptoeing around her like she might come apart at any moment, like she might crack when she realized what she'd done. She was even more eager now to see the rest of them dead than she had been before. They'd made her this way; it was only fair they got a taste of the monster they'd created.

Shoving the covers back, she crossed to the open door and stepped onto the balcony. The breeze off the water was cooler at this hour, but she ignored the goosebumps that raised on her arms and leaned on the railing. The stars were faint under the glow of city lights, and she searched for the ones she recognized.

Her mother began studying the stars when she got sick and was unable to sleep. Carina would sit up with her until the early hours of the morning, listening to her mother point out the constellations and recite the myths for each one.

Cassiopeia, who angered Poseidon by claiming to be more beautiful than the sea nymphs. Cetus, the monster sent by Poseidon to teach the vain Cassiopeia a lesson. Cepheus, Cassiopeia's husband, who tried to sacrifice his own daughter to save himself from Poseidon's wrath. Andromeda was really someone Carina could relate to.

If she closed her eyes, she could almost hear the lyrical sound of her mother's voice over the gentle crashing of the waves, weaving each tale, her finger tracing the shapes in the sky. Carina had wondered many times over the years if her mother would be proud of or disappointed by the woman she'd become.

What would Vittoria Bianchi have said seeing her daughter covered in blood and hungry for more of it? Her mother had always been so kind. Such a stark contrast to her father, who never bothered to be kind to anyone.

As a girl, she'd thought each of them balanced the other, that they were in love and this was just their way. As a woman, she wondered if instead her father had slowly crushed her mother's spirit under his iron fist.

Maybe her mother had been fiery and passionate and outspoken once, and the embers of that fire had been doused by the same man who had tried to crush Carina's own spirit as a girl. A man who might have succeeded if not for her mother, always willing to step in and defend her.

Carina shook her head. These were questions orphans could never have answers to. It hardly mattered anyway. Her mother's opinion of her wouldn't stop her from seeking revenge. Perhaps she was more like her father than she wanted to admit.

She smelled him, that faint scent of spice that could only be him, seconds before Alexei's arms wrapped around her from behind. He rested his chin on her shoulder, pressing a kiss to her jaw.

"Why aren't you sleeping?" he asked softly.

"I woke up, and you weren't there."

He straightened, turning her slowly in his arms, and cupped her face in his hands. "Did you have a nightmare?"

Reaching up to grip his wrists, she smiled. He'd been terribly concerned with whether she was having those too. "No. I just woke up alone. I used to enjoy that. Now look at me."

His mouth quirked up at the corner, and he pressed a long kiss to her forehead. "I'd apologize, but we'd both know I didn't mean it. Since you're up, how do you feel about talking to Matteo?"

"At this hour?" He nodded. "What time is it?"

"Late. Almost three."

She worried her bottom lip between her teeth. "What does he make of all those papers?"

Sliding his hand down her arm, Alexei captured hers, lacing their fingers together. "Why don't you come downstairs and see? I think you'll find it as interesting as I do."

He led her from the room and down the stairs. Alexei had been sitting in on more meetings with her brothers as of late, and she wondered if that was because Matteo was finally coming around and pulling him in closer or if Alexei wasn't giving him much choice in the matter.

The lights were on in the study, and she heard the faint hum of low voices before they stepped into the doorway and the conversation died. Luca's eyebrows shot up when he saw her, and Matteo appraised her with a searching stare.

"I couldn't sleep."

Irritation simmered in her chest when no one spoke, and she lifted her chin. They'd been treating her like a breakable doll since the day she'd gone to the bank, and she was tired of it. If she hadn't proven herself to them by now, she didn't know what the fuck else it was going to take.

She gave Alexei's hand a squeeze and then disentangled herself, claiming a spot next to Dom and looking at Matteo. "What have you discovered?"

Matteo's eyes drifted over her head to look at Alexei, and her temper snapped. "I'm right here, Matteo. Alexei might share my bed, but he is not my keeper. If I haven't earned the right to know your plans by now, tell me, and I'll take matters into my own hands."

There was a beat of silence, then Matteo sat forward and plucked a paper off a stack, holding it out to her. "The Romano holdings are under an impressive amount of debt. Not just loans from Varda, but bank loans against their clubs and private property."

Carina glanced down at her brother's scribbled notes. It was a detailed list of each property and how much debt had been stacked against it. It totaled in the billions. Far more than Elio would get out of their paltry deal.

"So that's it? He's already sunk?"

Luca shook his head. "Not quite. Debt like this operates differently. That's why he was able to collect so much of it. He can bet the financial health of the clubs' profits against what he owes and then pit profits against debt to reduce payments and tax burdens."

"And then he can coast along in the red indefinitely." She tossed the paper on the table and rubbed her temple. "Meaning we're no closer to having him than we were before I was almost raped and murdered."

Alexei sank down onto the arm of the sofa and rubbed a

hand over her back, gripping her neck and giving it a gentle squeeze. She leaned into his warmth, ignoring Matteo's disapproving frown.

"Not necessarily," Matteo replied. "Whoever owns the debt owns the property. And Elio isn't worried about paying off the banks."

"Right," she replied. "And?"

"And if someone else owns the property and demands payment," Matteo said, "he's got a problem on his hands."

She tilted her head and glanced down at the paper again. "And how do you propose to do that? Do we have enough liquid capital to buy that much debt?"

Matteo shared a glance with Dom and Luca, and she barely bit back a sigh. "The casinos don't. Or Bianchi businesses in general don't." He paused. "But I do."

"What do you mean?" She scooted to the edge of the cushion, her fingers gripping the soft leather. "How do you have that much money?"

"I didn't hop around the world doing nothing for the last seven years, Carina," Matteo replied, and she rolled her eyes.

"Do enlighten me. Since everyone else seems to know already."

"I did everything Father wasn't interested in. I made foreign connections across Europe and in the States, invested profits back into different businesses, set up shell companies to move money more easily. I amassed quite a fortune."

Her eyes narrowed on his face when he sat back, looking proud of himself. "You let everyone think you'd have to sell off Bianchi assets to pay Elio back when all this time you could have just written him a fucking check?"

"It isn't that simple, Carina." Matteo dismissed her like she was a child, and her irritation boiled into anger.

"I'm not an idiot, brother. And I would appreciate it if you'd stop treating me like one."

"That's not what I—"

"Quiet," she snapped, enjoying the dark look on Matteo's face at being ordered about by his baby sister. "You might have everyone here eating out of the palm of your hand when you snap your fingers, but you have yet to give me what I've asked for. And I'm bored with listening to you talk in half-truths and unfinished stories while you bring your vision to life at my expense."

"I'm doing what's best for—"

"The family. Yes. I'm bored with listening to that too. What do you plan to do with this?" She spread her arms out, indicating the papers displayed in front of them. "This information apparently only I could get for you. The truth, Matteo. And all of it before I get angry."

A muscle ticked in Matteo's jaw as he studied her, but he ultimately relented. "I plan on using it to assume an owner's stake in Elio's companies by purchasing the debt."

"Control the debt, control the business," she repeated, and Matteo nodded. "And then you'll, what? Demand payments he can't make?"

"Something like that. I'll run the purchase through a shell company, so he doesn't know I'm—*we*—are the ones who bought it. When he can't pay, we go through the steps of foreclosing on the property and take full, legal ownership."

"And then I can kill him."

Matteo huffed out a breath. "I don't remember you being quite so bloodthirsty before I left. But yes, then you can kill him. Or Alexei can."

Carina glanced up at Alexei, who gave her a knowing look. He wouldn't leave her out of this. She didn't need Matteo's approval to be involved in killing the Romanos, but she wouldn't mind avoiding his lectures if he found out.

"Speaking of killing." Matteo shifted his gaze to Alexei. "I want Elio distracted when I make my purchase. I've already heard rumblings from my spies about him not being able to find Lepera. He isn't happy about that. Let's throw him off a little more by taking out a beloved family member. He's close to Vincenzo, isn't he?"

Alexei's hand tightened on Carina's neck before she could speak, and she decided to hold her tongue to see how he would handle it. "He is, but I think Giovanni is a better target."

Matteo frowned. "Why?"

"They're closer. And Giovanni is a confidant and advisor to Elio. It would be a bigger blow to him personally and financially."

"That's true," Dom agreed. "Elio's always been closer to his uncle than his father."

Matteo looked to Carina, who nodded her agreement. "Giuseppe didn't like Elio much. Considered him weak. Giovanni was constantly using that to his advantage to get Elio to do what he wanted."

"Fine. Giovanni then. But I want it to look like an accident. I don't want Elio to know I'm coming for him. Yet."

Alexei inclined his head. "Accidents are my specialty."

Carina glanced up at him, something in his tone snagging at the edge of her consciousness. But he offered her a small smile and brushed his thumb over her cheek, and she shook it off.

Alexei was a lethal weapon; she'd always known that. And now she was going to get to watch him in action.

Chapter Twenty-Three

Alexei lined the vials of clear liquid they needed on the counter in a neat row. Two doses for Giovanni's glass. One should do it, but if something happened, he wanted to make sure they had an extra. Three of accelerant. If their plan didn't work, he wanted a backup for that too. He wasn't leaving anything up to chance tonight.

Carina stepped out of his bedroom dressed in a skintight silver sheath dress. It sparkled when she moved. She'd paired the low-cut outfit with a lace pushup bra, the edges of it just visible above the sweeping neckline, and it made him want to drag her back inside his room and have his way with her.

But he'd already done that. Twice. And they were going to be late if he attempted it a third time. Especially now that she'd fixed the blonde wig into place, the long straight tresses skimming her waist. He much preferred her as a brunette, but Giovanni liked blondes, and she needed to get close enough to him tonight to tip the vial into his drink.

He wasn't keen on this part of the plan, but they'd had men sitting on Giovanni for almost a week, and it would be the best way to slip him something without being caught. The goal was to make it look like an accident, after all.

The planning on this one was precise, and if he pulled it off—if *they* pulled it off—it would be a very satisfying kill to add to his list.

"Ready?" Carina asked.

He couldn't tell if she was nervous or excited. Or both. He'd asked her multiple times over the last week, since Matteo had given them the green light on Giovanni, if she wanted to back out. She was adamant she wanted to do this, giddy even. She'd been anticipating tonight's kill almost as much as he had. Maybe that was why he couldn't keep his hands off her.

"Tell me the plan again."

She rolled her eyes, expertly applying lipstick on her full lips with a handheld mirror. "Sit next to Giovanni at the bar where he likes to have two glasses of scotch before going home to his awful wife, Maria. Flirt with him enough to keep him distracted."

Gesturing with her chin toward the vials on the counter, she slipped her lipstick and mirror into her clutch. "Add one vial of that to his drink and wait ten minutes before suggesting we get out of there."

"And then?"

"Then load him into his car, tell him to follow me back to my place, and get in the car with you to handle the rest. We've gone over this a thousand times, Alexei. Don't you trust me not to fuck it up?"

He reached for her hand and tugged her up against his chest, curling a strand of fake hair around his finger. "Of course I trust you. It's Giovanni I don't trust. Don't let him touch you."

She waved his words away, and he scowled. "I'll let him

touch whatever he wants as long as he ends up dead at the end of it. You really think he'll hit the wall hard enough?"

"Depends on how eager he is to fuck you."

Leaning back to get a good look at his face, she raised a brow. "You think he won't be?"

"I think any man who lays eyes on you tonight will want you. Myself included." He pressed a quick kiss to her lips, smiling against her fingers when she wiped at the lipstick left behind. "I'm more worried about him recognizing you."

She stepped out of his arms and moved toward the door. "None of them ever really noticed me. It'll be dark in there. I'll be a faceless blonde in a tight dress flirting with an old man. Besides"—she peeked at him over her shoulder and grinned—"you'll be watching."

He pocketed the vials from the counter and followed her out to the car, a beautiful Ferrari V12 Spider on loan from the Bianchi car collection. There was plenty to say about Lorenzo Bianchi, but the son of a bitch had good taste in cars. The top was already down, exposing the rich black leather interior.

Opening the door for Carina, he slid his hand down to squeeze her ass before she slipped inside, and she grinned. Then he rounded the hood and slid behind the wheel, biting back a groan as the car growled to life. He gunned the engine just because he could, and Carina laughed.

"Matteo is going to kill you if you crash this car."

He reached for her hand and brought her knuckles to his lips. "You and this car are safe with me tonight. Ready?"

She nodded, and he gave into his desire to gun it down the driveway and take the turn onto the road at speeds that made his heart race. He expected to look over at Carina and see her clutching the dash, but instead she had her arms up, laughing as the air blew her hair back over the headrest.

Everything about her took his breath away, and he had to

stamp down the sudden urge to whip the car around, take her back to his cottage, and keep her in his bed for days.

Refocusing on the road, he reached for the radio, satisfied when thumping bass pounded out of the speakers. Knowing Matteo, Alexei half expected opera or some shit.

They drove south, crossing into Varda territory. Alexei had argued with Matteo about this part of the plan for days. With their most recent excursion into Romano territory, he didn't want anyone who might be watching a little too closely to see them coming from Bianchi land.

Tensions were escalating with Varda after Matteo refused to meet with the Don about what he called territory disputes. But Varda's hurt feelings were tomorrow's problem. Tonight, Alexei was only worried about getting Carina safely into and out of Romano land with one less Romano bastard left breathing. He'd failed her on their last trip. It wouldn't happen again.

Keeping close to the border, he crossed it and wound a lazy path to the bar Giovanni had been spotted in every night this week. It was already dark when they pulled into the parking lot, and he dropped the vials into Carina's open bag before getting out and opening her door. Now they'd pretend not to know each other until Giovanni was in his car, hoping to get laid.

Carina jogged ahead of him, running her fingers through her blonde tresses. The man at the door gave her a leering once over before letting her in without checking for ID. But Alexei's was scrutinized with a flashlight before he could follow Carina inside. His heartbeat quickened until she was in his sights again.

Like clockwork, Giovanni was already here, occupying a seat at the end of the polished bar. Likely on scotch number one at this hour, he glanced at Carina when she sat down.

Alexei watched for signs of recognition, but there weren't any, not even when Carina turned to smile at him.

He leaned forward to say something, and Carina laughed, laying her hand on his arm when she did, and Alexei clenched his hands into fists before shoving them into his pockets. Just because he knew it was for show didn't mean he liked to watch it.

She laid her bag on the bar close to his drink and waved away his offer to buy her a drink before finally relenting. Alexei moved closer to try and hear what they were saying, taking a seat at a table as close to them as he could get without drawing suspicion.

"Let me catch up with you," Giovanni said, tossing back the rest of his scotch and signaling the bartender for another.

"I think I'm the one who should be catching up with you." Carina grinned, slipping her fingers into her bag and pulling them out again, an invisible vial clenched in her fist.

"I'll stay here as long as you need, my dear."

She giggled and laid her hand on his arm again. When she pulled away to reach for her drink, she swept her hand over the bar and knocked her purse onto the floor.

"Oh God. I'm so clumsy. Let me just…"

She started to push away from her chair, and Giovanni waved her away, stooping down to retrieve her bag. Alexei watched Carina upend the vial into his waiting scotch and bit back a grin. She was fucking perfect.

"A beautiful bag for a beautiful woman." Giovanni laid the clutch on the bar and rubbed his knuckles over her cheek, chuckling when she blushed. "And so modest. I do love that in a woman."

She reached for her drink and held it aloft. "What should we toast to?"

Giovanni considered, matching her pose. "To happy accidents and chance meetings." He gave her a flirtatious wink. "You never know where they might lead."

Her eyes darted first to Alexei and then to her phone to check the time. Ten minutes. He watched them flirt. Giovanni wasn't particularly good at it. Alexei wasn't sure if it was the drugs or if the man was entirely inept. He imagined most women went home with him because they saw dollar signs.

At ten minutes exactly, Carina leaned in close, her lips brushing Giovanni's cheek and her arm stroking his shoulder. Whatever she said had him sitting up straight and gulping the rest of his scotch before reaching for her hand.

Alexei waited a beat before following them out to the parking lot. Waiting by the car, he watched Giovanni slide his hands all over Carina, squeezing her ass, tugging her against him so hard she wobbled on her impossibly thin heels. When they finally reached Giovanni's car, he pushed her back against it, but he was unsteady on his feet from the drugs, and he fell against her.

Gritting his teeth, Alexei watched Giovanni fumble his hand over Carina's breast before she was able to get him behind the wheel of his car. She leaned down in such a way Alexei knew Giovanni was getting a generous view of her cleavage, then stood and shut the door for him.

Alexei climbed behind the wheel while she sauntered across the parking lot toward him at a leisurely pace, careful not to draw too much attention to herself. Her face was lit with a grin when she climbed in next to him, and it took everything he had not to yank her up against him and take her mouth.

"He's hot for it. I told him I'd honk so he knew which one was me," she said, sweeping her long hair over one shoulder. "Ready?"

He nodded and revved the engine. This was the part of their plan that could be hit or miss. It all depended on how good his driving skills were and how slow the drugs had made Giovanni.

Pulling the car to the edge of the parking lot, he honked once, being sure to stay low in his seat. He didn't think Giovanni would be lucid enough at this rate to notice if someone taller than Carina was driving the car, but no need to take too many chances at being made.

Giovanni swerved on the road behind them as Alexei led them away from the bar toward a less populated area. As businesses faded into houses and houses into trees, he navigated onto the highway and picked up speed, glancing in the rearview to make sure Giovanni was still keeping pace with them.

He glanced at Carina and saw her watching the car behind them intently in the side mirror. Taking the next curve at breakneck speed, he pressed the gas, the car growling with the effort of pushing the speed limit. There it was. The cliff face.

Aiming right for it, he prayed Giovanni's reflexes were slow enough that he'd plow right into it instead of swerving like Alexei was about to do. He kept the gas to the floor, and Giovanni clearly did the same. Alexei's fingers were tight on the steering wheel as he aimed for the solid wall of rock.

Her hands gripping the edge of her seat, Carina tensed when Alexei downshifted and slammed on the brakes, veering the car to the right to avoid the wall. They fishtailed, his heart racing, before the car ultimately righted itself and slowed. Seconds later, he heard the unmistakable sound of metal meeting stone and then a deafening explosion.

He looked up when Carina gasped and saw her twisted in her seat to see. Looping the car around, he pulled behind a squat row of bushes that gave them the perfect vantage point to watch.

Orange flames licked at the sky from the hunk of metal

sitting at the base of the rock face. If he'd survived the impact, Giovanni wouldn't survive the fire. It was silent, no screaming, and Alexei grappled with the disappointment that Giovanni likely wasn't burning alive before their eyes. It's what he deserved for the marks he put on Carina. But at least the fucker was dead.

He felt Carina boost herself up on her knees in the passenger seat, and then she was draped over his shoulders, her lips hot on his neck and ear. "You did it," she whispered, voice breathy.

Turning his head, he met her lips with his and grinned. "We did it. You were fantastic."

"I have to admit, I wasn't entirely sure it would work." She glanced back at the flames, and he watched them dance in her eyes. "I guess Matteo has his distraction."

He nipped her jaw. "And you your revenge."

She looked back at him, and he turned to pull her into his lap so he could capture her lips again, hungry, desperate for her. Her hands skated along his shoulders and into his hair, gripping it tightly while his fingers teased the lace edges of her bra and danced across the tops of her breasts.

Pulling back, she cupped his face in her hands and leaned her forehead against his. He felt her breath against his lips when she spoke. "Thank you. For giving it to me."

He reached up to grip her throat, giving it a rough squeeze and grinning at the way she moaned for him. "Anything for you, Carina."

Chapter Twenty-Four

Carina pressed her fingers to the newspaper's edges to keep it from flying away and scanned the article on the front page.

Giovanni Romano has been identified as the victim of a single-car accident. Other drivers called in a car fire, and an unknown victim, later identified as Romano, was pronounced dead at the scene. After a brief investigation, authorities have concluded Romano was driving under the influence of alcohol and drugs and failed to take a sharp turn. He is survived by...

She sat back in the chair with a grin. One down, two to go. Matteo had moved his chess pieces and now owned enough debt to effectively control about 60 percent of the Romano empire. He'd purchased debt levied against all but two of the clubs as well as the villa in Cefalù that she hoped he burned to the fucking ground when he finally took possession of it.

The only thing he hadn't managed to get his hands on were drug sale profits. But according to him, their sales were dwindling due to the product he'd been slowly tainting and buyers randomly disappearing. Plus, once Elio didn't have the clubs to launder money through, his business would get even slower. The Romano empire was a sinking ship, and Elio didn't even know it yet.

Kicking off her sandals, she lowered herself to the edge of the pool and stuck her feet in the water, tipping her face up to catch the sun. Everything was coming together nicely.

Matteo was amassing the power he'd always craved, and the Romano men were falling. It wouldn't be long before Vincenzo and Elio were dead and buried next to Giovanni and Giuseppe. The idea of it warmed her.

She'd been dreaming of this moment for five years. Of the day when she'd be free from all the men who'd tormented her for so long. Her father's death had set this whole thing in motion. The bastard finally did something for her after all.

Footsteps ground against the stone, and she looked toward the sound to see Luca making his way toward her. He handed her a cocktail with a twist of lemon in it, and she raised a brow, sniffing it delicately.

He dropped into the chair she'd vacated and chuckled. "It's Limoncello. Your favorite."

She took a sip, closing her eyes at the bright burst of citrus on her tongue, and shifted so she could both look at her brother and keep one foot dangling in the water. He glanced down at the paper and back up at her.

"You did it." His eyes were hidden behind a pair of sunglasses, but there was something in his tone.

She nodded. "I did. Well, we did. Alexei and I."

"I didn't think you had it in you."

"You didn't spend five years with them." She took another sip, studying him over the rim of her glass. "Did Matteo ask you to come talk to me? Try and get me to back down?"

Luca drank from the wineglass in his hand. "He did." She snorted. "But I'm not going to do that."

"No? And why not?"

"Because you're not a delicate little doll, Carina. Whatever

Matteo wants to think, whatever he's chosen to remember of you, you've always had steel in your spine."

"Have I?" She wasn't so sure.

"You don't think so?"

She shrugged. "It's not like I put up a fight in marrying Giuseppe. Wouldn't someone with steel in their spine put up a fight?"

"It's not always about fighting." He set his glass down and leaned forward to rest his elbows on his knees. "At least not like that. You survived it. That counts for something."

"Maybe." She took another sip and set her glass on the edge of the pool. "A lot of things could be different if we'd all made different choices. But these are the ones we're left with. These are the pieces we have to collect. And this is how I want to collect them."

"By killing these men."

"And what's wrong with that?" she snapped, sitting up straight. "The three of you can plot and plan and scheme. Dom can order a hit on whoever he wants, and Matteo can take out unsuspecting drug addicts to toy with Elio, and it's fine because there's money waiting for you at the end?"

"I didn't say there was anything wrong with it. I think Matteo is trying to reconcile the girl you were with the woman you are, that's all."

"Well, I wish he'd hurry up."

Luca studied her for a long moment before asking, "Are you still planning on leaving Sicily when it's all said and done?"

"What?" She jerked around to look at him, nearly knocking over her glass. "Who said I wanted to leave?"

Another beat of silence. "Alexei."

"I didn't realize you two were so close," she said, trying to keep her voice casual.

"He mentioned it. In passing." Luca relaxed back in his

seat and took another sip of wine. "He didn't seem all that keen on the idea."

Carina blinked. She hadn't spoken about her plans to leave with Alexei again. Not since her confession over her scars. He hadn't brought it up since, never mentioned not wanting her to go.

The idea that he would want her to stay both soothed an ache and sparked worry. An aching desire to be wanted, needed, cared for. Worry over being so far gone for him she lost herself. This was what she was afraid of. Getting in so deep with him she couldn't get out again.

Luca stood, drawing her attention. "After everything you've been through in the name of family, you deserve to have whatever you want. Whether that's Elio in pieces or something else or both. I'll make sure Matteo doesn't take that away from you."

She smiled up at him, watching him round the pool and disappear through the patio doors. Whatever she wanted. She used to know what that was. It was all the Romanos dead by her hand and then freedom from Sicily and the men who would control her.

But with her father gone, her brothers showing no signs of using her as a pawn to move as it suited them, and Elio nearing his end, who was left? The only man in her life after that was Alexei, and if Luca was right, he didn't want her to leave.

She had to admit, she'd stopped actively planning on leaving weeks ago. The idea barely flitted through her mind these days. She assumed it was because her head was too full plotting revenge, staying up late into the night to talk with Alexei about the best ways to do it. He'd insisted on fire for Giovanni, but he'd been open to her suggestions on Vincenzo. But what if it was something else?

She was content to share a bed with him, to fall asleep in

the warmth and safety of his arms every night, to plot and plan. Alexei had never asked her to be anything other than who and what she was. He didn't just recognize the darkness in her. He coaxed it out; he fed it.

He worshipped it.

Unlike Matteo, he hadn't tried to change who she'd become. He reveled in it. He suited her. She couldn't deny that. And he didn't just want her. He saw all of her jagged edges and fit them to his own.

But what if he wanted more than that? As often as he assured her he didn't really mean what he'd said about her carrying his son, it still sat heavy at the back of her mind. What if he really did want marriage and babies and tying her to him forever?

After Giuseppe, she swore she'd never let herself be trapped by a man again. She didn't want to ever be at the mercy of someone else. Even someone as perfect for her as Alexei.

Chapter Twenty-Five

The shrill noises from the casino floor faded with every step until all he heard was the steady hum of the air conditioning blowing through the vents. Following the looping maze of hallways, Alexei made the last turn for his office and unlocked the door.

Dropping the bag of cash in the center of his desk, he settled into the chair and upended it, corralling the stacks as they toppled onto the cold metal surface. Between plotting Giovanni's death, keeping up to date with Matteo's plans for world domination, and spending as much time in Carina's bed as he could get away with, he hadn't had much time to collect and catalog casino debt payments.

Not that Berto minded picking up the slack. He enjoyed the rush of a fist to the face and the crunch of bone as much as Alexei enjoyed the feel of a blade drawing through flesh and blood on his fingers.

Pulling the ledger from the shelf overhead, he flipped it open to the right page, dragging his finger down the column of names. Still three more payments to collect this week. Berto would love that. Separating the bills by denomination, he began to count them.

Unlike the Romanos, the Bianchis were more than flush with cash. Both from everyday business and from the infusion Matteo had supplied from his private coffers. Alexei knew from Luca that Matteo intended to update some of the casinos with more modern machines and better security.

He also wanted to build a few high-stakes poker lounges above the casinos meant to cater to the super rich. Something Luca had pushed Lorenzo to do for years. Big buy-ins and an even bigger pot would draw serious players, which meant a hefty profit for the house.

All of it would be great cover for absorbing the Romano drug trade Matteo had been purposefully sabotaging over the last several weeks. Tainted supply that sent people to the hospital with Romano brands all over it was bad for business. And Matteo had been quietly flooding the streets with his own product. Business was beginning to boom.

Alexei knew because he heard the men talking about their increased cut of the profits. Inspiring loyalty by sharing the wealth was the best way to do it. Since Matteo's return, the men had gone from concerned rumblings to measured interest to enthusiastic support. Matteo was making a name for himself as Don, with his men and with Sicily.

It was obvious the other Dons were taking notice. Varda and Lorenzo had been enemies for decades, and if the whispers were true, Varda was preparing his own strike against the new Bianchi Don. But Dom was counting on that, infiltrating the territory with well-paid spies. If Varda made a move, Matteo would almost certainly know about it first.

In any case, the men were primed for the war that seemed to be brewing. And Matteo appeared just as hungry for it. It was as if he'd planned his whole life for this moment and not just arrived back on the island by happenstance. Perhaps he had always been waiting for this day. The day his father would die and he'd finally be able to claim Sicily's throne.

But Varda, Gallo, Antonetti, Sicily's seat of power, they were Matteo's problem. Alexei was still focused on the Romanos and the two bodies they had left to drop. Vincenzo and Elio.

He knew Elio well. A pompous asshole who was desperate to earn his father's approval. Something that always eluded him. Vincenzo he knew only by reputation, and it wasn't a good one.

Elio's oldest cousin liked to beat the women he slept with, and he wasn't shy about taking as many of them as possible to bed. Whatever he'd done to Carina, whatever she'd seen him do to others, fixed a faraway look in her eyes whenever he brought up the man's name. Alexei was determined to make Vincenzo's death a long and painful one.

He'd yet to make a final decision on Giovanni's younger son, Davide. Carina insisted he'd stayed away from the villa in Cefalù, preferring to spend his free time with his lover, Sergio. She didn't seem all that interested in whether Davide lived or died. But Alexei was still letting possibilities simmer in the back of his mind where Davide was concerned. Just in case.

Once he'd finished counting the bills, he marked them against the debts owed in the ledger. Some men were a handful of payments away from being free from their weekly visits. Then they'd be monitored closely for a few months to ensure they didn't do anything stupid. Like go to the cops.

He was stuffing the money back into the bag to take downstairs when the door to his office flew open and ricocheted off the wall with a bang, leaving behind a hole in the plaster. Alexei paused, lifting a single brow at the figure in the doorway.

"Are you too dense to understand what knocking is? Or too arrogant?"

Matteo strode in without invitation, his eyes sweeping the small space with a calculating gaze. "I own the place."

Alexei snorted, resuming his work of stacking bills and cinching the top of the bag closed. "You sound exactly like your father when you say shit like that."

"Mmm," Matteo murmured. "Why is your office so small? And buried in the back of the building? I'm sure there's a bigger one around here somewhere."

"I'm sure there is. But I don't spend much time in here, and I don't like interruptions when I do." He gave Matteo a pointed stare. "What do you want?"

"I wanted to see how debt collections were going."

Alexei leaned back in his chair and tilted his head. "You drove all the way here to ask about numbers you could get with a text message?" Matteo raised a brow, waiting. "They're fine. We're all caught up. A few will make their last payments in the coming weeks."

Matteo nodded. "And we still surveil to make sure—"

"They don't rat. Yes. If that's all, I—"

"Actually, I'd like to ask your opinion about Varda."

"Really," Alexei replied. "Since when do you care about my opinion on Varda or anything else to do with your grand scheme?"

Matteo waved Alexei's suspicion away and stepped further into the office, closing the door behind him. He searched the space for a chair and, finding none, shoved his hands into his pockets and leaned back against the wall.

"Dom has given me his opinion as boots on the ground, and now I want yours." Alexei waved a hand for Matteo to continue. "Would you say Varda's control of his men is slipping?"

Tilting his head, Alexei considered the question. "The younger ones, maybe. Not the older ones."

"Why not?"

"The older ones are too loyal. They've got history. The younger ones are easily bought. They follow the money every time. That's why they make excellent spies."

Matteo nodded. "Dom said the same."

Alexei cast his eyes to the ceiling, tired of the games. "Why don't you say what you really came for, Matteo? Save us both some time."

Clearing his throat, Matteo pinned Alexei with a hard stare. "I want to talk to you about Carina."

"Christ," Alexei muttered. "What now?"

"I want you to convince her to pull back from all of this business with the Romanos."

"And why would I do that?"

Matteo scowled and took a step forward. "Because I'm telling you to."

Alexei laughed, and Matteo's frown deepened. "We've been over this already. I don't take orders from you where your sister is concerned."

"She helped kill Giovanni, was forced to kill Lepera. That should be enough blood for her." Matteo twisted his watch around his wrist. "She'll listen to you if you ask her to stop."

Pushing back from the desk, Alexei shelved the ledger and crossed his arms over his chest. "You're only here because Luca already failed."

A muscle ticked in Matteo's jaw. "She isn't cut out for this, and you know it."

"I don't know that. The only one who doesn't know how capable she is of this, how much she wants it...no. Fuck that. How much she fucking *deserves* this. Is you."

"Carina is—"

"Stronger than you give her credit for."

"She isn't," Matteo spat. "Whatever you want to believe you've seen in her these last few weeks, I know my sister better than you. I've known her longer. She's like our mother. Sweet, with a tender heart. One day she'll wake up and regret the things she's done. She'll regret being like y—"

Alexei's grin was cold. "Like me? Tell me, Matteo. What am I like?"

"You know what I mean," Matteo growled. "One day, she'll wake up and regret the amount of blood on her hands."

"The only thing she'll regret is trusting you if you keep dangling the promise of revenge in front of her and then yanking it back when you get cold feet. If you don't have the balls to take out Elio Romano, then say that. And stop laying the blame around Carina's neck."

"You fucking prick." Matteo surged forward and shoved Alexei back against the safe, gripping him by the front of his shirt. "I'm trying to protect her."

"Careful, Matteo. You'll ruin your pretty suit." Alexei squeezed Matteo's fingers in a vise grip until Matteo finally released him and stepped back. "Carina will have her revenge, because even if you won't give it to her, I will. I've seen the scars on her body. I know what they did to her. And if you cared half as much as you claim to, you'd let her bathe in their blood until there wasn't a drop left."

Stepping around Matteo, Alexei stalked to the door and yanked it open. "Why don't you do us both a favor and stick to what you're good at? You can both have what you want, but don't pretend you're doing it for her, to protect her virtue or whatever you have to tell yourself."

"Then we're doing this my way," Matteo said through gritted teeth.

"No. I told you weeks ago Elio, Giovanni, and Vincenzo Romano would be dead when this was all said and done, whether you wanted them to be or not. You're the one who keeps trying to resurrect them despite what they did to the woman you're supposedly trying to protect. Ask yourself why that is."

Alexei turned on his heel and left Matteo standing alone in the middle of his office. He didn't know why Matteo continued to flip-flop on killing Elio and letting Carina have a hand in it. Alexei suspected it had nothing to do with Carina's purity. If Matteo cared so much about that, he wouldn't have left in the first place.

Whatever Matteo's resistance, the end result would be the same. Because the only person Alexei cared about in this scenario was Carina. And he'd make damn sure she got every single thing she wanted before this was all said and done.

Chapter Twenty-Six

After dropping off the cash in the basement for their accountants to deal with and touching base with Berto about the debts still needing to be collected, Alexei drove home. At this time of day, Carina was likely lying out by the pool, her body stretched out on one of the loungers, bronze skin glowing in the sunlight.

She wasn't comfortable in bikinis yet, still preferring to keep her scars hidden from prying eyes. But she'd long since stopped hiding from him, stopped flinching when his fingertips grazed one of them or he pressed his lips to one.

Parking in the lower garage, he wound around the stone path to his cottage. He hadn't used the pool in years, but he still had an old suit lying around somewhere. Maybe he could coax her into the water and then coax her into something else. Work out some of these frustrations Matteo had stirred up with his bullshit.

He didn't expect to see Carina waiting for him when he opened the door. Or, not waiting for him so much as sitting there on his couch like she belonged, like there was nowhere else she'd rather be.

She had a pad of paper perched on her knee, and she was tapping her chin lightly with the pen in her hand, staring off into the distance, deep in thought. He stepped in, and she looked up, the smile that lit up her face arrowing straight to his heart.

"Hi. I hope it's okay I let myself in. There were too many people at the house, and I needed somewhere quiet to think." She studied him for a moment, then tilted her head in question. "What's wrong?"

He closed the door behind him and leaned against it. "What makes you think something's wrong?"

"I don't know." She lifted a shoulder. "Something about that look. You usually look happier to see me." Her smile faltered as another idea occurred to her. "I didn't mean to intrude. I'll go."

Closing the distance between them, he leaned down to capture her lips before she could get up, dropping next to her on the couch and draping an arm over her shoulders to keep her in place. "You're not intruding. I got distracted thinking how much I liked seeing you here."

She relaxed, leaning into his side. "Then what was that look when you first walked in?"

"Matteo came to see me at my office."

"What were you two arguing about this time?" She drew light circles on his thigh with her manicured fingernail.

He pulled her closer and pressed a kiss to her temple. "You."

"Christ. He's not going on about us sleeping together again, is he? Because that is not something I plan on giving up any time soon."

Alexei grinned, trailing his fingertips down her side and making her squirm. "No?"

"No." Carina moved to straddle his thigh, wrapping her

arms around his neck. "He's lucky we're not fucking all over the house."

His hands moved to her hips, lifting his thigh to increase the pressure against her core as he rocked her back and forth. "I thought the same. But it wasn't about that."

She bit her bottom lip and let it drag through her teeth. He could tell she was debating whether to find out more or let him distract them both. In the end, her curiosity won out.

"What were you arguing about, then?"

"He wanted me to ask you to stop your vendetta."

Her arms fell to her sides, and fury etched itself onto her face. "He what?" Her voice was hard and cold.

"I told him no, for the record."

Carina's hands curled into fists against her thighs. "Let me guess. He said I was too young and immature to really understand what this all meant."

"No." Alexei's eyes narrowed. "Did he say that to you?"

"When sending Luca failed, he came to speak to me himself." She clenched and unclenched her fists. "Said I couldn't possibly understand the ramifications of what I was getting myself into."

The condescending bastard. "He told me you were too pure and innocent to have so much blood on your hands."

On a strangled scream of rage, she leapt out of Alexei's lap. "Pure and innocent?! If he was so worried about my purity, maybe he should have stayed and made sure my father didn't marry me off to the highest fucking bidder!"

Alexei grinned despite himself.

"What's so funny?" she snapped.

"I had pretty much the same thought." He reached for her, frowning when she didn't retake her position on his lap. "I've already told you what Matteo wants doesn't matter."

"It matters to me. I'm tired of being underestimated and shoved into the background by the men in my life."

"I'm not shoving you into the background, Carina. Or underestimating you."

She softened, relaxing her shoulders. "I know you're not. You are apparently the only one. Luca might have refused to talk me out of it, but he still takes his orders from Matteo. And Dom…Dom is complicated."

"Matteo seems to think you might regret the blood on your hands one day."

"I didn't regret it the first time," she muttered. "Why would I regret it now?"

"What do you mean you didn't regret it the first time?" Alexei pushed off the couch and moved to stand in front of her. "Was Lepera not your first kill?"

"What? No," she said quickly. "I misspoke."

"Carina." He slid his hand into her hair, fisting the strands in his fingers and forcing her to meet his gaze. There was only one other person she could mean. "Did you kill your husband?"

She dragged her tongue over her bottom lip. He could see the battle in her eyes over whether to tell him the truth. Tightening his hand in her hair, he stepped closer.

"I would have preferred something a little bloodier," she said. "But a flavorless liquid slipped into his morning espresso to stop his heart did the job."

The words barely left her lips before he claimed her mouth, yanking her roughly onto her toes until she crashed into the hard plane of his chest. He molded their bodies together, taking from her lips until she rewarded him with a soft moan. His little Carina was more familiar with death than he realized.

"Why didn't you tell me?" he demanded, reaching for her shirt and tugging it roughly over her head.

"I wanted to. I didn't know how." Her fingers made quick

work of his jeans while he slipped out of his shirt and tossed it to the floor.

"Tell me." He released the front catch of her bra and filled his hands with her breasts. "Every detail." He dipped his head to swirl his tongue over her nipple, dragging his teeth against it. "Don't leave anything out."

"I used to fantasize about killing him all the time. Within" —her breath hitched when he closed his teeth around the sensitive bud—"a year of getting married. We'd have dinner, and I'd imagine walking from my end of the table to his and jabbing my knife into the side of his neck."

He growled as he kissed from one breast to the other. "But you didn't."

"No." Her hands roamed over his shoulders and down his back. "Always so many people around. I didn't think I'd make it out alive if I did something like that. And I still wanted to live then."

Jerking upright, Alexei smoothed her hair off her face. "There was a moment when you didn't?"

She shrugged, but he read the heaviness in her gaze. "There were many moments."

He lifted her into his arms and carried her into the bedroom, laying her gently on the bed. "Keep going," he said, dropping to his knees and working open the button of her shorts, then peeling down the zipper.

"I was toying with the idea of sacrificing myself." She lifted her hips at his urging so he could slide her shorts and panties off. "I was okay with letting them kill me if it meant Giuseppe would be dead too."

The realization that he had come so close to losing her had rage heating his blood until he vibrated from it. "What changed your mind?"

He pressed slow, methodical kisses up the inside of her thigh, grinning when her hips jerked but not changing his pace. She pushed onto her elbows to watch him, reaching down to run her fingers through his hair.

"Elio's wife."

Alexei's brows shot up. "She told you to kill Giuseppe?"

"No." She shook her head, using her hand to guide his lips back to her skin. "She'd given Elio two daughters, and he was desperate for a son. She wasn't used to sharing a bed with him so often. One day we were having tea in the garden, and she mentioned wanting to drug him so he'd leave her alone."

Her hips jerked when he blew a warm breath against her core, and when he dragged his tongue up the length of her slit, she dropped her head back between her shoulders with a groan.

"Then what did you do?" he prompted, flicking his tongue against her clit.

"I started researching. It was slow. Someone was"—her breath caught when he sucked her clit into his mouth and slid one finger inside her—"always watching me."

"Mhmm," he hummed against her clit, pumping his finger slowly in and out.

"Eventually, I found a podcast about high doses of potassium chloride causing heart attacks. Oh God." She groaned when he added a second finger, speeding up his thrusts. "Alexei."

"Keep going," he commanded, curling his fingers up and rubbing against her g-spot.

"I can't."

He sat back to watch her, her hand falling from his head and moving up to pinch and twist her nipple. "Carina, look at me." Her eyes shot open and locked onto his. "Tell me the rest of it."

He didn't let up the pace, and her breath came in sharp pants when she spoke again. "You can buy it anywhere. As a supplement. Virtually undetectable on an autopsy. Fuck," she gasped when his thumb pressed against her clit. "I dissolved the powder from several pills in some water."

"And slipped it into his espresso."

"Yes," she whimpered, hips rocking against his hand.

"Good girl," he replied, voice hoarse. "Now you can come for me."

He drove into her faster, using his thumb to rub rough circles over her clit, pushing her closer and closer to the peak of her release and loving the way she sobbed his name when she came on his fingers.

"Eyes on me."

He stood up, sliding his fingers into his mouth to lick them clean while she watched him, then stepping out of his jeans and boxers. Motioning her back, he climbed on the bed between her thighs and rubbed his cock up and down her slit, grinning when he brushed her clit and she hissed.

"I love watching you take my cock," he said, sliding in to the hilt and reaching down to rub her clit with his fingers.

"Alexei," she said, her voice barely above a whisper while her fingernails trailed up his arms and down his chest.

"Yes, baby."

"There's more." She groaned when he pressed her thighs wider apart and changed the angle, sinking deeper inside her. "About…about…"

"About Giuseppe?" She nodded frantically. "Tell me."

"I watched him." Her back bowed when he pinched her clit, his cock still working in and out of her. "Die."

"Fuck," he moaned, hips slapping against her. "You stood there and watched him die and did nothing?"

"Yes," she whimpered as he pounded her. "I didn't know how much to give him." Her fingernails raked down his biceps as she writhed under him. "I wanted to make sure I gave him enough so—oh God—so I stayed. And I watched. And…"

"And what?" he demanded, wanting to hear the words from her lips before he let her come again, before he gave in to his own need.

"And I liked it."

Fuck. He slammed into her so hard she cried out, pounding her relentlessly until she had no choice but to come around his cock and drag him over the edge with her until he saw stars.

Slumping on top of her, he barely held himself up on his forearms, face buried against her neck. He pressed his lips against her hot, sweaty skin and rocked his hips into hers, making her shudder.

"Jesus Christ, Carina." He rolled onto his back and stared up at the ceiling, smiling when she shifted on the bed beside him and her face filled his vision.

"Are you mad I didn't tell you? I should have done it sooner."

He pulled her in for a kiss, deepening it by degrees until she moaned softly against his lips. "I'm glad you told me, and I'm not mad," he assured her.

She frowned. "You're sure?"

"I'm sure." He traced a finger down the column of her throat and over her clavicle, dragging it against her nipple and delighting in the way she twitched against his hold. "I'm also sure you keep getting better and better in all the best ways. Kill anyone else I should know about?"

Unable to contain a grin, she bit her lip. "Not yet. But do you want to hear about my ideas for killing Vincenzo?"

"Absolutely." He repositioned her to straddle his waist, pulling her down until she took his length deep inside her again. "Don't leave anything out."

Chapter Twenty-Seven

Carina stood on the sidewalk in front of the address Alexei had given her and rolled her eyes. His wry grin as he scribbled it on a scrap of paper suddenly made sense. He knew what she didn't. That Matteo had bought himself a fucking office building with his mysterious fortune.

Not for the first time, Carina wondered how in the hell he'd amassed so much money in such a short amount of time. Especially after leaving home with precious few connections. She imagined what they could see was only the tip of the iceberg. He was undoubtedly sitting on plenty more cash he hadn't shared with them yet. And she still wasn't sure how wary of him she needed to be.

Dom respected him enough to follow orders, or at least respected his plans for the Bianchi organization and the power they would eventually wield. Luca, with his brilliant head for numbers, was happy to finally have someone to talk to whose business vision matched his own. At least Alexei seemed to be on her side in this.

Matteo had secrets, and until he was willing to share

them, his opinions on how she lived her life, on her stupid fucking purity, were none of his damn business. She'd killed three times now, and she didn't regret any of them for a second. She wouldn't regret Vincenzo either. Or Elio. He looked so much like his father. She would thoroughly enjoy killing Elio.

After waiting for a group of businessmen in suits to look her up and down and stroll past, she darted to the looming glass door and stepped inside. The lobby was empty, the sound of her heels echoing in the soaring atrium. What she assumed was a guard desk sat empty against the back wall, and she wondered if Matteo would eventually staff it.

Crossing to the elevator, she pressed the button to call it and watched the numbers tick down until the doors opened with a cheerful ding. Once inside, she punched the button for the top floor as instructed, clasping her hands in front of her when the car lurched into motion.

Matteo had been avoiding her since Alexei told her about their little chat, since she'd confessed to killing Giuseppe. She didn't know if Matteo's absence was intentional, and frankly, she didn't care. She was tired of being ignored and treated like a child. Matteo didn't know who she was anymore, he'd been gone too long, but he was about to find out. He'd left a shy wallflower behind, and he'd come home to someone else entirely.

The elevator announced the floor in a pleasant female voice that startled her out of her thoughts, and she stepped off onto rich carpet. This floor was just as empty as the lobby, with walls of windows showing off the monochrome of Palermo's business district and the colorful houses beyond.

Did Matteo really need such an obscenely large office building for a single office and no other staff? What the hell would he even do out of this building anyway? Invite their men to discuss drug deals and count the blood money Dom and Alexei were responsible for collecting?

Hearing noise from somewhere in the recesses of the space, back where she assumed a corner office might be, she wandered down the wide main hallway until she found a woman sitting at a desk. She was maybe a few years younger, fresh out of university by the looks of her.

The woman's hair was bright red and pulled back into an elegant bun, a few tendrils loose to frame a round face. Carina didn't recognize her, and with hair that red and skin that pale, she was unlikely to be the daughter of one of their capos. Unless she was illegitimate.

Carina cleared her throat, and the woman glanced up from her computer, a serene smile immediately painting itself across her full mouth.

"Hello. How may I help you?" the woman said, and Carina was surprised by the unfamiliar lilt of her accent.

"I'm here to see my brother." Carina nodded to the closed door over the woman's shoulder.

The woman swiveled in her chair, flipping through what looked like a calendar and tracing her fingernail down the page. "I don't see you here on his schedule."

"That's because I'm not." Carina fought hard not to roll her eyes. Not only had Matteo removed himself from the house to do his work, he'd hired himself a gatekeeper. "If you tell Matteo I'm here, I'm sure he'll make time to see me."

"One moment." The woman picked up the phone on her desk and pressed a button, waiting for a beat. "Yes, *Il Signore*, I have your sister here with me. She'd like to speak to you." Another beat of silence. "Of course, I'll send her right in."

Carina didn't wait for further instructions from the woman, stepping around the desk and letting herself in. She was right about the corner office, but she'd vastly underestimated the size. Two of the four walls were nothing but floor-to-ceiling windows with a view of Palermo that stretched to the sea and the fat white clouds that rolled lazily across the bright blue of the sky.

It was furnished well, with a big modern desk flanked by two oversized armchairs and plush carpet underfoot. Against one wall was a long sofa in rich black leather with a low coffee table in front of it. It was an impressive space, and the thought annoyed her.

"To what do I owe the unexpected surprise?" Matteo turned from the window and moved to his desk, propping a hip against it. "I wasn't aware you knew about these offices yet."

"Hard to know about things you choose not to share with me."

Matteo sighed. "I've been very busy."

"Mmm," Carina mumbled. "So I see."

Shoving away from the desk, Matteo moved to a cabinet. He opened it to reveal an impressive collection of liquors and spirits. He poured himself a glass, and she waved away his offer for her own drink. She wondered if he now required alcohol to get through a single meeting with her or if he was becoming more like their father with each passing second.

"You wanted to talk, Carina." He gestured at her with his glass before taking a sip. "So talk."

She peered over her shoulder at the closed door and then back at her brother. "You're sure your assistant isn't listening at the door?"

"Maeve? She knows about me. Everything about me," he added at Carina's raised eyebrow.

"Because you're sleeping with her?"

Matteo chuckled and set his glass down on the desk. "No, because her grandfather is the head of Dublin's Mob. And Eoghan Quinn and I have done business on more than one occasion."

Well, that explained the strange accent under her Italian. "If she's a Mob princess, what is she doing here? With you?"

"I guess she wanted to see the world. Did you come here to talk to me about Maeve or something else?"

She studied her brother and his blank expression. In his tailored suit with his expensive shoes and flashy watch, he looked more like the CEO of a large corporation than the Don of a crime family whose ties to Sicily dated back centuries. Everything she learned about her brother only served to pile on more questions instead of providing answers. Not that he'd offered up many since his arrival nearly a month ago.

But those questions were for another time. She did have business with him here today. And she might as well get it over with.

"Your deadline with Elio is almost up."

He shifted on the desk, but his expression didn't change. "It is."

"How are you planning on delivering the message that his money isn't coming?"

"We're still working out the details of a meeting." He cocked his head. "Why?"

"Because you don't need him or Vincenzo anymore." Anticipation sizzled in her blood until she felt electric with it. "Once he knows what you've done, we can get rid of him. Both of them."

His eyebrows winged up. "It isn't quite that simple."

"Well." She waved a hand in dismissal. "Whatever you need from him. Once you get it, he doesn't need to be alive anymore, does he?"

Matteo's brow furrowed, and he rounded the desk, dropping into the chair. "No, not technically. But I'm not interested in discussing this with you right now."

"I'm not leaving until you do." She crossed her arms over

her chest at his raised brow. "I'm not a child, and it's time you stopped treating me like one."

"I never said you were a child." He reached for a file folder, but she wouldn't be dismissed that easily.

"You've implied it every way you know how. Worried about my purity now, brother?" He dropped the folder in front of him with a smack and glared up at her. "Yes, Alexei told me what you said when you cornered him in his office. When you sent another messenger to try and talk me out of what you promised was already mine."

"It's not like they won't be dead at the end of it all. I promised to give you that, and I will. Isn't knowing that enough?"

"No. It isn't. Not for me."

"I'm worried you'll regret it."

"I won't." She held up a hand to silence his protests. "I won't regret this. And even if I did, that is my consequence to bear. I might have needed your protection once, but I don't anymore. I haven't for a long time."

"I know, and I'm trying to right some wrongs here, Carina."

"No." She shook her head and approached the desk, leaning her hands against the edge. "You're trying to ease your own guilt. Your feelings about what happened after you left are yours to deal with. And I won't be the excuse you use to do it."

"Why can't you trust I have your best interest at heart?"

"Why can't you trust I know myself better than you do?" She stood when he sighed and raised a brow. "I'm trying to trust you, Matteo. Trust that you want what's best for this family and not just yourself. But your misplaced white knight bullshit is making it impossible. We can work together on this, on what you want to build in Sicily, or we can be enemies."

His eyes narrowed on her face. "Don't threaten me, Carina. I'm still the head of this family."

"It's not a threat. It's a fact. I will not exist in the background anymore, smiling politely and marrying to suit your whims. I'm in this all the way, starting with these Romano kills. I promise I can be a far better asset than an enemy."

"You wouldn't turn on me, on this family."

A smile spread slowly across her face. "Are you willing to bet everything on that, Matteo? Who do you think Alexei will choose if you force him to pick sides? Mine? Or yours? Don't pretend you don't need him to win this fight."

Matteo studied her for a long moment, her skin prickling under his intense gaze. She hadn't meant to come at him quite so hard, but he'd forced her hand. She'd already spoken to Alexei about the very real consequences of going against her brother if he put his foot down and what that might mean.

But with Alexei on her side, and she believed without a doubt he would stand with her whatever came, she had the upper hand in this. And Matteo was a fool if he didn't recognize it.

"Fine," he agreed at last. "I'm here to pull this family back together, not tear it apart. But when you wake up steeped in nightmares about what you've done, don't come crying to me."

With a smile, she claimed one of the chairs opposite his desk and crossed her legs. "Don't worry. I've slept like a baby every night since Giovanni died. I don't imagine it'll stop now."

Matteo shook his head and pinched the bridge of his nose. "I'm assuming you have some ideas then." She nodded. "What are they?"

"Insist on meeting with Elio face to face to do the transfer.

Alexei says Elio goes almost everywhere with Vincenzo now that his man is gone."

"Since you killed him, you mean."

She ignored her brother's tone. "Since he tried to rape me. Yes. You can have Elio do whatever you need him to do so you or Davide can assume control of Romano interests."

"Davide?"

"Yes. I've been trying to tell you for weeks he's very pliable. If you needed a pawn to do your bidding while still play acting as the head of the Romano territory, he'd be your best option."

Matteo swiveled in his chair, twisting his watch around his wrist. "What makes you so sure of that?"

"He's very committed to keeping his secret."

"What secret is that?"

She uncrossed and recrossed her legs, letting the silence stretch out for dramatic effect. "His lover, Sergio."

The spark in Matteo's eyes made her grin. If only he'd listened to her about all of this weeks ago. The plan would have been settled, and Elio might already be dead. But it didn't matter now. All she needed to focus on was the end goal. Whatever happened between now and Elio's slow and torturous death was Matteo's problem.

"Are we agreed?"

Tapping his fingers on the desktop, Matteo considered. "We are. I'll finalize something in the next day or two."

The thought she might have blood on her hands before the week was out made her pulse quicken. She was determined to savor every second of her last moments with Vincenzo and Elio Romano.

"Good." She pushed to her feet and turned for the door.

"What do you plan on doing to them?"

She paused in her reach for the knob and looked at her brother over her shoulder. "I haven't decided yet," she lied.

No need to tell Matteo all the gruesome details she and Alexei had laid out between them. The last thing she wanted to do was give him a reason to say no. Again. He nodded, and she slipped out the door, past Maeve, and down the hall.

The Romano empire was crumbling under her hand. And she meant what she told Matteo. She would have a hand in its rebuilding, in the new order Matteo had planned for Sicily. She had as much of a birthright to it as any of her brothers. It was high time she claimed it.

Chapter Twenty-Eight

"But I want to go with you."

"I know you do," Alexei replied, slipping an extra knife into his pocket and attaching the gun Dom insisted everyone carry today to the waistband of his jeans. "But you can't."

Carina pouted as she watched him get ready. "I went to the last meeting."

"Yes. In a club surrounded by people when we weren't preparing to tell them to go fuck themselves." He stepped between her thighs where she sat on the counter and pressed his lips to hers. "I can't guarantee your safety where we're going. So you stay here."

"I don't care if it's dangerous."

He kissed her again, gently nibbling her bottom lip until her body relaxed against his. "I do. You can be mad at me if you want, but I'm not going to risk you, *lyubimaya moya*."

Carina tilted her head, capturing his face in her hands before he could step away and running her thumb across his scar. "It's been so long since I've heard you speak Russian. What does it mean?"

"I'll tell you later." Alexei kissed her palm. "I have to go, or I'm going to be late meeting your brothers at the casino."

When he moved toward the door, she hopped off the counter and followed him. "If you take me with you, you could tell me what it means right now."

Hand on the doorknob, he chuckled. "You're nothing if not persistent. But no. Don't you trust me to bring Vincenzo and Elio back to you so you can have your way with them?"

"Of course I do, but—"

"No. No buts. Matteo and I are in agreement on this. When we have Elio and Vincenzo in a location we can control, then you can see them and do whatever you want to them. But not before. Understand?"

"Fine." She crossed her arms over her chest, that pout reappearing on her lips that made him want to haul her off to the bedroom and have his way with her. "But you'll call me as soon as it's done?"

"Of course." He claimed one last kiss from her lips before disappearing out the door and jogging around the path to his car.

As much as he thought Carina deserved to be part of this plan, he wouldn't do anything to jeopardize her safety, and meeting Elio in what amounted to an underground bunker was hardly secure enough to risk it. Alexei was a little skeptical of today's proposed meeting spot, but nothing about this part of the plan was without its risks.

As far as Alexei knew, Elio still had no idea Matteo owned a controlling share of the company's debt, but the rumors on the ground said soldiers were pushing back, if not outright defecting, because Elio couldn't pay. It was likely Romano was too desperate for any kind of infusion of cash to fuck this up today, but that didn't mean Alexei wanted to take the chance. Desperate men did desperate things.

The brothers and an escort were already waiting for him

when he pulled up in front of the casino nearest the house. The weight of the gun at his hip felt unnatural as he crossed the lot to the waiting SUV, but he could see the wisdom in it. Elio preferred guns, and bringing a knife to a gunfight, no matter how much more skilled he was with it, was asking for trouble. He was a decent enough shot to hold his own.

"Sorry I'm late."

Luca twisted in his seat and grinned. "I'm surprised Carina didn't stow away in your trunk."

"She tried valiantly to the last second," Alexei admitted. "Everything still a go?"

"It is," Dom said from the driver's seat.

Matteo checked his watch. "Then let's roll out."

They drove in silence, winding through the streets of Palermo toward the meeting spot Elio had chosen. It was an odd location for a funds transfer. Not entirely in Romano or Bianchi territory, but rather at the border where both of their lands met with Varda territory. It was the deciding factor in leaving Carina at home.

Dom hadn't heard about a possible Varda-sanctioned ambush from his spies, but that didn't mean it was impossible. Varda had a vested interest in Elio getting paid today. This particular move could bring Varda against them as easily as it brought Elio. Only time would tell.

The lead car pulled into the abandoned parking garage and wound down the maze of ramps to the basement level. They were out of sight of the street but also sitting ducks. Matteo had stationed extra men close by, but Elio was just as likely to have done the same.

Alexei and Dom shared a look in the rearview mirror as they parked across from a single black SUV with tinted windows. Nobody moved until the other door opened and Vincenzo Romano stepped out from the backseat, a laptop tucked under his arm. Two men got out from the front and flanked him. Alexei noted the silhouette of the guns at their hips, hidden beneath long shirts.

Matteo climbed out of the car first and asked the one question Alexei imagined they were all thinking. "Where's Elio? He asked for this meeting a week ahead of schedule and can't even be bothered to show up?"

Vincenzo inclined his head. "My cousin apologizes for his absence. He had some urgent family business to take care of."

Matteo swept his gaze over the three of them standing there and toward the car with the rest of their men. Alexei read the distrust in his gaze and nodded. He shared it. There's no reason Elio wouldn't be here. And it meant they wouldn't be able to take them both. Something that could have consequences far beyond Carina not getting her revenge. They didn't want to give Elio enough time to regroup.

"Shall we get this over with?" Vincenzo opened up the laptop and typed quickly with one hand.

When he turned the laptop around, it displayed a funds transfer screen. If Matteo was actually going to be transferring one billion euros into Elio's offshore account, he'd type in an account number and a secure access code, and the money would travel through the mysterious tunnels of the internet from one account to the other.

At a glance from Matteo, Luca stepped forward and took the laptop from Vincenzo's hands, carrying it to his brother. Matteo brought his hand to the keyboard, then paused.

"What if I'd rather wait until Elio can meet me face to face?"

"Then you'll be waiting a long time," Vincenzo snarled. "There's nothing in this stupid contract that requires Elio to be here. If you don't have the money"—Vincenzo took a menacing step forward, pausing when Dom did the same— "then that's a different issue to resolve."

"I have the money." Matteo paused, and Alexei wondered if he was hesitating, recalculating the plan, deciding on a different course of action that meant they wouldn't leave here with even one Romano bastard today.

"Good, then do it and stop playing games."

Matteo nodded, raising his hand to type and then pausing again. "I was sorry to hear about your father. Terrible accident."

Vincenzo jerked and, for the first time, looked unsettled. "The money, Bianchi. Now," he said through gritted teeth.

"You know." Matteo closed the laptop, smiling when Vincenzo's eyes narrowed. "I don't think I will. I wish Elio would have bothered to show up for this. It would have been nice to see his face when I told him."

"Told him what?" Vincenzo snapped.

"That he owes me more money than I owe him. Several billion more."

Vincenzo scoffed. "Does he? And how do you figure?"

"Because while you were burying your beloved father, I was quietly buying up the considerable debt that's been borrowed against your clubs. And if Elio can't pay—and I suspect he can't—then 60 percent of Romano assets belong to me."

"You're bluffing."

"I assure you, I'm not. Now, since your men won't be leaving this garage alive and you'll be coming with us, why don't you tell me where Elio is so he and I can have a little chat?"

The men at Vincenzo's side drew their weapons, but Dom and Luca were faster, taking each down with a single shot before their fingers even touched the trigger. But the sound of gunfire opened a floodgate. Romano men poured from the stairwell over their left shoulder, exchanging rapid fire with

Dom and Luca while Alexei drew his own weapon and dove with Matteo behind a nearby SUV.

Their men piled out of the second car, but none of them moved to flank Vincenzo. Alexei was torn between making sure Vincenzo didn't leave here and holding back the Romano shooters until backup could arrive. He decided to try for both. The Bianchis couldn't afford to lose another Don, not so soon after Lorenzo, but he'd do everything in his power to make sure Carina got what she deserved.

He moved around the side of the SUV, where he had a clear view of Vincenzo, now surrounded by his own men while he yelled something Alexei couldn't hear into a phone. The guys buffering Vincenzo were squeezing off shots of their own, and Alexei took careful aim, dropping the man closest to him. Vincenzo didn't even glance in his direction. Alexei considered that a bonus.

Another man stepped forward, slightly away from the man he was guarding, and that left Alexei with enough room to get a clear shot. Satisfaction rippled through him when the man collapsed to the ground. When tires squealed behind them, Alexei spun, weapon raised.

"Ours!" Matteo shouted, making a crouched run toward the additional SUVs as they screeched to a stop.

True to Matteo's word, their men descended in earnest, surrounding the Romano soldiers, and Alexei watched them fall. He tracked his gaze back to Vincenzo and saw him kick at the flat tire of their only getaway vehicle. When he caught Alexei's eye, he took off at a dead run toward the stairs. Alexei gave chase, aiming shots that went wide and lodged themselves into the concrete by Vincenzo's head as he pushed through the door to the stairwell.

The banging of the door echoed in the silo when Alexei shoved in behind him, and he sprinted up the stairs after

Vincenzo. He expected Vincenzo to go for the street level, maybe to meet a waiting car he'd called as backup, but he continued to climb. Alexei's lungs burned as he followed him up and up until there was nowhere but the top deck of the garage to go.

He burst through the door into the bright sunshine, blinking against the blinding light. But Vincenzo was nowhere to be seen. Not sprinting across the vacant lot, not crouched beside the little shed hiding the stair access from view. Alexei couldn't even see a shadow creeping across the bleached surface.

The sound of approaching footsteps reached his ears too late, and then Vincenzo slammed into him from behind with a grunt, knocking them both to the ground. The gun fell from his fingers and clattered across the concrete. Fuck it. He was better with a knife at this distance, anyway.

Bringing his elbow back into Vincenzo's face, he rolled away from his haphazard punches and dug out the knife in his pocket. Vincenzo didn't have a weapon, only his fists raised to protect his head when Alexei spun to face him.

"You're not leaving here a free man," Alexei said, circling him. "You might as well make this easy on yourself."

"I'd rather leave here a dead one. I imagine the result would be the same either way. And at least this way it'll involve less torture."

Alexei grinned. "You underestimate how much I can make this hurt, Vincenzo."

"So do you."

He saw Vincenzo's muscles bunch before he charged, and he stepped out of the way, reaching out with his blade and catching Vincenzo in the side. Vincenzo hissed and spun away, putting more distance between them. Alexei's goal wasn't to kill him, at least not here. He wanted Vincenzo tired and weak. He'd be much easier to overpower that way.

This meant his cuts didn't have to be precise. They didn't

even have to hurt. All he needed to do was inflict enough of them to create a decent amount of blood loss that would leech the fight right out of Vincenzo's body. A game he could play for hours.

When Vincenzo took another run at him, Alexei held his ground, spinning at the last moment and catching the man in the bicep this time. He knew he must have nicked deep with the way Vincenzo stumbled toward the railing at the edge of the lot.

He gripped it, blood from the cut on his arm already welling up and racing toward his wrist. But Alexei let himself get too comfortable, and Vincenzo's swing caught him off guard, allowing him to land a blow to Alexei's jaw that snapped his head to the side.

Pain radiated up into his temple and down into his neck, and he gave Vincenzo a moment to savor his victory before twisting and dragging the knife across his chest. It tore through the material of his shirt, and Vincenzo collapsed back against the waist-high wall rimming the open level of the garage.

Vincenzo pressed his hand to the wound, pulling it away to stare down at the blood coating his fingers. Alexei was surprised by how quickly he seemed to be giving up. It was almost too easy, and his eyes darted to nearby structures to check for snipers, wondering if Vincenzo had lured him up here for a reason.

The stairwell door banged open, and they both turned toward the sound, Alexei forcing his heart rate to slow, his breathing to steady. Shutting out everything but the threat was the only way he'd survive the onslaught of an attack. Or at least put up a hell of a good fight before they killed him.

But it wasn't Romano men who burst through the door. It was Bianchi soldiers, looking harried but no worse for wear.

Alexei turned back to Vincenzo in time to see him hoist himself onto the narrow ledge, arms held out to his side.

"Don't," Alexei growled.

Vincenzo smiled slowly. *"La lealtà richiede sacrifici."*

Alexei darted forward, grasping for Vincenzo's shirt to pull him off the ledge, but he was already falling backward, his body plummeting toward the alley below. He reached the wall in time to watch Vincenzo make contact with the pavement, his arms splayed out beside him, his legs twisted at an odd angle like a macabre recreation of Christ on the cross.

"Son of a fucking bitch!"

Dom was beside him in seconds, breath sawing in and out of his lungs. "What the fuck did you let him do that for?"

"You think I invited him to jump off the fucking building when I wanted him alive?"

Casting him a sideways glance, Dom pulled his phone out of his pocket and dialed. "Matteo, Vincenzo swan dived off the top of the garage. He's in the alley between this structure and the pink building on the west side. Looks dead from up here."

It wasn't long before men were in the alley, surrounding the body and confirming Vincenzo was dead. Matteo barked out orders that were impossible to hear and then glanced up at where they were still peeking over the side.

"He wants us to meet him back at the cars," Dom said, glancing down at his phone when a text message came through.

Wiping the knife on his thigh to clean it and shoving it back into his pocket, Alexei followed Dom and the rest of their men inside and jogged down to the basement level. Much easier going down the endless flights of stairs than up. Matteo was waiting for them when they stepped through the door, and he caught a glimpse of Vincenzo's body being loaded into the back of his own SUV.

"Want to tell me exactly how that went horribly wrong? We were supposed to take him alive."

"We were supposed to take them both alive," Alexei replied. "It's not like I shoved him off the goddamn thing myself. Fucker jumped. Said *la lealtà richiede sacrifici* right before he went over."

"Loyalty requires sacrifice." Matteo's mouth thinned into a hard line. "Well, he certainly did that. I don't want Elio getting wind of this and disappearing or, worse, mobilizing against me. He doesn't appear to be inspiring much loyalty right now, but even his men will want to protect their own if they think they're under direct attack from us."

Matteo flicked a glance at Dom before pinning Alexei with a hard stare. "Find him and bring him to me."

Chapter Twenty-Nine

"Your eyes are going to cross if you keep staring at those notes."

Carina looked up to see Alexei standing in the doorway to her bedroom. It had been two days since the meeting with the Romanos went sideways and Alexei came home empty-handed. Matteo's quick appeal to Davide—at her insistence—was the only thing stemming the tide of all-out war erupting between the two families.

"There's got to be something I'm missing about where he could be. Something Giuseppe said." She rubbed two fingers against her temple. "I just have to remember."

"We're doing everything we can to find him."

"I know. But does that mean I can't help?"

He stepped into the room, easing the door shut behind him. "Of course not. But you've been holed up in this room obsessing about it for days. You need a break." He tugged his shirt off over his head and grinned down at her. "Let me distract you."

"You really think a distraction would help?" Pushing onto

her knees, she inched toward the edge of the bed, skimming her fingertips up his chest to his shoulders.

"I do." He flipped open the button on his jeans. "Take your mind off it for a while."

Her eyes followed her fingers along the side of his neck and across his jaw, then she slowly traced the length of his scar. "How did you get this?"

He caught her wrist but didn't pull her hand away from his face. The look in his eyes was serious now instead of playful. It was an impulsive question, but he said she needed a distraction. She swallowed around the lump in her throat, wondering if she'd made him angry, and his gaze dipped to her neck and back up to her face.

"You've never asked me that before."

"That's not true," she replied, scooting forward until her chest brushed his. "I asked you once. When I was nine and you were bleeding all over the front hallway. You wouldn't tell me then. You said—"

"It wasn't your kind of story." His gaze swept over her shoulder to the wall as if he was recalling that day as clearly as she was. "I remember."

"You said it didn't have a happy ending." She laid her palms flat against his chest, searching for the steady beat of his heart. "Is that still true?" she whispered.

He stepped away from her suddenly, and her heart sank. She'd pushed too far. Alexei had always refused to talk about his past, about who he was and how he ended up in Naples for her father to scoop up off the street. It wasn't something she thought much about. Not until recently, when he'd taken to whispering in Russian against her skin. Words he'd yet to translate for her but wound around her soul in ways she couldn't explain.

Settling into one of the chairs in front of the fireplace, he held his hand out for her, and she went to him. He didn't look at her when she crossed the room, but when she tried to sink down into the chair beside his, he took her hand and pulled her into his lap, settling her until she was seated on his thighs with her knees on either side of his hips.

His hands rested on her waist, his thumbs drawing absent circles over her stomach through her loose cotton dress. Emotions danced across his face one after another while he stared at her shoulder. When he brought his green eyes up to meet hers, they were filled with them.

"I was born in Russia. In this shitty little town where everyone was poor and hungry and barely surviving. I don't remember much about my parents when I was young. My father was never around, and my mother dumped me with my grandparents one day and never came back."

She rested her hands on his forearms, waiting for him to share whatever felt important to disclose. Whatever he had to say, she wouldn't push him for anything beyond what he was willing to give.

"They were good people, my grandparents. They loved each other in their way, intense and unforgiving. They tried to make sure I had enough, that I went to school and studied hard so I could get out of that life. When I was eight, my mother randomly showed up."

He huffed out a dry laugh, his fingers flexing on her waist. "She'd come back from traveling the world or some shit. Hooked herself a new man, one with money this time. She wasn't staying, but she wanted to take me with her. Wanted to be a family."

"Did you want to go?"

"No." He shook his head. "But my grandparents didn't have money to fight her, and she had a new rich husband who was content to bankroll her every whim. It wasn't bad for a while. I missed my grandparents, but you can get used to luxury pretty fast when all you've known is poverty and an empty belly."

His eyes darkened, and his brows knit together. "Then she got pregnant when we were living in Toulon, and suddenly being a family didn't include me. One night, a few months after my sister was born, she called my grandparents to ask about sending me back."

"What did they say?" Carina prompted when he didn't continue.

"Nothing. They were dead." His arms circled her waist when she gasped, and he leaned in to press a kiss to her jaw. "She wouldn't say how. It ate me up that I hadn't been able to say goodbye."

"How did you end up in Italy if you were living in France?"

He sighed, his chest heaving with the force of it. "They dumped me here. Or at an orphanage in Naples."

She jerked in shock. "They what?"

"We took a trip to Rome for my stepfather's birthday. One day he and I drove down to Naples. I'd always wanted to see Mount Vesuvius. But instead of going on the hike up the volcano, he took me to an orphanage. Told them I was a problem child, a liar, a danger to his daughter, shoved some fake papers at them, and left."

Tears pricked the edge of her vision, and she slid her hands up the side of his neck to cup his face, pressing her forehead against his. "I'm so sorry."

"I spent three years there. I got jumped a lot in the beginning because I didn't speak much Italian. My mother had only been teaching me French. I ran away whenever I could and taught myself how to fight so no one would ever get the jump on me again. I got pretty good at it."

A wry chuckle rumbled through him. "When your father found me, I'd been on the streets about two weeks after running away again. I'd just been in a fight, and someone had caught me in the face with a broken bottle."

When she tilted his head to study his scar, he let her, and she leaned in to press her lips to the top of it by his eyebrow. "And he brought you home just like that?"

"He asked me what shape the other boys were in. I told him worse and hopefully dead by morning. He smiled at me in that way he had."

"The one that let you know he was up to something."

Alexei nodded. "Then he asked me if I wanted a job. A job that would make sure no one got the better of me ever again."

"And you said yes."

"And I said yes." He sighed.

"Why did you stay once you knew who and what we were?"

"Instead of running again, you mean?" She nodded, heart beating slow and thick in her chest at the look in his eye. "I met this girl. She had dark brown eyes and brown hair streaked with red and gold. And she was nice to me. She didn't shy away from my injury or my scar or the monster I became. I thought it was her light that called to the darkness in me." He tucked a strand of hair behind her ear. "But I think now it was something else."

"What was it?" Carina whispered, voice hoarse.

"I think there was darkness in her too. A darkness that mirrored my own. And that's why she was the only person who ever really saw me."

She claimed his lips then, nipping them roughly with her teeth while he tightened his hold on her waist and pulled her chest flush with his. His hands skimmed down to the hem of her dress, tugging it up over her body and sending a wave of goosebumps over her skin where his fingertips brushed.

Pulling her dress over her head, he dropped it on the floor and leaned in to feast on her neck, skimming his teeth across her pulse and pressing a kiss against it. She rocked her hips against him, nothing between them but the fabric of his jeans.

He slipped a hand between their bodies, fingers sliding down the length of her slit and pulling a desperate moan from her lips. "I have to say," he murmured against her skin, "your distaste for wearing panties is one of my favorite things about you."

Rocking her hips against his hand, she laughed softly. "It's for entirely selfish reasons. I promise."

His lips curved into a grin against her throat, and he nibbled across her jaw to her earlobe. "I didn't understand it at first, the way I was drawn to you. Not until I was older and you were sent away to school."

"I didn't understand it either." She groaned when he pressed his fingertips roughly against her clit. "Except for my mother, I didn't really miss my family when I was away. But I missed you. Every opportunity I had to be near you when I was home, I took it. You were my obsession."

"And you're mine," he growled against her skin, lifting her as he stood and carrying her to the bed.

Laying her across it, he stepped out of his jeans and covered her body with his. He slid easily inside her, groaning softly when she wrapped her legs around his waist and rocked against him. The friction on her clit sent shockwaves through her. The weight of him, of where their bodies made contact, buzzed like electricity along her skin.

He pressed a kiss to her lips, reaching up to wrap a hand around her throat and squeezing until she sighed. "You are everything, Carina," he promised as he slowly moved his cock in and out. "I should have protected you sooner."

"Oh God," she whimpered as he picked up the pace, his hips slapping against her with each urgent thrust. "What do you mean?"

"I should have done more to stop your marriage."

"What could you have done?" she wondered.

But he didn't answer, increasing the pressure on her throat until blood pounded in her ears and pleasure mingled with pain while he thrust hard and deep inside her. He reared up to look down at her, his grip steady on her throat as he fucked her faster until she shuddered under him, at the mercy of his desire and on fire from it.

"Do you want to come for me, Carina?"

She nodded as much as his hand on her throat would allow. She felt the orgasm building inside her, tingling down her spine and racing along her nerve endings with each brutal thrust of his hips, each thump of her pulse under his fingers.

Gritting his teeth, Alexei leaned down to brush his lips against the shell of her ear. "Now, baby. Come all over my cock."

The words had barely left him before she obliged his command, his name a hoarse whisper on her lips, her fingernails biting into the skin of his hips as he thrust deep inside her and followed her over the edge.

Sliding her hands up his back and into his hair, she brought his mouth down to hers for a kiss as he loosened his grip on her throat and pushed himself up onto his hands. She groaned when the movement shifted his cock inside her, and he grinned.

"Alexei? What did you mean when you said you should have done more to stop my marriage?"

He rolled off her suddenly, shifting to lean back against the pillows, and she bit the inside of her cheek. There was something about her question that felt heavy. Her heart pounded in her chest with his silence. He didn't speak for so long she thought he would refuse to answer.

"I should have killed him sooner," he whispered.

She froze, eyes glued to the ceiling. He started to move

away from her, but her hand shot out to grab his elbow, pulling him back on the bed against her side.

"What did you do?"

Tracing his fingertips over her wrist and palm, he took a deep breath. "I told you your father wanted to send you back to the Romanos to be Elio's mistress."

"Yes. But that was when I first arrived. After Giuseppe's funeral."

"That's right. I thwarted that idea for weeks. And apparently, it inspired him to try and make a new deal." His fingers stilled when her hand jerked under his.

"A new deal. He was going to bargain with me again?"

"He'd already started."

The revelation made her sick to her stomach. "Who?" she demanded.

"Gallo's second son."

Carina shuddered. Dante was worse than Elio. And far richer and younger than Giuseppe. It would have been a match her father would have been happy to secure.

"I found out he'd set up a meeting with Gallo to make the offer. I couldn't let him do it. I couldn't watch…" He sighed, long and deep. "I couldn't watch him sell you again."

Shifting, she pushed onto her knees to stare down at him, but he refused to meet her gaze until she gripped his chin and forced him to look at her. "You saved me. If not for you I'd be dead. Because if my father had made that match, I would have killed myself."

Alexei sat up suddenly, drawing her into his lap. "I lost you once. I made the mistake of letting you walk down the aisle to that fuck Giuseppe. I couldn't lose you again. But I didn't know it would set all this off with the Romanos."

"In a way, you gave me more of what I needed." She cupped his face in her hands and pressed her lips to his. "Thank you."

"There is nothing I wouldn't do for you." He pulled her in for another kiss, trailing his hands down to the curve of her ass and giving it a rough squeeze. "I was worried you'd be angry."

"My father was a monster. He deserved worse. So much worse than a single bullet to the brain."

"You are everything, Carina," he repeated, wrapping his hand around her throat and squeezing gently while he rocked her against his cock. "*Lyubimaya moya.*"

She moaned low in her throat, shifting to slide his hardening length against her slit. "What does that mean?"

He smiled, using his hand on her throat to guide her onto her back and positioning himself between her thighs. "My love."

"*Amore mio,*" she sighed, trailing her hands up over his abs and around his hips to his ass, squeezing as he slid his cock in to the hilt. "Alexei," she groaned as he thrust slow and deep inside her. "You are everything."

Chapter Thirty

"He can't tell us anything if you break his fucking jaw," Alexei snapped, gripping Dom's arm before he could land another blow on the man they'd cornered in an alley on the edge of Romano territory.

"He hasn't exactly been forthcoming so far," Dom retorted, wrenching his arm from Alexei's grasp and stalking a few paces away. "Would you prefer to ask him nicely where Elio is hiding?"

"I would have preferred to take him and his buddies back to my workshop in the casino and wring every answer I could out of them." Alexei gestured to the three men already dead on the ground. "But you made sure that wasn't an option. Do you want bodies or information?"

"I want Elio. Our position isn't secure until he's dead."

"I want Elio too. But if you keep pummeling everyone who might be able to give us some answers, Elio will keep twisting in the wind, a threat to your brother's reign."

"I-I don't know anything about Elio," the man said, drawing Alexei's attention. "I swear."

His left eye was swollen shut, and a cut on his right cheek wept blood, sliding down to his chin to drip off onto the collar of his shirt. Alexei might have believed him if the source that led them in this direction wasn't a credible one. One of their own spies who'd infiltrated lower Romano ranks since Matteo's return to the island had set their long-term plans in motion.

"Then why were you seen coming and going from the villa in Cefalù?"

"His wife and daughters are still there," the man explained. "I was taking them supplies. That's it."

Dom took a step forward, fist raised, but Alexei shifted to block Dom's path, removing a knife from his pocket and flipping out the blade with a flick of his wrist. The man tracked its movement with wide eyes.

"Tell me, what use does Elio's wife have for guns? Are his daughters going to fire them at invaders from the balconies?"

"G-guns? What guns?"

Raising his fist, Alexei buried the knife into the man's shoulder, covering his mouth with his hand to muffle the scream. "Don't lie to me about things I already know are true. Or I'll let him kill you with his fists." Alexei jerked his chin at Dom, who stood with his arms crossed over his chest. "I'll ask again. Why were you delivering guns to the Romano estate?"

Alexei removed his hand, and the man whimpered but didn't speak. Impatient, he twisted the blade until the man let loose an anguished cry, shuddering with the pain.

"We were just following orders," he insisted, voice strained.

"Whose orders?" Alexei pushed the knife in to the hilt when the man paused again.

"Baranello," the man panted. "One of his loyal capos. He doesn't have many left. The Baranello family has been connected to the Romanos for generations. He instructed me to bring the weapons from the docks to the villa and leave them in the courtyard. He paid me well. That's all I cared about."

"A common refrain from Romano's men." Alexei looked over his shoulder at Dom. "Where do you think Baranello is getting the cash from? Elio?"

"If he's that loyal, he could be funding from his own pockets on the promise of repayment."

Alexei snorted. "He's a fool if that's true." He turned back to the man, easing off the constant pressure on the blade but leaving it embedded. "Who else besides Baranello is still loyal?"

The man shook his head. "Not many. Payments have been dwindling since Giuseppe died, and a month or so ago, they stopped. Elio has been stringing people along with empty promises. But people have been grumbling for a long time."

With a nod, Alexei flicked the blade of the knife and made the man wince. "Since you've been so helpful, you can decide how you die. I can bury my knife in your skull, or he can snap your neck." He gestured over his shoulder at Dom with two fingers. "Both relatively fast ways to put you out of your misery."

The man whimpered, shrinking away from Dom when he took a step forward. "If you let me live," he said quickly, "I'll give you another piece of information. A better one."

"I'm listening," Alexei said, ignoring Dom's grunt of displeasure. Alexei motioned for the man to continue.

"You want to know where Elio is hiding, yes?"

Alexei pinned the man with a dry stare. "Let me guess. You, a low-level gun runner, know where that is?"

"No, no," the man pleaded when Alexei reached for his knife. "I don't. Not exactly. But I did hear that a few years before he died, Giuseppe bought a bunch of shitty, rundown buildings. Rumor was they all had underground tunnels and safe houses. They said he never did anything with the buildings themselves, but he outfitted the bunkers with supplies and state-of-the-art shit. So he could use them to escape if he ever needed to."

"We're supposed to take your word on a well-known rumor?" Dom shook his head and scoffed. "Give me something better, some proof, or I'm taking your choice from you."

The man trembled, looking at Alexei to intervene, but Alexei remained silent, too focused on how close the man's theory was to something Carina had said the night before.

"I didn't think so," Dom said, lurching forward to grip the man's jaw and head in his hands. He twisted at a sharp angle until the man's neck snapped and he fell to the ground in a heap.

"Jesus Christ," Alexei muttered, crouching to retrieve his knife from the man's shoulder and using a clean bit of shirt to wipe the blade.

"What? I told him I wasn't going to give him a choice if he didn't have more."

"You're like a bull in a china shop with your kills. So clumsy and inelegant."

Dom rolled his eyes as Alexei stood. "We don't always have time for your methodical prodding. We needed answers, and we got them."

"*I* got them," Alexei reminded him, trailing Dom to the car as their men moved in to dispose of the bodies littering the alley. "With my methodical prodding."

"Whatever. Now we know for sure Baranello is one of seemingly only three or four capos still left helping Elio. The rest have defected to Davide, who has so far been willing to operate under Matteo's discretion."

"It's still early yet. Things could take a turn."

Dom started the car and pulled away from the alley toward home. "You sound like you want a war."

"I don't. I only want Elio."

"Right," Dom replied with a knowing nod. "So you and my sister can torture him to death."

"Something like that. She deserves the closure."

"I don't disagree." Dom paused, eyes intent on the road ahead of them. "But what if she doesn't get it?"

Alexei turned to look at Dom, a frown drawing a deep crease between his brows. "What?"

"What if we can't find Elio? Or we have to kill him when we try to take him alive? Or he kills himself like Vincenzo did? What will she do then? Will it be enough that he's dead? Or will she be left empty and wanting?"

Alexei didn't answer. He couldn't. He hadn't let himself entertain the idea that they wouldn't find Elio and bring him in alive. He'd be as content as anyone else to kill him on sight wherever he turned up and end the threat of this war that was brewing. Only Carina's desire to watch him die, to have a hand in it, had him pushing back on every scenario that didn't end with Elio being taken prisoner.

But like the confrontation with Vincenzo, there were a million different ways this could end. With Elio dead long before Carina got what she wanted. And if she didn't, would she blame him? Would she leave Sicily like she'd talked about weeks ago to start over?

Something had unlocked between them when he told her the story of his life before Sicily. A sense of possibility. But possibilities had never been something he could rely on. He didn't waste much time thinking about the future. It was hardly certain.

But the more time he spent with her, the more he wanted to. He had no idea what lay on the other side of this for them, especially not if she missed out on her chance to kill Elio.

Which is why he was determined to do everything in his power to help her get it.

"You think he was lying about the tunnels?" Alexei wondered into the silence.

"Of course I do. We haven't been able to find any sort of property like that in his name or any of his holdings. And if he was hurting so badly for cash, why would he keep them?"

"If he was hurting so badly for cash, why didn't he do a lot of things?" He rolled the idea around in his mind, unable to let it go. "What if he put them in someone else's name?"

"Like who? We didn't find anything like that in Giovanni or Elio's names either."

Alexei chewed on the pad of his thumb. Last night, as she went over her notes for the millionth time, Carina remembered having to sign some paperwork maybe two years or so before Giuseppe's death. When she asked him what it was for, he said insurance against attack.

She'd assumed at the time he meant actual life insurance. But if the gun runner they'd cornered in the alley was right, maybe she'd been signing paperwork for the sale of those buildings. Buildings that would be in her name and not show up on a property records search for Giuseppe.

But he was wary of sharing that information with Dom. It would only get back to Matteo, and the Bianchi Don had made it very clear he didn't care if Elio was brought in alive or dead as long as he was taken care of. Things were going well enough with Davide that they didn't need Elio anymore, and Matteo had hardly proven to be reliable when it came to holding up his end of the bargain in this.

No, if Alexei wanted to make sure this ended right for Carina, he would have to chase down this lead himself. Let the Bianchis busy themselves with raising their banner over Romano lands and ushering Davide and his soldiers into the

fold with the promise of money and protection and partnership.

He would focus on searching for these properties and
rooting out Elio himself. Then he'd haul him back for Carina
and let her use every tool in his tool kit to exact her revenge.
He couldn't wait to watch her work.

Chapter Thirty-One

The warm water cradled her body as she sliced through it, punishing herself with laps from one end of the pool to the other. Anything to help channel this anxiety and tension and anger until her real target was in her sights. It had been nearly a week since Elio slipped through their fingers, and with each passing day, Matteo seemed less and less focused on his manhunt and more interested in rebuilding the Romano empire in his image.

Things were going well with Davide, as she suspected they would. The youngest cousin had never thought to hold much power, content mostly with staying in the background to not draw his father's wrath. He had no plans, no desire to make waves.

He wanted only money and the time and space to do what suited him. Matteo was willing to give him all three in exchange for a controlling say in what happened in Romano businesses and a decent share of the profits.

But power was not money. Romano coffers were empty, and it would take time and skill to build them back up again.

Matteo was playing the long game, and he'd already set his sights on his next target. Varda was making it an easy decision with the way he kept making a run at them along the border, trying to distract them with petty skirmishes.

The distraction was working for one thing. Matteo was constantly using it as an excuse to give her the runaround when she asked for updates about finding Elio. The men were looking, they were doing everything they could, she needed to be patient. Alexei echoed her brother's sentiments, and that gave her at least a small measure of comfort. But the waiting was driving her crazy.

She'd begun to catch herself in quiet moments wondering what she would do if her revenge against Elio was never satisfied. If she never got to watch the life drain from his eyes, if she never got to be the one to inflict the fatal blow. Would she be able to cope with that?

She'd devoted so many years to imagining Giuseppe's death. All the painful and bloody ways he could die. In the end, she'd been robbed of that too, forced to settle for a simple heart attack.

Elio, who looked and acted and sounded so much like his father—he was her chance at redemption. But what if that chance never came?

Could she move on with Alexei and have a life with him? Despite his revelations the other day and the way it had seemed to open up something between them, they hadn't talked about the future. She had no idea what he wanted after this was all said and done, no idea if his obsession would wane when they didn't have this shared cause and desire knitting them together.

And beyond that, she wasn't entirely sure what she wanted either. She'd already been tied to a man once. Did she want to be tied to another? She couldn't compare Alexei to Giuseppe; it would be cruel and unfair. Giuseppe had sucked the life out of her, and Alexei had killed to protect her. They were worlds apart in every way.

But in her limited experience with love and marriage, it never seemed to do anything but drain the woman until she had nothing left to give. Until she was a shell of her former self while the man gave nothing, lost nothing, changed nothing.

She couldn't do that again. Couldn't sacrifice herself like that. The way her mother had, the way every Romano woman had in service to their men. As much as she wanted Alexei, as much as she loved him, she'd rather be alone than slowly wither away.

The thought brought her up short, and she nearly crashed into the side of the pool, putting her hand out to stop her and breaking the surface of the water with a gasp. Did she love Alexei? Is that what this feeling was?

It was embarrassing to realize how unfamiliar she was with the sensation. She hadn't had much experience with boys before her father married her off to Giuseppe. She hadn't been given the freedom to find out, always kept close to home when she wasn't at school or under supervision when she was. And there was certainly no love in her marriage.

Resting her forearm against the edge of the pool, the rough stone scratching her skin, she leaned her forehead against it. She'd asked her mother once about love, if she was in love with her husband. Her mother had smiled and said love was different for everyone.

Sometimes it was instantaneous and unpredictable, like a lightning strike on a clear day. Sometimes it was slow and methodical, like a storm moving inland from the sea. Sometimes it grew out of something unexpected, like a flower that flourishes through a crack in the sidewalk, pushing its way up from impossible odds to blossom. And no matter how love arrived, if you found it, it was worth protecting.

But maybe the thing no one wanted to admit was the act of protecting that love is what drained the life out of you. Shoving away from the side of the pool, she floated onto her back, closing her eyes and willing her mind to still. She didn't have to think about any of that now, didn't have to wonder if she was or wasn't in love.

Instead she could focus on Alexei and the way the sound of his voice calmed her nerves, the way the feel of his body warm against hers in the dark helped her sleep, the way he listened to her speak without interrupting, as if whatever she had to say was the most important thing he could hear all day. She didn't know if that was love, but it felt nice, and she would hold on to that as tight as she could for as long as she could.

She was contemplating getting out and letting the sun warm her, the breeze dry her skin, when something soft smacked her in the face. She jerked, sucking in a mouthful of pool water when she shouted in surprise. Shoving it away, she paddled toward the shallow end, coughing and wheezing the water out of her lungs.

"I'm so sorry, Signora," came Giulia's apologetic voice from the side of the pool. "I was shouting your name, and you didn't hear me."

Carina boosted herself out of the water, her coughing subsiding as she sent the maid a hard look. "So you tried to drown me?"

"No! No, of course not, Signora. I would never—"

Waving away her protestations, Carina stood, taking the second towel she offered and running it over her body. "What was so important then?"

"Your brothers have just arrived home." Her face was

bright red with embarrassment and panic. "You said you wanted to know right away."

"I did." Carina used the damp towel to wring as much moisture from her hair as she could. "How long have they been back?"

"Only about ten minutes." Giulia handed her another towel and reached for her wrap where it lay on the end of a lounger. "They're in the study."

Carina quickly squeezed water from her suit with the fresh towel and let Giulia help her into her wrap, belting it at the waist. "Thank you, Giulia. Just make sure you get that towel out of the pool before my brother sees."

Giulia's eyes widened, and she nodded in agreement. Carina left the woman to her task, quickly braiding her hair and clearing the last of the pool water from her throat as she crossed the patio and let herself inside. She heard voices drifting out from the back of the house, loud ones, and she set off in that direction.

When she stepped into the doorway, Matteo was seated behind the desk, his favorite spot when he wanted to remind everyone who was in charge. Dom and Luca were positioned across from it, Luca sprawled in one of the chairs and Dom leaning against the other from behind. Alexei was reclined against the bookcases on the far wall, his eyes smiling when they met hers. It was Dom and Matteo who were shouting at each other.

"You can't ignore this forever just because you have other things you'd rather be focusing on!"

"I'm not ignoring it," Matteo assured him. "Just because I'm not addressing the Varda issue exactly the way you want doesn't mean it isn't being handled."

"Handled," Dom sneered. "Not everything can be settled with a meeting over drinks, Matteo. Sometimes you have to bloody your pristine knuckles."

Matteo's lip curled back over his teeth. "Why don't you worry less about what I'm capable of and more about the task you've failed to complete? I've asked for Elio's head, and I still don't see it."

At that, Alexei cleared his throat, and conversation stalled instantly. She frowned. Had Matteo rescinded his promise to bring her Elio alive? And if he had, why was Alexei covering for him?

Matteo glanced at Alexei, following his gaze to where she was standing in the doorway. Dom shoved away from the chair at the sight of her and stalked over to the bookcases to stand beside Alexei.

"Did you need something, Carina?"

Carina dragged her gaze away from where Dom and Alexei had their heads bent together, Alexei's eyes still on her while they spoke, and turned to face Matteo. "I was wondering what updates you had."

Matteo sighed loudly, as if her very presence was a nuisance, and anger sparked in her chest. But it was twined with something else. She darted a look at Alexei again. Something like betrayal. She expected her brothers to keep things from her, but if Alexei was doing the same now, she had no one left on her side.

"We're still looking. He has more allies than I thought. He might even have sought shelter with another Don."

"Varda?" she wondered, but her brother waved a dismissive hand.

"Possibly. After all, Varda is out a lot of money if Elio is dead. But our spies think it's unlikely."

"Why?"

Pinching the bridge of his nose, Matteo sat back in his chair. "Varda has his own problems where I'm concerned. I can't imagine he wants to make them worse by harboring Elio, knowing we're looking for him."

"Looking to execute him, you mean."

Matteo's stare was unflinching. "That's what you said you wanted."

"Yes," she said softly. "In a manner of speaking."

"If you don't mind," Matteo said before she could say anything else. "We have a lot of work to do."

The dismissal was clear in his tone, and when no one intervened or offered any other information, she swept each of them with a look of disappointment, lingering on Alexei for a beat longer than the others, and turned on her heel, disappearing into the hallway.

"Carina, wait." Alexei followed her to the stairs, grasping her elbow before she could climb them. "What are you thinking?"

She hated the tears burning her eyes, hated the feeling of abandonment that sat heavy on her heart, especially from the man standing in front of her with that imploring look in his eyes.

"I'm not thinking anything," she lied.

"I'm doing the best I can to get you what you want, Carina. What I promised you."

"Are you? Because more and more, you seem to be on Matteo's side. At his beck and call."

He frowned. "You know that isn't true. How could you think that?"

"What's being done to recover Elio, Alexei? Will you tell me that? And not the company line. The truth."

His green eyes searched hers, and she read the hesitation in them, in the loosening of his grip on her arm. He opened his mouth and closed it again, no doubt unsure of how best to lie to her. In that moment, she felt like an idiot. Here she was, wondering about tomorrows like some lovesick schoolgirl, and he was moving further and further away from her toward the power and money Matteo promised.

"Right." She pulled her arm from his grasp and turned to climb the stairs.

"Carina—"

"Don't. You'll only insult us both when you lie to me. I should have known it would come to this. Pretending it wouldn't was my mistake."

"That isn't fair," Alexei said, voice gruff with an underlying note of hurt. "You said you trusted me."

"I did trust you," she replied without turning around. "And look where it's gotten me."

He didn't follow her when she jogged up the rest of the way, didn't pound his fist on her door when she locked it behind her. That in and of itself felt like its own kind of proof. Its own sort of confirmation that none of what existed between them was what it seemed.

It was better to realize it now, before things went too far and she found herself trapped. But it didn't make it sting any less.

Chapter Thirty-Two

Alexei watched her from under one of the shade trees at the edge of the courtyard. She sat at the small table on the overlook, one of her mother's favorite spots, twirling pasta around the tines of her fork. He could only see her from behind, but every so often, she would look out to sea and stare for a few moments. He wanted desperately to know what she was thinking. But she wouldn't talk to him.

He'd tried last night when he came to bed. After threatening to break down the door if she didn't let him in, he'd attempted, unsuccessfully, to draw her into a conversation, to explain why he was handling this situation with kid gloves. It hadn't worked. She'd rolled over and gone to sleep and left him staring at the ceiling most of the night. It was infuriating.

Dom's words about what could happen if Carina didn't get her closure rang truer to him now. Worry over whether she might pack up and leave if she didn't get to exact her revenge sat like a lead weight around his shoulders. He could not—would not—let that happen. She was his. And he would do whatever it took to lay the world at her feet or help her burn it to the ground.

"I can feel you staring at me," she said, startling him out of his thoughts. "Go away."

Steeling himself, he crossed the grass and claimed the chair opposite hers. "You were right."

The look she fixed him with was distant, her brown eyes blank. "I'm sure I was. What was I right about this time?"

This was either going to be the dumbest thing he'd ever done or the smartest. But he couldn't stand that look in her eyes, not when it was aimed at him. He dropped a folder next to her plate and nudged it forward with his fingers.

"About that paperwork Giuseppe had you sign."

She glanced down at the folder, taking a bite and chewing slowly before flipping it open and picking up the first page. It was a list of properties purchased under a shell company with her signature. The company was in her name, along with an offshore bank account she probably didn't know about.

She arched a brow as she read, and he fought the urge to reach across the table and haul her into his lap. She had no idea how quickly she could undo him with a look. Her gaze snapped up to meet his, and her eyes were full of questions. He much preferred that to her blank stare.

"I own buildings?"

"You do. Among other things." He pulled the next page off the stack and set it on top of the first in her hands. "Six houses, possibly with some kind of tunnel system. We cornered someone the other day off a tip from one of our spies. He thought giving us information about some purchases Giuseppe made might save his life."

Her lips twitched at the corners. "Did it?"

"No." He grinned. "But it did give me a thread to pull."

"You should have told me."

"Yes," he agreed, and she looked up at him in surprise. "I should have. I didn't want to get your hopes up. But I've discovered I'd rather that than the way you looked at me last night. And just now."

Dropping her eyes to the stack, she picked up the next paper, this one outlining the details he'd been able to find out about the shell company in his limited search. "What way is that?"

"Like this thing between us is finished."

Her eyes slowly found his again, and she swallowed hard. "And if it was? Finished, I mean."

"It isn't."

"You sound awfully sure of that."

He shrugged, but every sense was on high alert as he spoke. "I am. You're mine, Carina. If you think I'm letting you go that easily, or at all, you haven't been paying attention."

"I'm not a plaything, a toy for you to pick up and discard when you feel like it." Her chin ticked up. "I've lived through that once and—"

"I am not Giuseppe fucking Romano," Alexei growled, gripping her wrist and tugging her out of her chair and into his lap. "Is that what you think you are to me? A plaything?"

"I...No," she admitted, her hands braced against his shoulders.

"No." He cinched his arm around her waist. "You are mine in the same way I'm yours. You know it as well as I do, even if you aren't willing to admit it."

"And if I leave Sicily?"

"Then I would follow you. To the ends of the fucking earth."

She slid her hands up to the back of his neck, fingernails biting into the skin, and brought her lips down against his, greedily taking from his mouth while he slid a hand down to cup and squeeze her ass.

Her tongue swept against his, and he nipped it lightly, making her moan low in her throat. When she shifted in his lap, her thigh pressed against his hardening cock, and he would have lifted her onto the edge of the table and taken her right there if she hadn't pulled back.

"I want to go," she said.

"Away from Sicily? What about Elio?"

"No." She shook her head and reached behind her for one of the papers. "I want to go check these out. I want to see them for myself."

"You're insane." He plucked the paper from her hand and slammed it down on the table. "I'm not letting you wander through Romano territory looking for Elio's hiding spot. We don't even know if these properties are set up to act as safe houses or not. It's just a hunch."

"I know." She retrieved the paper and studied it. "The only way to find out is to go there and look."

"Yeah. And I will do that. Not you." She held the paper out of his reach when he grabbed for it, and he scowled. "Do you remember what happened the last time I took you into Romano territory?"

"I do. I remember I bashed that asshole's face in with a rock."

"Not until after he attacked and tried to rape you." Alexei shook his head at her narrowed gaze. "It's too dangerous. Elio is a wild card. Let me investigate, see what I can find. Then I can take some guys and bring him in."

She pushed out of his lap and paced away, then back again, glancing down at the stack of papers before propping her hands on her hips. "If you don't take me, I'll go by myself."

Alexei growled, shooting out of his chair and gripping her elbows to haul her up against his chest. "That's not funny, Carina."

"I'm not joking. It's taken too long already. And the longer it takes, the higher the chance Matteo gets what he wants. I know he doesn't care how Elio dies. Only I do. Only *we* do," she corrected at his sharp look. "Please, Alexei."

"This is a terrible idea." She squealed with excitement, pushing up onto her tiptoes to press a kiss to his jaw. "Go put on pants and decent shoes," he said, releasing her and watching her bound away.

This was absolute insanity. But if the alternative was her sneaking off on her own to investigate—and he had no doubt she would do just that—then at least he'd be there to keep an eye on her. If Elio really was hiding at one of these properties, he wouldn't be thrilled to find any of them poking around.

Alexei was slipping an extra knife into his pocket when Carina came bouncing down the stairs in jeans and a tight tank top. She spent most of her time in dresses, which he loved, but he had to admit he didn't mind what jeans did for her curves. Except now all he could think about was peeling them off her later.

"Stop looking at me like that."

"Like what?" he replied, opening the car door and helping her inside.

"Like you're thinking about me naked."

He grinned, tracing a fingertip around her nipple through her clothes. "But I am." Laughing when she bit her lip and her cheeks colored, he rounded the hood and climbed behind the wheel.

The properties were clustered, which gave even more credibility to the idea that they were linked by tunnels. Two sat close to the main villa, two more backed up against a more rural side of the territory, and the last two in the small town where Vincenzo had taken a header off the parking garage.

He would not, under any circumstances, be taking her to

the ones near the villa. Not without a fully armed guard. But they had time to check out the other two locations. And she was practically vibrating in her seat when they pulled up outside the ones near the parking garage.

"This is where Vincenzo killed himself?"

She stood on the sidewalk in front of the first building, her face half hidden by big sunglasses, staring up at the crumbling facade. The second house was at the end of this block.

"About three blocks that way." He gestured to their right.

"This could be a good candidate, then. Especially since Matteo let Elio pick the meeting location and then he didn't show. Maybe he was watching from here."

"I thought the same. But I don't think he stayed."

"Why not?"

She moved to where he'd crouched at the edge of the sidewalk as it turned into a dirt path for cars. Between the overgrown bushes and trees was the corner of a little shed, most likely for hiding vehicles from the street.

"The weeds here aren't flat. I'd guess no one has driven into or out of this place in a while."

"But you said there could be tunnels, right?" She stood up and looked toward the other house. "Maybe they're delivering supplies there and bringing them here in the tunnels?"

They drove up to the other house, but it looked as abandoned as the first one. No disturbed vegetation, no compacted dirt to suggest anyone had been driving in and out to bring supplies. At her pleading, they drove to the second set of houses.

These were in a far less populated area, on the edge of a small town that faded into miles and miles of farmland. The entire street was completely deserted. It was the perfect place to hide if you wanted to go unnoticed. Something about this one made him feel uneasy, and he refused to let go of her hand once they'd parked in a nearby spot and gotten out.

"This one looks promising," she said, voice hushed with excitement.

"I'd rather go and come back with several men," he said, eyes roving for the source of the sensation prickling the back of his neck. "An army of them, to be exact."

"The weeds are flattened here," she said, pulling him toward a similarly hidden shed.

"We need to get out of here."

She looked up at the bite in his tone and pushed her sunglasses onto her head. "What's wrong?"

"I'm not sure." He couldn't shake the feeling that they were being watched, that they were in danger. "But I don't want you out here anymore. It isn't safe. Let me take you home, and I'll—"

His body jerked when her hand was wrenched from his grasp, and he turned in time to see a man easily three times her size wrap his hand over her mouth to keep her from screaming. Her sunglasses were on the ground, one lens cracked, and her eyes were wide with fear as she fought uselessly against the man holding her.

Alexei slid his hand into his pocket, drawing a knife out as Elio stepped from behind the trees, flanked by three more men with guns drawn.

"I wouldn't get any wild ideas," Elio warned. "If we have to shoot you, we might miss and hit pretty little Carina." He dragged his fingertips down the side of Carina's face. "You wouldn't want to give her a scar as hideous as yours, would you?"

Carina screamed uselessly against the hand covering her mouth, flailing out with her legs until she caught Elio in the back of the knee and he nearly buckled.

"Let her go and I'll kill you quickly, Elio."

Alexei flipped out the blade and twirled it once in his fingers. He might not be able to take out Carina's captor, but

Elio was close enough for him to land a deadly blow before they got off a good shot. How loyal could four men be when their Don was dead?

"Kill me and she dies."

The man holding Carina tightened his grip until her thrashing stopped.

"Okay! Okay." Alexei raised both hands.

"Toss the knife there," Elio said with a tilt of his chin, and Alexei threw it into the overgrown yard. "Good. I've been trying to figure out how to get my hands on this bitch to use her for ransom. Between you and Matteo, I figured you'd pay a pretty penny to get her back. Or at the very least get your fucking noses out of my business. And here you are, waltzing right into my hands." Elio's eyes glittered. "Lucky me."

"Take me," Alexei demanded, taking a step forward and jerking to a stop when the man holding Carina growled in warning. "I can't promise you Matteo will pay to get her back, but he'll pay for me."

Elio rolled his eyes. "Please. What kind of fool do you take me for? Tell Matteo I'll be in touch. If you live that long."

Elio had barely gotten the words out before a car screeched to a halt next to them and Carina was shoved into the backseat. Alexei heard her hoarse, terrified shouts before the door closed and the car sped off. Two men remained, both with their guns aimed at his chest while he went over his options in his head. Take out the big one first, then the thin one. Once that was done, call Matteo and find Carina.

Fishing the second knife from his pocket, grateful he'd thought to grab it, he lunged for the big one to throw him off balance. Sidestepping at the last minute, he swung around and drew a deep gash down the guy's shooting arm with his blade.

The man let out a strangled scream, his gun hanging limply from his fingers. He tried to regain his grip, but his fingers wouldn't close all the way. Alexei must have severed tendons in the forearm. Good.

At the sound of feet scraping on pavement, Alexei pivoted, but not before the thinner of the two got off a shot. Pain exploded in his side and radiated into his chest when the bullet found its target. Gritting his teeth against it, he dodged a second shot and drove his knife into the fucker's bicep, twisting until the man dropped the gun with a pained gasp.

Panting, Alexei kicked it into the tall grass. The knife was slick in his hand, and he took a fraction of a second to wipe it on his pants. The distraction gave the big one enough time to attempt to rush him, but Alexei was faster.

Darting to the side, he wrapped his arm around the guy's beefy neck and plunged the knife into his side once, twice, a third time. The guy grunted and fell to his knees, bracing himself with one hand on the pavement while the gun fell from his other one and skittered away a few feet down the sidewalk.

Alexei twirled the knife in his fingers, leaving his friend to spit blood into the grass and circling the remaining man. This one was more patient, but Alexei could outlast him. As long as he could shove down the fear for Carina.

Taking a deep breath, he shut everything out and focused only on his opponent. If he let his fear punch through, he'd end up dead, and fuck knew what Elio would do to her then. So he packed it into a box and shoved the box into the back of his mind, focusing instead on circling the man staring him down, inching closer with each revolution.

The thinner man's eyes darted over Alexei's shoulder seconds before he lunged, not for Alexei but for the gun on the pavement. Alexei dove for the guy at the same moment, poised to strike when the shot sounded off like the pop of a firecracker.

The pain was blinding, unbearable, and he went to his knees.

"You might be good with a blade," the thin man said, grinning wildly and pressing the warm muzzle of the gun against Alexei's temple. "But didn't anybody ever tell you not to bring a knife to a gunfight?"

"I guess I missed that lesson," Alexei said, breath hissing out between pursed lips. "Lucky for me, I'm smarter and faster than you."

The fucker opened his mouth to hurl another insult, but he didn't get a word out before Alexei knocked the gun away from his head and drove his blade into the side of the man's neck.

As soon as he collapsed, Alexei rolled on top of him, pulling the knife free and drawing it across his throat to make sure he was dead. He enjoyed watching the life drain from his eyes, body going slack.

The second man coughed, drawing Alexei's gaze. He ignored the pain in his hip and shoulder, crawling on hands and knees to where the other man was lying on his back, staring up at the sky.

"Where is she?" Alexei said through gritted teeth, holding the knife dripping with blood in front of the man's face.

"I'm dying anyway. Why would I tell you?"

"Because I can fill your last minutes on this earth with indescribable pain. Tell me." He slammed the blade deep into the man's belly and twisted. "Now."

The man coughed, blood spraying out of his mouth, and groaned. "Fuck. You."

Pulling the knife out, Alexei jammed it in again, catching himself on his palm when he swayed. "I can do this all fucking day."

The man hesitated, so Alexei drew his knife out again and prepared for another blow.

"Wait! Fuck." He coughed up more blood. "There's a cabin. It's…" He dissolved into a coughing fit before his eyes rolled back in his head and he began to convulse.

"No, no, no. You stupid fucker." Alexei inched closer, gritting his teeth against the sharp pain so hard he thought they'd crack. "Wake up, you bastard, and tell me where the cabin is."

But it was too late. He was already dead. Falling back onto his ass, Alexei fought the wave of nausea, squeezing his eyes shut when everything went blurry. He needed to get it together. He had to find her.

He rolled onto his hands and knees, his shoulder screaming in pain at the movement, but he couldn't make himself stand. Biting the inside of his cheek until he tasted blood, he collapsed to the sidewalk and rolled onto his back, fishing his phone out of his pocket.

Bringing it up to his face with trembling hands, he squinted at the screen, his fingers leaving bloody smears across the glass. The edges of his vision dimmed, his blood leeching out onto the sidewalk and soaking into the concrete, but he forced himself to concentrate.

Contacts. Berto. Mayday ping. Send.

The phone fell from his fingers and clattered onto the ground, and he reached his good arm up to press roughly against the wound in his shoulder. It seemed to be the one bleeding the worst right now. He hoped Berto got here fast. The more time Elio spent alone with Carina, the worse it would be for her.

Carina. Her deep brown eyes were the last thing he saw before everything went black.

Chapter Thirty-Three

The sound of car doors slamming reverberated through his skull, and the scrape of shoes on asphalt was like nails on a chalkboard. But the feeling of hands on his body shoved him fully conscious, his body pulsing with pain.

"Son of a fucking bitch, man." Berto. Thank fucking Christ. "What the hell happened?"

"Carina," Alexei croaked, but he wasn't sure if he'd said it loud enough for anyone to hear. "Elio took her."

"Fuck. Call Matteo!" Berto yelled before reaching down to grip the hem of Alexei's shirt and ripping the fabric away from his body. "Through and through in the shoulder. Just grazed the side. Hang on. I'm going to clean it."

That was all the warning he got before Berto doused him with some kind of antiseptic that made him want to die, pain stabbing around the opening of his wounds like tiny knives. Alexei grit his teeth when Berto pressed something hard against his shoulder. A gauze pad. It didn't take long before it was soaked through with blood and he was applying another.

"We need to get you up and to the doctor," Berto said,

gripping the hand on his good arm and dragging him upright.

Alexei waited for the dizziness to subside and slowly shook his head. "No. Pack it and give me something for the pain."

"You're insane. You need stitches. We'll find her."

Grabbing Berto by the collar, he yanked him closer until they were nose to nose. "I'm not sitting in a doctor's office while she's out there. Pack the fucking wound and help me up. I have to find her."

"Fine." Berto shoved Alexei's hand away and helped him lean back against the tire of the SUV. "This is going to hurt."

"Shut up and do it."

Berto paused long enough to suck in a sharp breath and then ripped open a fresh pack of gauze, using his fingers to shove it deep into the wound. Alexei shuddered, forcing air through his lips against the searing pain to keep from passing out. Hands pressed on his shoulder from behind while Berto bore down from the front. When blood stopped soaking so quickly through the bandages, they wrapped his shoulder in more gauze and secured it with medical tape.

Gripping Berto's hand, he let the man haul him to his feet, collapsing back against the SUV when the world spun and his stomach churned.

"Are you sure you're in any shape to go after her?"

"Since I'm going either way, it's pointless for you to ask the question. Doesn't your kit have pain meds?"

Squeezing his eyes shut, Alexei held out his hand and dry swallowed the pills Berto laid in his palm. He didn't care if it killed him; he wasn't going to limp away to lick his wounds with Carina out there.

A few minutes later another car arrived, and Matteo, Dom, and Luca jumped out. None of them looked particularly pleased, and Matteo, to his credit, looked especially stricken. Alexei wasn't sure Matteo really cared that much about his sister. At least not until now.

"What the fuck happened?"

"You were dragging your heels on finding Elio, and your sister insisted on taking matters into her own hands," Alexei said, leaning back against the side of the SUV. "I'm pretty sure these are safe houses." He gestured at the seemingly abandoned building behind them.

"Like the guy said."

Alexei nodded at Dom. "Right. They're all in Carina's name. Or a shell company in her name. That's why they didn't come up on any property searches for the Romano men."

"The clever fuck," Luca mumbled.

"That's great," Matteo ground out. "What's that got to do with my sister being missing?"

"Elio said he wanted to use her for ransom." The pain meds were starting to kick in, the fogginess in his brain receding.

"And because you brought her here instead of keeping her at home, he got his hostage."

Guilt surfaced, hot and bright, and Alexei stuffed it down. It would be about as useful to him as the fear. And he couldn't afford any distractions. "Yes. We can fight about it later. Once we have her back."

"Any idea where they took her?"

Alexei looked at Luca. "They said something about a cabin. Anything like that come up in your records searches?"

"A cabin." Luca frowned, digging his phone out of his pocket and tapping furiously across the screen. "They own a piece of property near Calcarelli. It looks like farmland, but it could have a cabin on it."

"Then let's go."

He reached for the handle on the car door, irritated when

Matteo's arm shot out and gripped his wrist. "Where the hell do you think you're going?"

"If you think I'm going to sit this one out, you're fucking insane."

"You're going to get yourself killed," Luca pointed out.

"I don't care," Alexei spat. "As long as she's alive at the end of it. Now, we can go, or we can waste time on an argument you'll lose. It's up to you."

Matteo studied him a moment longer before releasing his wrist. "Fine. But we're not going in blind. If we do," he continued over Alexei's protests, "we only end up putting Carina at greater risk. It's not like we want her getting caught in the crossfire. Agreed?"

Matteo waited for murmured words of agreement, then nodded. "Good. Dom, choose twelve of our best men for this. We want them quiet, efficient, and good with a gun at long range. Have them meet us at the strip club closest to Calcarelli. There's one maybe twenty minutes from there, isn't there?"

"There is," Luca confirmed as Dom hurried off to make his calls. "I'll get some guys out here for cleanup," Luca added, gesturing to the blood and bodies littering the ground.

When they were alone, Matteo sent Alexei a scathing look before crossing to the car he'd arrived in and slamming into the backseat. Alexei didn't care how much Matteo hated him, disapproved of what he'd done, or wanted him dead. He cared only about making sure Carina was okay.

He stripped out of his ruined shirt, grateful the pain had subsided to a persistent ache. He'd have to be careful with it, though. One wrong move and he was liable to permanently fuck something up. Just because he couldn't feel it didn't mean he couldn't do damage. He rounded the hood of the SUV, pausing at the door.

"What are you doing?"

"You think I'm going to let you drive with your arm all shot to hell like that?" Berto gestured to Alexei's bandaged shoulder. "You'll get us both killed. Get in. I've got an extra shirt for you."

Climbing into the passenger side, Alexei carefully pulled the shirt on over his head, wincing when he worked his arm into the sleeve. There was a thin sheen of sweat on his forehead by the time he was done.

"Don't," he said when Berto took a breath.

"Don't what?"

"Don't ask me if I'm sure I want to go after her."

There was a beat of silence, then Berto reached for the key to turn the ignition over. "All right then."

He pulled away from the curb to follow the rest of their group out, and they drove away from the Varda border toward the strip club. Alexei played the events of the last hour over and over in his mind. The terror in Carina's eyes, the way her body went limp when the man holding her squeezed too tight, the sound of her voice when they shoved her into the car. She was screaming his name, screaming for help he hadn't given. He pressed the heel of his hand against his eye to try and drown out the sound of it ringing in his ears.

If they killed her… No. He couldn't let his mind go there. Elio wanted her for ransom. They wouldn't kill her. But there were a lot of ways to hurt someone without killing them.

"We're going to find her," Berto said into the heavy quiet.

"We have to," Alexei whispered.

Chapter Thirty-Four

Carina breathed through the panic fluttering behind her sternum while the man who'd shoved her into the car bound her wrists in front of her with coarse rope. She hissed when he pulled the knot tight and the material scraped against sensitive skin.

Trees whizzed past the windows, briefly giving way to buildings while the car sped away from where they'd left Alexei. She prayed he was okay, that he was coming after her.

"You're dumber than I thought, Elio."

He didn't rise to the bait, ignoring her in favor of whatever he was doing on his phone. At this distance, she could see how pale he was with dark circles under his eyes, like he hadn't been sleeping. It gave her a small sense of satisfaction that a man as vain as Elio could look like absolute shit.

He wore his usual suit, but it was wrinkled and hung oddly on his frame. The stress of the last few months, of trying to right his father's sinking ship, had taken a toll on him. He looked tired, gaunt.

The village streets again turned into trees and gently rolling hills as they drove further and further away from the town. They took a sharp turn, and she fell into the big man who'd grabbed her with a grunt, wriggling quickly away from him when his fingers brushed too close to her breast.

Elio might want to ransom her, but that didn't mean he had to return her whole, in body or mind. Matteo would pay; Alexei would make sure of it. Assuming he was still alive— and she had to believe he was. But who knew how long it might take him. Or how Elio and his men might choose to entertain themselves in the meantime.

The idea of what Elio might do to her between now and when he had his money made her stomach tighten, and she blinked up at the roof of the car to keep the tears at bay.

The car jostled as the road narrowed, turning from pavement to gravel and finally to dirt before a squat house came into view. It was overgrown with brush, the gray, sun-bleached logs barely visible through the thick vines. The car slowed in its approach, pulling around the house out of sight of the makeshift road.

She wasn't expecting him to take her somewhere more isolated. She'd have bet money on them going to the safe houses closest to the villa. But that wouldn't make sense now that Elio was aware they knew about them. Then again, if Elio had this place, why the fuck had he been staying in those safe houses at all? Unless he hadn't been.

She squeezed her eyes shut when the driver cut the engine and the two men in the front got out, leaving her alone with Elio and his big bodyguard in the backseat. If he had eyes on the houses, he would have seen them visit the first two and could have made an easy guess on where they would go next, meeting them there and taking them by surprise.

What an idiot she was. Her impatience had played right into Elio's hands and given him the perfect opportunity to try and cut a deal to save his skin. She'd have to apologize to Alexei about that later. Once she managed not to die.

Someone knocked on the window, and Elio reached for the handle, pausing. "If you run, I'll shoot you."

She glared at him in the fading light. "You can't collect a ransom on a dead body. Matteo won't pay without proof of life."

His grin was sinister, and it made her blood run cold. "Who said I'd shoot to kill?"

Elio slid from the car, but she hesitated, her mind frantically, uselessly searching for a way out of this. But there wasn't one. All she could do was survive until Alexei and her brothers found her. Or paid for her. Whichever came first.

When the man at her back poked two fingers roughly into her shoulder, she glared at him and wriggled unceremoniously from the car. She slipped on the dewy grass and was suddenly grateful Alexei insisted she put on jeans. She didn't want to think about where hands might wander if she was in a dress.

The man gripped her arm so hard it stung and dragged her toward the small cabin. She stumbled along at his side, barely able to keep up with his long strides, the rope biting into her skin.

The cabin was comprised of just two rooms—a big living space and what she could only assume was a bedroom beyond. And if the candles and lanterns burning on every surface were any indication, there wasn't any electricity. It surprised her that Elio was choosing to live like this. Not that Matteo had given him much of a choice. The takeover had been swift and merciless.

The man shoved her into a chair, kneeling in front of her to bind her legs to the wood, cinching the rope tighter than was necessary to hold her in place.

"Ow," she said through gritted teeth.

He ran his hands up the back of her calves and down again, caressing them with a sick, smug smile on his face. If her legs were free, she'd have kicked his teeth in. He groped her thighs, and she recoiled as much as her bindings would allow, the chair scraping across the floor.

"Enough, Baranello," Elio said, barely glancing up from his phone. "You can have a taste later."

Carina shuddered at the implication, but Baranello stood and backed away, still staring at her, eyes dropping to her breasts and lingering there far too long. He licked his lips. She would die before she let this man have a taste of anything.

"Smile, bitch." Elio raised his phone and took a picture of her, the strobe of the flash forcing her to blink against the brightness. "Let's see if your big brother is willing to pay up."

Elio finished typing and then settled onto a ratty, sunken couch, crossing his legs like it was the most expensive piece of furniture he'd ever touched. He looked even worse by candlelight, the harsh light casting the lines in his face in sharp relief. She was going to enjoy killing him.

She'd been planning how to do it for weeks, since the day Alexei showed her all the tools in his kit. The scalpels and picks and tweezers. He hadn't spared a detail about what each thing could do, how it could be used to prolong someone's pain and suffering until you were ready to end it and not before.

She wondered if Elio would scream while she carved him up, while his blood pooled underneath his body. She wondered how much of it he could lose before he passed out. She imagined the light draining out of his eyes, imagined his cold, unseeing stare, and a smile played at the corner of her mouth.

"What's so fucking funny?" he demanded, ruining her fantasy.

"I was just thinking about how much I'm going to enjoy killing you."

Baranello scoffed, and Elio's eyes narrowed.

"Your brother tried that once, and look where it got you."

"It's not my brother you need to worry about."

Elio's phone rang, and he held it out to her, displaying Matteo's name on the screen. "Speak of the devil." He connected the call and put it on speaker. "Matteo. Good of you to get in touch."

"If you harm one hair on her fucking head—"

"Don't start with me. She's fine." Elio flicked a hand at Carina. "Go on, tell him."

"Matteo! I'm here."

"Carina. You're okay? They didn't hurt you?"

She looked from Elio to his man. "No. Not yet. Is Alexei all right? I didn't—"

"This is hardly time for idle chitchat," Elio scolded. "Let's get back to the topic at hand."

"What do you want?" Matteo bit out.

"I want the money you owe me. This might have all been avoided if you'd just paid me what was due and moved on with your pathetic little life. Now it'll cost you extra."

"How much?"

"Five billion euros. I know you're good for it. If you have enough to buy up as much debt as you did, no doubt you can cover this. You have two hours."

"I can't get five billion together in two hours."

Elio shot Baranello a look, and he crossed the floor, bringing his hand down across Carina's face and snapping her head back. She whimpered, squeezing her eyes shut against the pain as it raced across her jaw, leaching into her temple and down her neck.

"Son of a bitch! If you touch her again, I will fucking kill you!"

Her eyes were still closed, but there was a grin in Elio's voice when he spoke again. "You're hardly in the position to be making demands of me. One hour and fifty-nine minutes.

Don't be late, or I'll let my men take their frustrations out on her in whatever ways they please."

Matteo's shouts were cut off, and when a hand brushed her cheek, she thought she would be sick. She leaned as far away from it as she could, nearly toppling sideways before strong hands righted the chair again. Baranello leaned in and closed his teeth around her earlobe, biting it hard enough to make her yelp.

"We're going to have so much fun together, slut."

"Fuck you," she snarled, but he only laughed.

"Already eager for me, I see." He stood up and gripped his crotch, thrusting his hips lewdly toward her face. "You won't be able to scream with my dick in your throat."

"No. But I'll be able to bite it off."

"Enough," Elio barked when Baranello raised his hand to strike her again. "Matteo is right. He won't be able to get that kind of money together in two hours. You can have your fun with her later when he misses his deadline."

A heavy breath shuddered through her lips. "You gave him an impossible deadline?"

"I did. You didn't think I'd waste my opportunity to exact my own revenge, did you?"

"Revenge for what?"

"For the way you ruined my life."

"Oh, please," she sneered, "tell me how a twenty-year-old girl traded like livestock to a man three times her age ruined your privileged little life."

Elio shot out of his seat and wrenched her head back by her hair. "My relationship with my father was fine before you came along and whispered in his ear. Then all of a sudden, he was talking about babies and new heirs and splitting responsibilities. As if I wanted to share my birthright with your brats."

"You think that was me with those dreams? I did everything possible to avoid having his child growing inside me. Do you have any idea what he would have done if he found out I was on birth control? I risked my life to ensure you were an only child."

"You're lying."

"I can give you the number of a little old lady in Mazzaforno," she replied. "I paid her a thousand euros to take care of the first and only brat your father ever managed to plant in my belly. I was much more careful after that."

Elio released her, stalking away and back again.

"If your father didn't trust you to take over, it had nothing to do with me. Maybe he finally saw how weak and pathetic you were."

"I am not weak!" Elio screamed, rushing forward and hitting her across the face so hard she fell backward, head bouncing against the floor when she landed.

Twisting his fingers through her hair, he used it to pull her upright. The pain of it had white spots erupting across her vision. Even with that mad look in his eyes, the way his breath puffed against her cheek, she couldn't help but goad him.

"I don't know if Elio has what it takes to build the empire back up. Another son to raise and put in Elio's place would be better."

"What is that?" Elio snarled, jerking her head.

"It's what your father said to me the last night he climbed on top of me. Hoping he'd finally managed to replace you with another."

His hand was around her throat in an instant, squeezing until she coughed. "You lying bitch. For that, I won't wait until your brother gets here with my money. I'll kill you and take it anyway."

Her heart pounded in her chest as he tightened his fingers. She tried to shove him away, but he was standing at an odd angle, and between his hand on her neck and her legs tied to the chair, she couldn't twist her body far enough to force him off. So she did the next best thing she could do. She played dead.

His fingers loosened when she went limp, and she fought the urge to suck in a deep breath of air. Better for him to think she passed out. He slapped her face a few times, and she heard him call her name over the blood rushing in her ears.

Then there was another sound. The unmistakable rumble of a car engine carrying over the hills, drawing closer. To her left, Baranello stiffened, and then footsteps pounded past her, shaking the floor. When the door slammed shut, she knew she was alone with Elio.

He was breathing heavily, standing maybe a few feet away, probably in front of the window, and pacing across the floor. He moved closer and stopped in front of her.

"Your brother's an idiot for coming here instead of getting my money and waiting for my instructions. It's like he doesn't care if you live or die."

He tried to sound nonchalant, but she could hear the underlying tremble in his voice. Elio hadn't planned on a direct confrontation, hadn't realized he was easier to find than he thought. He was afraid.

Checking one more time to ensure she was out cold, he crouched in front of her and began to untie her legs from the chair. That seemed like a mistake, but she waited to see what he would do, holding her breath.

He gripped the first one once it was free, then started untying the second. When he shoved them together and fed the rope behind her ankles, she finally realized what he was doing. Preparing to move her to a different location. She couldn't let that happen.

Jerking his head up at the pop of gunshots, his task temporarily forgotten, she seized on his distraction, bringing her knee up hard to connect with his face. He fell onto his ass, gripping his chin as he glared at her.

"You fucking bitch."

He lunged at her, but with her legs free, she was able to roll out of the chair, landing on her still-bound arms with a grunt. He was behind her in an instant, his hands gripping her ankle and tugging. She kicked against his hold, desperate to get her arms out from under her so she could fight back.

Then his arm was around her waist, and he was hauling her to her feet. The movement threw them both off balance, and when he stumbled back a step, she lunged for the closest weapon she could find. A candle.

Closing her fingers around the thin taper, she hissed as the hot wax spilled onto her skin with the sudden movement. Elio was advancing when she turned and shoved the candle into his eye, ramming it into the socket with as much force as she could.

He screamed, his hand reaching up to shield the burned and reddening skin as the candle fell to the floor. She didn't wait for him to recover, spinning and darting around him to the front door. But he was faster than she expected, his hand gripping enough of her hair to pull her back against his chest before she could get free.

"I should have let them rape you," he snarled in her ear. "It's no less than a cunt like you deserves." More gunfire made them both jerk toward the door. "If they make it through this, I'll let them take as many turns as they like on you."

"Go to hell, Elio."

"Only if I can take you with me," he whispered in her ear, wrapping his arm around her neck and squeezing.

"Be my guest," she gasped, inching her toe forward until she kicked over a lantern onto one of the chairs.

The dry wood and fabric went up in seconds, flames

licking the ceiling and spreading to the couch where he'd been sitting only minutes before. Once the couch caught, the chair on the other side of it did too, and then the curtains, burning a path to the front door and the only way she knew in and out of the cabin. Well, if she was going to die, at least she knew Elio was going to die too.

Shock had him loosening his hold, and she pushed away from him, scrambling to undo the bindings on her wrists and using her arm to protect her mouth and nose from the worst of the smoke. She heard shouts from outside moments before the front wall ignited and the entire cabin became an inferno.

Elio stood rooted in place, whether in fear or disbelief or resignation, she wasn't sure, but if he had forgotten about her, she wasn't going to remind him. Her eyes, stinging from the billowing smoke, searched for another exit, a window, anything. Then they landed on a knife.

Something they probably used for chopping up vegetables. And it was right there. It wouldn't take much to bury it in Elio's back. To be sure he didn't make it out of this alive. She debated a second more and then grabbed it tight in her fist.

"Elio!" she croaked, smiling when he whirled to face her. "Tell your father I said hello."

She drove the knife into his chest as hard as she could, twisting it in her fist until he screamed and dropped to his knees. Pushing her foot against his stomach to shove him onto his back and pull the knife free, she moved forward to stab him again. She had to make sure.

But the flames were climbing over the ceiling now, racing toward her, and as much as she wanted to watch Elio bleed out and burn and cease to exist, she didn't want to be next. After plunging the knife into his stomach, she spun, propelled by his agonized screams as the fire took over his body, and raced into the other room.

The smoke was thick in this room too, but at least it wasn't on fire. There was only one window in here, but it was high off the floor, and the bed was too heavy for her to push underneath it. The only other furniture in the room was a solid wooden dresser.

Closing the door against the smoke and the flames, she shoved her shoulder against the side of the dresser, ignoring the thump of something against the wall from the outside. If she was still in here when the roof collapsed, she was dead.

Coughing as the smoke invaded her lungs, she nearly cried with relief when the dresser began to scoot across the floor. She angled it under the window and boosted herself on top. But when she gripped the frame to slide it open, it wouldn't budge. Nailed shut.

"No," she whispered, clawing at the frame in her desperate attempt to escape.

Another thump against the wall was followed by a splintering crack, and she covered her face with her hand and shoved her elbow through the glass. She felt it scrape along her skin, the blood welling and oozing down her arm. She did her best to clear out all the pieces to avoid getting cut. It would have been a tight squeeze even if she'd managed to get the window open. Now it was going to be a painful one.

Gritting her teeth, she braced her hands on the ledge to hoist herself through. Another sharp crack sounded, and a hole splintered in the wall. She stuck her head through the window, and a sob escaped her. Alexei and Luca pounded furiously against the side of the cabin with axes.

"Alexei."

He looked up at the sound of her voice, and relief washed over her. He was okay. He was alive. They were going to make it.

"Get me something I can stand on," Alexei ordered, but Luca was already moving away.

"Here," Luca grunted, dragging over a stump they must have used for chopping firewood.

Alexei jumped onto it, his face level with the window now, and reached in to hook his hands under her arms, helping her slide through the opening. A stray shard of glass dragged along her side, but it was better than the intense heat of the room behind her. The bedroom door wasn't going to hold back the fire much longer.

Pulling her legs through, she braced her feet on the side of the house and awkwardly jumped down to the stump, tears rolling down her face when Alexei's arms wrapped around her, holding her close.

"You're okay," he soothed, his hand running over her hair and down her back. "Come on. We need to get back. It won't be much longer before it goes."

He stepped down and helped her jump, wrapping his arm tight around her shoulders and hauling her up against his side. No sooner had they backed away from the side of the house than flames erupted from the window, reaching greedily for the sky. Within minutes, the house buckled and then collapsed in on itself.

"Carina, thank God," Matteo said when they rounded the house, running his hands over her head and shoulders and pressing a kiss to her forehead. "I thought we were going to lose you. Where's Elio?"

"Dead." She nodded toward the burning heap. "You'll find his body in the main room, badly burned with a knife in his stomach."

Alexei gave her shoulder a squeeze. "That's my girl." He looked to Matteo. "What about everyone else?"

"Two dead. One got away across the fields. I've got guys looking for him now."

"Which one?" she demanded.

"Big guy, dark hair."

"Baranello."

Alexei tilted her chin up so her eyes met his. His voice was rough when he spoke. "What did he do?"

"He got a little handsy. Would've done more if you hadn't shown up when you did."

A murderous glint lit Alexei's eyes, and he glanced at Matteo. "He'll have to pay for that."

"We'll get him," Matteo agreed, stepping away when someone shouted his name.

"You found me," she said to Alexei when they were alone, voice breaking on a sob.

He turned her in his arms and leaned down to press a gentle kiss to her lips. "I will always find you. Always. I told you, you're mine, Carina. Forever."

Chapter Thirty-Five

He lay stretched out on one of the couches on the wide balcony, the sun filtering through the shade trees behind his eyelids. The air was thick with summer, and every so often, he caught the faint sound of voices from the workers in the fields behind the villa.

They'd been holed up in the Marsala house going on two weeks now. After being rescued from the fire and confirming Elio's death, Carina had insisted she needed time away. He'd assumed that meant away from him. Until he found her in his cottage, packing his things into a bag as if it had been obvious from the start he was going with her.

It took her days to tell him everything that happened when she was with Elio, and when she finished, he made love to her on the balcony until the sun dipped below the horizon. It felt like a claiming, a promise, a possession. She was his and he was hers, and nothing would come between them again.

They hadn't talked about the future or what it held for them yet. But he had an idea. And if she didn't like it, well, he could think of plenty of ways to make her come around. She would in the end. He would make sure of it.

The breeze rustled through the vines and carried her scent to his nose, warm and delicate. He heard her soft footfalls across the stone and smiled.

"You're not supposed to take this off, you know."

She sank down beside him, and he opened his eyes to see her holding up the brace for his arm. Seventeen stitches to sew up his shoulder but no lasting damage, according to the doctor. A miracle after the way he swung that axe through the wall trying to get to her, trying to make sure she didn't burn alive in that fucking cabin.

"Unless I'm sleeping. And I was sleeping."

"You weren't." She braced her hands on either side of his chest, careful of his shoulder, and leaned down until her hair curtained their faces. "I can tell when you're sleeping, *amore*."

"Maybe I was falling asleep and you woke me up."

She tilted her head thoughtfully, then pressed her lips against his. "Were you?"

He grinned. "No."

Sitting up, she laughed, brushing her hair off her face and moving to sit on the edge of the low table between the two couches. "I talked to Matteo."

Alexei swept his eyes up to stare at the ceiling. He'd escaped Matteo's wrath thus far. He deserved every bit of it for what happened to Carina, for how bad it had almost been. But he wasn't ready to pop the bubble with her yet. To leave her and go back and take his lumps.

"Did you?"

"There's a meeting he wants you to attend next week."

"A meeting or a public flogging?"

"I don't think they do those anymore."

He glanced over at her, arching a brow at the grin on her face.

"Don't look at me like that," she said. "I told him to go easy on you. Reminded him it was my fault we were there in the first place."

"But I should have—"

"We're not having that argument again. You're fine." She ran her fingertips lightly over his shoulder. "I'm fine. And Elio is dead. That's all I really care about." She looked out over the fields, then back at him. "But I have been thinking."

"Have you?" He reached out to play with the hem of her dress when it fluttered in the wind. "About what?"

"About leaving Palermo. Now that Elio is dead and it's done."

His fingers stilled, and he looked up at her, but her expression gave nothing away. "Leaving Palermo."

"Yes. Striking out on my own. Buying a house, even."

Pushing himself up, he rolled the stiffness out of his shoulder and turned to face her. "When?"

"As soon as possible." She crossed her legs and leaned back on her palms.

He studied her for a long moment. The rich tan of her skin, the deep brown of her eyes set in a heart-shaped face. Tendrils of hair blew across her forehead, and he reached up to brush them behind her ear. He hadn't expected she'd want to leave Sicily so soon. He really hoped she wouldn't want to leave at all.

The Romano territory was cowed after the death of their Don, but war was brewing with Varda, and Matteo would need as much help as he could get to win it. But none of that mattered, not if Carina wanted to leave and never look back.

With a nod, he shoved to his feet and moved toward the door.

"Where are you going?"

He looked over his shoulder, eyebrow raised. "I'm going to pack."

"What?" She frowned. "Why?"

"You said you wanted to leave Sicily." He turned to face her, crossing his arms over his chest and ignoring the twinge in his shoulder. "Did you think I was joking when I said I would follow you anywhere?"

She laughed, warm and full, and it was his turn to frown. "Come here," she said, holding her hand out to him. He reclaimed his seat and pulled her into his lap. "I don't want to leave Sicily. Just Palermo."

"Oh. Okay. Where do you want to go?"

"Here. I offered to buy the house from Matteo. I want to live here. With you." She cupped his face in her hands. "I have enough money from that offshore account and my inheritances to staff it. We won't have to worry about anything. We can just be for a while."

"I have money." Her eyebrows shot up. "It's not like I've been working for free for the past sixteen years."

"Is that a yes, then?"

"Yes." He slid his hands up her thighs, pushing her dress up as he did. "On one condition."

"What condition is that?" she asked, squirming as his fingers roamed higher.

"Marry me."

"Alexei." She sighed and tried to move off his lap, but he anticipated her, wrapping his arms around her waist and holding her in place. "I've done that before. I don't want to do it again."

"You haven't done it with me. Forever, remember?"

"You don't need rings and priests for forever."

He pressed firmly against her back to draw her closer, leaning up to nip and kiss her chin. "I know, but I want that kind of forever with you."

"I can't give you what you want. I can't give you children."

"You are all I want. I'll tell you as often as I need to until you believe me."

"And if I say no?"

"Then I'll keep asking until you say yes. Let me make you mine, Carina. In every way possible."

She chewed her bottom lip while she considered, but he knew she'd say yes. He could tell by the look on her face.

Finally, she asked, "Do I get a ring?"

"Of course you do. I'm not an animal."

Grinning, she leaned in and captured his lips, nibbling his bottom lip with her teeth. "I get to pick it out. No diamonds. And you have to ask me properly. Down on one knee and everything."

He chuckled. "You can have whatever you want, *lyubimaya moya.*"

"Mmm," she hummed, leaning in to kiss him again. "I love when you say that to me."

He laughed, scooting her back when his phone buzzed in his pocket. A text message from Dom. His fingers tightened on her waist, and she shifted on his lap.

"I have another present for you."

"Already? You haven't even gotten me a ring yet." He turned his phone around to show her the picture from Dom, and she squinted at the figure bound to a chair, face bloody. "Is that…"

"Baranello. Why don't we grab my tool kit and pay him a visit? Then when you're done with him, I'll bring you back home—to our home—and fuck you until you can't breathe."

Her eyes darkened, her hand sliding up until it gripped his throat, fingers flexing on his skin. "Promise?"

He shifted closer and whispered against her lips, "Anything for you, Carina."

A Note for the Reader

Dear Reader,

From the very bottom of my heart, thank you. Out of all the billions of books available to read you choose mine. I had so much fun diving into the dark side of Mafia life in this book and I'm so excited for what comes next for the Bianchi family. I hope you enjoyed Carina and Alexei's story and I'm deeply grateful that you took the time out of your life to come along on their journey.

If you enjoyed this book, I would really appreciate a little more of your time in the form of a review on Goodreads or Amazon or wherever you purchased it.

I couldn't do this writing thing I love so much without you. This is the first book in the Sicilian Mafia Wars Series but I'm not done telling stories yet. In the next book we get to know Domenico, the second Bianchi son, and his perfect, passionate match, Emilia.

For exclusive sneak peeks, updates, release dates, and more, sign up for my newsletter at https://meaghanpierce.com/newsletter or follow me on TikTok.

All my love,
Meaghan

tiktok.com/@meaghanpierceauthor

Also by Meaghan Pierce

Callahan Syndicate Series

Sweet Revenge

Bitter Betrayal

Deadly Obsession

Dark Secrets